PRAISE FOR RODERICK ANSCOMBE AND
THE INTERVIEW ROOM

"The most original thriller I have read in a long, long time, with pacing and cutting-edge medicine that will keep you up late into the night. Roderick Anscombe is a welcome new voice in suspense. His writing is lean and sharp, with characters that matter, and ideas that are totally fresh." —Michael Palmer,
New York Times bestselling author of *The Society* and *Extreme Measures*

"Plan to stay up late. *The Interview Room* provides honest-to-goodness chills." —*Detroit Free Press*

"Anscombe, a forensic psychiatrist himself, delivers precise, perfectly calibrated thrills one after another in an implosive story that takes oedipal struggle to the breaking point."
—*Publishers Weekly*

"Riveting . . . the kind of mainstream appeal associated with Harlan Coben and Jonathan Kellerman . . . don't wait for the movie." —*Booklist*

"*The Interview Room* is a new kind of thriller—provocative, entertaining, and morally chilling, for people who like their justice subtle. A sly shocker that will invade your psyche and shake up your beliefs about good people and how bad they can get, it's an absorbing novel." —Perri O'Shaughnessy, *New York Times* bestselling author of *Unlucky in Law* and *Presumption of Death*

"Along with steadily mounting tension, Anscombe provides enough exquisitely turned therapeutic dialogues to create a heaven for connoisseurs of mind games." —*Kirkus Reviews*

"That Roderick Anscombe perfectly captures both worlds, that of a forensic psychiatrist as well as a sociopathic stalker, isn't surprising. But that he manages to convey the intersection of those worlds with such a gripping, gritty realism is astonishing and makes for a totally engrossing read." —Doreen Orion, M.D., forensic psychiatrist and author of *I Know You Really Love Me*

ST. MARTIN'S PAPERBACKS TITLES
BY RODERICK ANSCOMBE

THE INTERVIEW ROOM
VIRGIN LIES

VIRGIN LIES

RODERICK ANSCOMBE

St. Martin's Paperbacks

This is a work of fiction. All of the characters, organizations, and events portrayed in this novel are either products of the author's imagination or are used fictitiously.

VIRGIN LIES

Copyright © 2007 by Roderick Anscombe.

Library of Congress Catalog Card Number: 2006050597

ISBN: 0-312-94750-X
EAN: 978-0-312-94750-7

Printed in the United States of America

St. Martin's Press hardcover edition / March 2007
St. Martin's Paperbacks edition / March 2008

St. Martin's Paperbacks are published by St. Martin's Press, 175 Fifth Avenue, New York, NY 10010.

10 9 8 7 6 5 4 3 2 1

VIRGIN
LIES

10:45 A.M.

The tiger cages were hard to take, even for those of us used to maximum security. It was Kovacs who came up with their name—not that any of the clinical staff wanted one, far less a reference to the human rights violations of a repressive regime. Kovacs had seen the originals, he said, on one of his tours of duty in Vietnam, and once the name stuck we couldn't get rid of it.

Each of the four cages sat at the periphery of an imaginary five-spoked wheel, with a gap where I sat. Around us, the cavernous space of a disused cell block had been soundproofed at great expense, so that however loudly the participants in the group yelled—as Sammy Fields, brain-damaged child killer, was doing now, in full moralistic rant at the man in the cage beside him for a crime much like his own—the confidentiality of these outpourings would be maintained.

With each patient individually confined, nothing could get out of control. But this sound clinical rationale didn't make me feel any better about the cages. When you're surrounded by the routine exercise of raw power, you are never free of the nagging question of whether you are part of a repressive regime. In prison, so many of the ethical stop signs have been removed that you can't ever be entirely sure you have the right of way.

It was hard enough to keep my concentration without interruptions.

"Phone call, Dr. Lucas."

"Okay," I said without turning. "I'll call them back."

But Lieutenant Kovacs remained standing behind me. "You're going to want to take this call," he said.

"How so?"

"It's from your wife."

A call from the doctor's wife was a signal event. The Sanders Institute wasn't the kind of place where family of staff called for a chat. For one thing, Security would likely be monitoring the call. More than that, you did everything you could to insulate your family life from Sanders.

I walked quickly along the short corridor that joined the tiger cages to the control center, where two officers lounged in chairs, occasionally checking the bank of monitors. A telephone receiver lay on the console.

"Is this you?" Abby asked. "Thank God! It's been so awful!" There was a catch in her voice that alarmed me. Abby at the brink of tears at work wasn't something I'd encountered before. I had the sinking feeling that one of her clients had suicided. "They wouldn't put me through at first. They didn't believe who I was."

"That's normal operating procedure."

"Danielle's missing, Paul."

I was supposed to know who Danielle was, and I racked my brains to remember when, during one of our all-too-sparse dinner conversations, Abby had mentioned her. Was she a social worker at the agency? No one came to mind. I was grateful she'd called me at this time of crisis; I didn't want to fail the test, even if it was only putting a name to a face.

"When did you last see her?" I asked, playing for time.

"We sent her on her regular coffee run around nine o'clock. She does this every day for us. She's only a young girl, but it's less than three hundred yards."

Fragments coalesced in memory. Danielle's mother was a graduate of New Beginnings, the agency that Abby directed for pregnant teenagers and young mothers. The kid was going to spend the summer hanging around on the street and sooner or later getting into trouble, and Abby had arranged for her to work as a volunteer at the agency. She'd taken Danielle under her wing. That Danielle.

Abby dropped her voice almost to a whisper. "Please come, Paul."

No command could have been more compelling.

Abby's agency was housed in a large Victorian on a street undergoing sporadic gentrification. A three-decker two houses farther down Eastern Boulevard had gone condo and sported a crimson paint job with sparkling white trim; but plastic siding on the houses between hung loose at the corners, fast-food wrappers clung to front-yard chain-link fences, and the neighborhood still had a down-at-heel air.

It was eleven-thirty, and the heat of the summer morning hit me as I stepped out of the air-conditioning of my car. By the time I'd climbed to the top of the granite steps and reached for the door, I was already sweating.

Inside, the reception area of the agency was unusually crowded. The young women kept their children close at hand, and the kids themselves seemed subdued and watchful. Several uniformed cops were taking down details in notebooks, and a couple of male detectives were questioning a woman holding a baby on her hip.

Off to the side, in a space made by people keeping a respectful distance, a large woman in shorts and a tank top was slumped in a chair, weeping uncontrollably as a member of Abby's staff tried to comfort her.

When I came through the door, people turned as if I might be the bearer of news, and even the woman I took to be Danielle's mother stopped sobbing to look up.

The truth was, I expected the girl to turn up at a friend's house or a movie theater, surprised at the fuss. I'd come for Abby, not because I'd be much use to the missing girl. I was here to rescue my marriage.

But the presence of the detectives was an ominous sign. I recognized Detective Wolpert and inadvertently caught his eye. I looked away and saw other faces that were less familiar, recalling them vaguely from holiday parties or tedious hours in courthouse lobbies. Finally, I saw Abby just as she spied me and started through the crowd.

She hugged me fiercely; her fingernails dug through the light cotton shirt I was wearing.

"I'm so glad you're here!" She sighed, her lips pressed close to my ear. And then, to my disappointment, she added a formal, "Thank you."

"I know," I murmured, already dropping into the cadence of someone comforting the bereaved. "I know." I rocked her for a long moment, wondering if this child would bring us together, thinking of our own child, Adrian, who had died.

Abby pulled away. "She's still alive," she said defiantly.

"Of course she is!"

"She's hardly been gone any time at all."

"Which makes it all the more likely that she's hiding out somewhere with a friend."

"That's not Danielle. She wouldn't pull a stunt like that."

"But she's a kid. Maybe one of her buddies came along with some pocket money. Maybe they took off for the mall."

"We know she picked up the coffee from the coffee shop. She was on her way back. She had change she had to return. She wouldn't have taken off."

I turned to look at the cops in the hallway. Someone had pulled a lot of manpower off the streets.

"She's been abducted, Paul."

"Someone witnessed this?" I asked with a sinking heart.

Abby shook her head. "No. She just disappeared."

"Okay. It doesn't do any harm to get an early start."

"We have to accept, one, that Danielle's been abducted. And two, that she's not dead." She angled her head back to scrutinize my face, and her blue eyes nailed me as if their intensity could make me a believer.

"No, she's not dead." I wouldn't tell her now what I knew from my clinical practice about people who snatched children. "You're right. We don't know."

But when you're a forensic psychiatrist and you hear that a child's been abducted, you automatically check off a chilling list of likely outcomes. This was different, though; this was close to home. Danielle was one of Abby's girls.

"She was only out of sight a few minutes," Abby said. "It was a regular coffee run that she did for the day care staff."

Regular, I thought, and therefore predictable. Regular, so that the perpetrator could plan and lie in wait. This wasn't an impulsive grab. He would have prepared the abduction. Therefore, he would have prepared the keeping place. The place where Danielle was now, confused, alone, scared out of her wits.

Abby said, "She's eight years old."

I nodded. An eight-year-old girl wouldn't have been able to put up much of a struggle, even if she'd wanted to. More likely, though, he lured her.

"But she has street smarts," Abby said. "She lives a couple of blocks from here. This is her neighborhood. She isn't some kid from the burbs."

Then the lure must have been more difficult. The lure was stronger, or Danielle's fear had been less. "Maybe she knew him," I suggested hopefully.

"That would be something. That might lead somewhere. The police are all over it. They've been great. They came down here like a SWAT team. But now they don't have any leads to follow up."

"This was when?"

"Just after nine."

"Nine o'clock on a Thursday morning—someone has to have seen something."

As Abby and I were talking, Brenda Gorn, the assistant DA, had approached us and was impatiently trying to make eye contact. Brenda and I had been colleagues for a decade, and friends within the boundaries of our professional loyalties. Those boundaries had been tested when I was the prime suspect in the murder of a state cop and Brenda had gone out on a limb for me. Whenever I'd tried to thank her, she'd steered the conversation away. Brenda wasn't an effusive person, but she was passionate about her work, zealous, even, in her pursuit of culprits. Her work was her life, particularly now, in her early fifties, with her daughters finished with college. She'd let her hair go gray; she'd put on some weight.

"Paul." She took my hand with both her own. "I need your help."

"Of course," I said. "Whatever I can do."

"It's been two and a half hours since Danielle went missing."

Terrible things could happen in 150 minutes. I prayed that the abduction hadn't been a spur-of-the-moment affair. If he'd planned it, if he'd laid out his agenda, fantasized for days or weeks or months, then he'd hold back. He'd feel secure. He'd accomplished the most dangerous part, the abduction, and he'd gotten away with it, insofar as he could tell. He wouldn't feel rushed. He'd wait. He'd want to wait, to stretch it out, to savor the anticipation. He'd stash her in the place he'd prepared and then return.

But if he'd snatched Danielle on the spur of the moment, a blitz attack, if he didn't have a safe house lined up, if he had to do his stuff now or never, if he hadn't taken the necessary precautions to prevent the girl from recognizing him . . . Memories of crime scene photos flashed through my mind. Bestial images.

Brenda said, "But we have some good news: We have a witness."

"That's great."

I knew it wasn't, otherwise all these cops wouldn't be

milling around in the stifling-hot foyer, waiting for direction.

"The bad news is," Brenda went on, "she's crazy."

From the way Brenda and Abby stared at me, waiting for my reply, I guessed they'd discussed beforehand how to pitch this to me.

"Sure," I agreed. "Anything."

"She's not a suspect," Brenda said hurriedly, already recognizing the conflict of interest that reared its head.

There were psychiatrists who'd say that at the moment I introduced myself to their witness as "Dr. Lucas" she became my patient and I owed her a whole host of special considerations, one being confidentiality.

"We're not asking you to interrogate her," Brenda said. "She's a person who can help us in our inquiries. You're a person who knows how to ask certain people questions. That's the extent of the relationship."

"And she's all you've got?"

Brenda nodded.

"But you think this person saw the abduction?"

She raised her hands in a gesture of uncertainty, then let them drop in frustration. "This is what's killing us. We don't know. Maybe she saw something. Maybe she even saw the vehicle. Maybe she even saw the abductor. Maybe she recognized him. But when she talks . . . she goes off on a tangent, she contradicts herself."

"Her name is Martha Kinnard," Abby said, all business. "She's schizophrenic."

"You know her, then?" This sounded more hopeful.

"She's a fixture in the neighborhood. She sleeps in Dracone Park, or in doorways, when the police roust her. Sometimes she'll accept clothes from us that people have donated. One of our social workers who used to work at the Methodist knows her from there."

"Give me whatever you've got."

"Early forties. First break when she was a graduate student at MIT. She's smart, but all that brainpower goes into her delusional system."

"But she saw something?"

They exchanged looks. Each waited for the other to answer, hoping she'd put a more positive spin on what could be nothing.

"She was there," Abby said. "She had to have seen something."

Brenda hooked her hand behind my arm. "Come with me," she said. She was tugging me back toward the door by which I'd just entered. I felt the urgency in her grasp.

We swept through a barrage of hostile glances from the cops. They made it clear that they didn't want me to be part of their investigation.

We passed through the heavy mahogany doors into the dazzling summer sun and had to hold our hands to our heads like visors as Brenda pointed out the landmarks. From the sidewalk of Eastern Boulevard we could view most of Corporal Eddy Dracone Park, a charmless triangle named for a local boy who'd been killed in Vietnam, formed where Eastern Boulevard intersected Hubbard Avenue. At the far end of the park ran Winslow Street.

Brenda pointed out the donut shop across the park. The sign above the entrance said DOOSY'S in cursive script the color of coffee.

It was an unpromising spot for an abduction. Two locust trees and five straggly bushes provided scant cover. The park was surrounded by a series of busy intersections. Someone in a vehicle stopped at the lights, or even slowing in traffic, would have noticed a struggle. A low-riding

Honda Civic passed us at a leisurely pace, the driver scanning us curiously. His windows were down to catch a breeze; even with the thudding bass of his stereo, he could have heard a girl scream nearby. He would have noticed a struggle.

She had been lured, then. Most likely, she was acquainted with the abductor. I prayed he was organized. It made the crime colder, more callous, more grisly, but it would buy time.

Danielle would have used the crosswalk by the traffic lights at the intersection of Hubbard Avenue and taken the black-topped path that cut two hundred feet across the park, past a pair of benches, to the other crosswalk on Winslow, almost opposite the donut shop. Then, returning . . .

"She bought the coffee?" I asked. "We know that for sure?"

"Right. They know her at the donut shop. A woman served her. A regular employee. She remembered the order because it was always the same. Three coffees. One large regular, no sugar. One medium black. One large, extra cream, two sugars. One coffee roll. She made change from a ten-dollar bill. The guy who usually worked with her was on break; she had to attend to the next customer, so she didn't notice Danielle leave. It was all routine."

"That was a lot for Danielle to carry—three coffees in a cardboard tray, and a coffee roll balanced on top. It would all have come crashing down if someone had made a grab at her."

"We've been over every square foot of dirt and blacktop. There's not a drop been spilled."

"Someone helpful came along: 'Hey, let me hold that for you.' Someone she trusted enough to pass over stuff that didn't belong to her, stuff she'd been entrusted with."

"Someone she knew."

"Or someone with status. Someone in uniform. A cop. A priest. A meter maid. Or someone with a different kind of credibility: a local gang leader."

"There isn't a lot of gang activity in this area. We think it was someone she knew. We're going with that."

"And the paranoid lady from MIT?"

"She was sitting on the first bench on the right. She was the only person in the park."

"The only one?"

"There's no shade for those benches until the sun comes around behind the trees in the afternoon. It's not a place where most people would want to hang out. On a day like today, anyone with any sense was home or at the mall—somewhere with air-conditioning."

"How do we know she was sitting there?"

"Because she was sitting there before Danielle disappeared and she was sitting there afterward. She'll take up station there for a couple of months, then she'll disappear. We don't think she had anything to do with the kidnapping. As far as we can tell, she's just a harmless crazy."

"Psychotic person," I corrected her.

"Anyway, she never attacked anyone. She's been committed to the Methodist a few times, but more because she wasn't looking after herself. There's no criminal record."

"But she could have scared Danielle."

I considered the edge of the park that was formed by Eastern Boulevard. The police had strung yellow tape to prevent vehicles from parking, but a couple remained from earlier in the morning, a Jeep at the curb level with the bench, and a blue subcompact farther down.

"If the bag lady spooked her, Danielle might have detoured to avoid her. She'd have gone off the path, closer to Eastern Boulevard where that Jeep is parked."

Brenda looked in the direction I was pointing. "Maybe." She sounded skeptical.

We went back inside. Though there was no air-conditioning, it was a relief to come out of the sun, and the oscillating fan that stood on the desk of Nan, the receptionist-cum-bouncer, stirred the air in the crowded lobby.

I had no taste for a confrontation with the cops waiting there, and I was looking down to avoid eye contact, so I didn't see the rushing approach of Danielle's mother.

"Is this the profiler?" she asked Brenda.

"This is Sasha McNeely," Brenda said. "Danielle's mother."

"I'm Doctor Lucas," I told her. "I'm not a profiler—"

"You're Abby's husband, though."

"Yes, I am. And I'm going to help the police any way I can to get Danielle back to you."

I looked down into Sasha's pleading, tear-stained face. She was in her mid-twenties, but within her plump face I could still glimpse the child, adrift, dependent, overwhelmed. Sasha had been one of Abby's girls, a client of the social work agency since she was a pregnant teen.

Sasha had grasped one of my hands. Abby was approaching, and I hoped she'd head off what was developing into a difficult scene.

"These are pictures of my Danielle." She thrust photos into my hand. "This one—look—was taken this summer."

It showed Danielle in a two-piece bathing suit, her hair wet from the garden hose in the background and stuck in strands to the side of her head: hand on hip, she hammed for the camera with what she imagined to be a supermodel pout.

"You'll find her, won't you, Doctor?"

A fresh onslaught of sobbing contorted her face.

"Yes," I said. "I'm sure we will."

I tried to extract my hand, but she'd tightened her grip, and then before I realized what she was doing, she tumbled clumsily to her knees.

Around us, the lobby had fallen silent. I couldn't get Sasha to her feet. I felt, but couldn't see, the cynical looks of cops. I crouched to bring my face to Sasha's.

"You'll find her, won't you, Doctor?" she pleaded.

"Yes," I promised her. "I'll find Danielle." I squeezed her hands in reassurance. "The police are good at this," I lied. And then I said, in expiation for my helplessness, "We'll do everything."

11:45 A.M.

Brenda had her hand on the back of my arm, propelling me up the stairs. Abby had handed Sasha off to another social worker and was running to catch up.

"We need a description of the kidnapper," Brenda told me. "Man/woman, age, height, clothes they wore—anything. We need the make and model of the vehicle. Assuming there was one."

"You have nothing?" I asked. "Nothing at all?"

"I can pull in twenty cops—like that." She snapped her fingers. "Get me something, Paul. Give me something to work with."

We turned the corner of the stairs and paused on the landing. A uniformed cop stood before the door to Abby's office.

"She's psychotic?" I asked Abby.

"She's as paranoid as we've ever seen her. She'll probably have to be hospitalized."

"But not right now," Brenda put in quickly. "Please, Abby."

She hesitated. "No, of course not."

"Do we know what her delusional system is?" I asked.

"It's all connected with her work at MIT. She seems to think her program was making chemical warfare agents. When she decompensates she calls up the police and the TV stations. Then she thinks the CIA and FBI are after her because she's blown the whistle."

"So she sees the police as allies or persecutors?" I asked.

"Right now, she sees everyone as against her," Abby said. "Even us."

"I really appreciate this, Paul," Brenda said. "I don't want to pressure you, and I know you have to work at your own pace, win trust and so on, but we're really up against it timewise."

"They're in my office," Abby said.

"They?"

Brenda took a deep breath. "Detective Dempsey's running the investigation." She brought her hands up in a gesture of helplessness, or it could have been acceptance of fate. "You're just going to have to deal with that as best you can."

Carol Dempsey had been in charge of the murder investigation of her colleague Lou Francone. The police had come within a whisker of arresting me, then shelved the case. As far as Detective Dempsey was concerned, I'd gotten away with murder.

I said, "I want her out of there."

"Can't do it," Brenda said. "This is a police investigation. We appreciate your help, we really do, but this is her show."

"You want me to interview someone with paranoid schizophrenia, who's already convinced the police are messing with her, in the presence of one of the most belligerent officers on the force?"

"Detective Dempsey isn't happy about the situation, either."

Abby's office was paneled in PVC fake wood from the 1960s, but she'd done her best to overcome this dispiriting background by covering much of it with paintings by children from the day care program and a fringed shawl from one of our trips to Oaxaca. Her desk in the right far corner from the door was piled with client files and paperwork. Seated at the desk, with the swivel chair tilted back to its fullest extent, was Carol Dempsey.

When you met Detective Dempsey for the first time, you had the feeling that you weren't entirely registering with her—a deceptive impression, because she was as astute an observer as I'd seen. She conveyed a world-weary indifference, as though countless encounters with bad people had worn her down, but worn her down to a hard, abrasive core that would take something off you if you pushed on her. She was in her mid-forties and her body was compact and hard, a physical presence that she was capable of using to convey a nuanced menace. Her hair was still a smoky blond, but she was wearing it shorter than when she had interrogated me less than a year ago.

The rotating fan by the window seemed to be blowing heated air in from the street, and Dempsey had been fanning herself with a manila client folder, the movement arrested as she caught sight of me standing in the doorway. Her face assumed an expression of truculent resignation as she turned away.

I'd visited Abby here a dozen times, but now I looked over the space with a professional eye. It was a large room, and that would help to prevent the paranoid woman now sitting on the corner of the sofa from feeling crowded. But the coffee table, the scatter of chairs around the sofa, the child's blackboard, and the stuffed animals cluttered escape routes.

Martha Kinnard sat bolt upright on the edge of the sofa. She was a woman in her early forties, though she looked ten years older, with tanned, windburned skin and hollows beneath her cheekbones showing a substantial degree of emaciation. A rough-cut fringe of her straight, graying hair protruded below a woolen cap. In spite of the heat, she appeared to be wearing two skirts as well as a khaki fatigue jacket, with layers beneath these that bulked her up and confounded any estimate of her true size.

She sat on the very edge of the sofa, her body arranged neatly—boots side by side, knees together, the hands in her lap disappearing into sleeves, elbows tucked in, gaze forward focused on the middle distance—so that every part of her was easily accounted for and protected.

She had avoided looking at me when I came in, but blinked repeatedly as she suppressed the automatic tendency of her eyes to fixate on the new object that had entered the space. She didn't want to betray interest, fear, hope, curiosity—anything that could be used against her. But during the first moments, when I talked briefly with Detective Dempsey, I glanced occasionally in her direction to sample her response and saw her eyes come swiftly up to me, linger on my face in an abnormally long fixation, then dart away, then return jerkily, wide-eyed and fearful.

These eye movements told of her disorganized perception. Her brain processing was too disrupted to make a sweeping, coordinated survey of her environment. Instead, her understanding of the scene was put together like a collage, each glance a fragment that was never entirely integrated with its predecessor, so that the picture her brain assembled contained gaps—blank, uncharacterized areas of vulnerability to be filled in with material extemporized from the worst-case scenario.

This was the person whose trust I had to win. The greater her fear, the more she'd fragment, with the shards of perception breaking into smaller and smaller pieces.

I seemed to have entered at a point of impasse. Any interview between Detective Dempsey and Martha Kinnard was destined to be one long impasse, a silent struggle interrupted by words.

I nodded to them both and introduced myself.

"I know who you are," Dempsey said in a tone of disdain.

An excellent response. Martha would take note of a hostile attitude that marked me as the detective's enemy. In the first exchange, Dempsey had bestowed on me a credential of sorts.

"If you're in the middle of something . . . ," I told Dempsey. I made a diffident, indecisive gesture of seeking permission.

"Be my guest," Dempsey said.

"The reason I want to make sure you're done," I told her, "is once I begin, I'm not going to appreciate being interrupted."

She made a shoveling movement of her open hand in Martha's direction, then resumed fanning herself indolently. Head down, she flipped pages of her notebook. I hoped that meant she'd stay out of my way.

Apart from a couple of quick glances, I'd avoided looking at Martha. Paranoid people feel transparent, as though others can see into their minds, so I wanted Martha to take a measure of me before the stressing moment when I turned my scrutiny on her.

I took a seat in the chair that made a diagonal with

the sofa, far enough not to impinge on her confused personal boundaries, but close enough for any discussion to have a sense of intimacy. I sat at an angle to her so that I could see her out of the corner of my eye without looking directly at her, and the two of us faced in approximately the same direction, outward, into open space, toward the common enemy. Detective Dempsey sat with her back to the window, the only source of light; Martha and I were both illuminated, our faces easily read, whereas Dempsey's face was in shadow, lowering and liable to misinterpretation.

It was going perfectly.

Now that I was close to her I noticed tiny movements of her lips, opening and closing as though in whispered speech, and I knew that she was hallucinating and that I would be one voice among several vying for her attention.

"I wanted to thank you," I said quietly, leaning forward, staring at the beige rug, park bench-style, four feet in front of me, "for helping us." I was feeling my way, hoping to find some point on which we could ally, whether it was saving the world from chemical weapons or a young girl from her abductor. "I'm sure there were several people who saw what you did. But you had the courage to come forward."

"Courage!" she scoffed. "That's not what it's about!"

I retreated into the impersonal, advertising my ignorance, my inability to see into minds. "I can't know what motivates people to do what they do. All I know is that you care about the world and the people in it. Enough to take a risk."

"What do you know about it?"

It wasn't an entirely rhetorical question. She stared at me, not with a suspicious glance that presupposed the worst, but with an appraising look of curiosity. I had the possibility of becoming a person, of being lifted out of the mass of *them*.

"I know some of the difficulties you've had in getting people to listen to you." I was searching for that small area where her reality and mine intersected. "It's been hard to get the bureaucrats to pay attention. The media are distracted by their own terrorist obsessions—"

"While there's an even greater threat right on our doorstep!"

I nodded agreement and let her go.

"No one's listening!"

For several minutes—precious time that I had to re-assure myself I wasn't squandering—my only action was to make sure she knew I was listening. It was a psychotic, disorganized rant against the agencies that persecuted her.

The CIA was reading her thoughts; her thoughts were being broadcast so that she was denied even the privacy of her own mind; some elements of the government believed that terrorists might tap into her thoughts to make weapons of mass destruction; she was afraid—here she dropped her voice and several times cast glances in the direction of Detective Dempsey—that extremists in law enforcement might take the law into their own hands and eliminate her as a threat.

As I listened, poised at that point of intersection of our worlds, I couldn't help but respect the enormous courage of this woman. Within her delusional world she risked her life on a daily basis; she underwent the most exquisite psychological torture to save the lives of a community of people who held her in contempt. You could say, clinically speaking, that her delusions were massively entrenched, rigidly held, proof against reason.

Or you could say that alone, reviled, against all odds, she kept the faith.

"Have you considered a sanctuary?" I asked. "A safe place where you can rest and regroup?"

She let her head loll as she briefly contemplated the luxury of such a line of thought. "But who can I trust?"

Her words contained a plea. She longed to come in from the cold world of suspicion. She would have liked to trust me.

"It's hard," I agreed. "It's hard to tell. The authorities—"

"Forget it!"

I aligned myself quickly with her mistrust. "A uniform. A badge. It doesn't mean anything."

"They come out of cereal boxes. A badge is no guarantee."

"It all comes down to the individual," I agreed.

She threw her head back and gave a bitter little laugh.

"You've been had before," I suggested.

"Oh yes."

"But you're not ready to write off the entire human race. Or you wouldn't be here. Trying to help. Ready to do your part."

She watched me stealthily, giving nothing away.

"There was a young girl taken this morning," I said. "She was in the park. Now we don't know where she is."

She cut me off with a hand raised like a traffic cop. "Don't think you can tug on my heartstrings."

But I thought I could. I said, "It was only her name I was going to say." She had turned away from me to protect herself from the humanity that was coming at her like the warm air from a grate on a wintry night. "Danielle."

She flared, paranoia and anger together. "Stop!" She

clutched her head to hold her thoughts together, to squeeze my influence out of her brain. "You think you can control me. You can't! You can't!"

I'd pushed too hard too fast. For several moments I lost Martha to the other voices. Detective Dempsey shifted in her seat restlessly. I cast her a warning glance.

When I looked back, Martha was staring at me with an unwavering gaze. I was a mannequin onto which she projected her delusional fears.

"There's something going on," I began, plunging recklessly into her delusional world. "I don't entirely know what it is." I held out a hand to forestall her. "I know you think I do, but I don't. Sure, I have some ideas. There's a war going on. Who knows who the terrorists are? Who knows what the government is really up to?"

Her expression changed at this. But I still hadn't declared where my loyalties lay, and she waited to see which way I'd go. One of us had to step across the line, and she wasn't going to join me in my reality.

"There are things you know," I said. "I don't need to know what they are. The main thing is that you feel you're in danger."

"I don't 'feel' it. It's not something I feel."

I'd feinted as though I were crossing the line, but delusional people are sticklers. They won't be bought off by lawyerly formulations. Not "seems"—"*is*." They demand that you commit.

For the first time, she looked directly into my eyes, as someone does who wants to convince the other person of what she's saying. She said, "I am being stalked by people from government agencies. They . . ." She looked away, shaking her head at the futility of trying to make me believe. "I know how it sounds."

"Yes. It sounds paranoid."

"It *sounds* paranoid," she agreed readily, eagerly. This is the wonder of paranoia: It *sounds* paranoid. "But . . ."

"But you live it."

She puffed her cheeks and blew off air in a derisory skepticism. "Every crazy person wheeling a shopping cart talks about government agencies, the CIA—all that conspiracy crap."

"In your case, though, it happens to be true."

Martha blinked, but otherwise she didn't give away her surprise at what I'd just acknowledged. I'd gotten it, finally. I'd crossed the line.

The only dissonant note came from the desk by the window, where Detective Dempsey noisily tossed the pages of her notebook, one at a time, ticking off seconds like a clock.

"It's a question of faith," I said. "It comes down to what you believe in. You've seen things I haven't seen. You know things I don't know."

"It's not just a question of what I see. Everybody knows what's going on. You can't shirk responsibility by laying it all on me."

I leaned forward reflectively, with my hands between my knees. I avoided looking at her and spoke into nothingness, rather like the astronomers who transmit mathematical symbols into deep space in case intelligent life exists out there.

"When no one believes you, and what you know is a matter of life and death, you're alone with this terrible knowledge."

"They're going to destroy the world. They're manufacturing weapons of mass destruction. Right here. In Cambridge. The chemistry's diabolical. Do you know—"

She was interrupted by a rhetorical sigh from Detective Dempsey. We'd forgotten about her, and her insertion into the flow of mistrust and disclosure only increased the general level of suspicion.

"They're everywhere," Martha said.

"There's a threat to the world," I said, to bring her back. "You're trying to save us."

"I'm the threat!"

"You?"

"I carry it inside me. Enough poison to kill the planet. They've altered my cells. I'm a walking biological warfare lab. They want to activate me. Sometimes I don't eat for a week because I know they're trying to infiltrate the substrate into my diet. If they do that I'll start producing."

"But they let you walk around? More or less freely?"

"Oh, yes," she said with bitter sarcasm, shaking her head at my naïveté. "Sure they do."

"Do they have some means to control you?"

"I'm like a cow at pasture: The cow goes into the pasture and eats the grass; then they bring the cow back to the barn and squeeze the milk out of its teats. Do they have to control the cow so that it eats the grass? Do they have to control the cow so that she chews the cud? Do they have to control the cow so she makes the milk?" When I didn't answer, she demanded, "Well, do they?"

"I guess not."

"I guess they don't!" she said with rising anger. "Don't you see? Milk is the product of a biochemical system. But it's good. It gives kids strong bones. I'm a biochemical system. I've been hijacked. They want to control my brain. But they don't need to. They just need to know where I am and what I'm eating."

"They watch you."

"They have spies. A system of spies. That's why I

like to sit in the park over there, where I can see people come and go."

"Why don't you get to the point, Doctor?" Dempsey said.

We ignored her. Our two agendas were becoming one.

"How can you tell?" I asked Martha. "People look like ordinary people . . . But really, they're spies."

"Exactly!"

Detective Dempsey shifted noisily in her seat. Evidently, she was uneasy with my alliance with the party of paranoia. "Whatever moves you've got," she said, "make them now. Because a little girl's running out of time. And, frankly, I'm running out of patience with this psychobabble."

Martha stared at her. "There's a look in their eyes," she said.

I looked hard at Detective Dempsey's face, too. "Yes," I said. "I think I know what you mean."

"After a while, it gets so you can recognize them at a glance."

"And there are regulars, I suppose. People you see coming and going in the park."

"I keep track of all of them."

That got Dempsey's attention.

"Did you keep track of the girl who was abducted?" Dempsey asked. I glared at Dempsey, and our eyes locked. I was going to tell her that I wouldn't be here if she hadn't already blown her chance, if the DA hadn't asked me, as a personal favor, to see what I could salvage from her fuckup. I was choosing my words when she looked away.

When I turned back to Martha, she was still staring at

the detective. She looked frightened, and I saw I'd have to work to get her back.

"People disappear all the time," she said.

Her eyes darted to my face—seemingly a casual gesture—but I knew she was checking me for complicity with the cop. She had granted me a provisional acceptance that she could rescind in an instant. She played me every bit as carefully as I played her. Even the stakes—a life, hers or Danielle's—were the same.

"People disappear all the time," I said. "But no one notices. No one's paying attention."

She weighed this. I had no illusions that she viewed me as a friend. She had no allies. There were none to be had.

I pushed forward gently. "But you notice," I said.

"Sometimes."

"Because you're paying attention."

"Sometimes."

"Always."

I'd gone too fast into areas I didn't understand, and Martha balked.

She snorted. "How can I pay attention all the time? How can I?" she asked plaintively. She sighed with exasperation and despair. "I can't be expected to save everyone on the planet!" She held her hands clenched, fists braced against the task that was being pushed toward her. "I can't be everywhere at once! I can't!"

I heard Detective Dempsey shift and prayed she wouldn't misread what was happening.

"It's too much," I agreed quietly.

"It's impossible!"

She'd turned her face, and in the shadow I couldn't make out whether the glints in her eyes were tears.

"You've been asked to do too much," I said gently.

The future of the human race rested on this frail, rejected woman's shoulders. It was crazy, of course, the idea that she must save the world, but at that moment the question of delusion versus reality seemed like an irrelevant detail as I momentarily entered her world and saw Martha's mission through her eyes. When you understand the purpose of the paranoid's life, the goal to which all her waking energy is directed, you are awed.

I said, almost in a whisper, as if I might disappear and become another voice within her head, "It's too much to do alone."

For the first time in the interview, she nodded in agreement. She hung her head. She was exhausted by her lonely struggle. She had the fortitude to go on alone, but the presence of another walking beside her weakened her.

"You were watching," I began again. "You chose a place where you had a clear view of people around you. A place in the park where you could take note of vehicles that hung around for no clear reason."

She was watching me as much as listening to what I said. I was on the right track.

"From that bench, you'd see the regulars come and go. You'd be able to spot newcomers."

"Correct."

"One of the regulars was a girl—I'm not going to say her name—eight years old, who came back carrying a tray of coffee from Doosy's."

"Three coffees: two large, one medium. And something like a Danish or a coffee roll."

"That's the person I'm thinking of."

"You call her a person."

"She seems just like an eight-year-old girl."

"She could take the path that leads straight from the

corner by the traffic light to the crossing by Doosy's. It's the most direct route, but she doesn't take it. She does the same thing on the way back."

I nodded with the puzzlement of partial understanding.

When I didn't show any sign of getting it, Martha said, "She goes around behind me. As though I wouldn't see her!"

"What do you make of that?"

"Isn't it obvious?"

It was a test. "It's open to a number of interpretations," I said.

"It is—" she paused for added sarcastic effect "—open to a number of interpretations. But there's a reason—one specific reason—she behaves the way she does."

"She's been sent to monitor you," I supplied, like a bright student who had learned his lesson: the world through Martha's eyes.

She looked at me levelly. Perhaps there was even a hint of approval in her eyes.

"Because there was uncertainty about what the girl—apparently—was about, I would think you'd track her fairly carefully."

"I did."

Dempsey's chair creaked.

"You saw her when she came out of Doosy's, carrying the coffee."

"Correct."

"She crossed at the crosswalk as usual, came up the path, then made her detour. But even though she was behind you, you still tracked her."

"I have ways of tracking people. I have to."

"Of course." I hoped the method wouldn't be something psychotic, like telepathy or monitoring the radar properties of their brain waves.

"I have a way of turning so that it seems I'm looking for something in my cart—nothing sudden, I just turn as though I've thought of something I need and I rummage a bit."

"And out of the corner of your eye . . ."

"I can see what's going on behind me."

I cast a quick, warning glance in Dempsey's direction, but I needn't have worried, because for the only time, Detective Dempsey and I were in tune. She sat forward in her seat, motionless, pen poised over the notebook whose flapping pages had been such an annoyance to me. In the silence, I became conscious of the whirring of the fan by the window as it rotated back and forth.

We strained telepathically to force an answer from Martha. *And then?* we urged silently. *And then?*

Outside the window, a truck rumbled by. A car horn sounded impatiently down the street.

"She disappeared," Martha said.

I was stunned. "How do you mean?" How could we have come all this way to arrive back at our starting point? "How do you mean, 'disappeared'?"

"She was gone," Martha said quietly.

Dempsey exploded. "Why have I been listening to this crap?" She threw the useless notebook on the desk. "There's a little girl out there with some pedophile breathing over her. She goes behind your back for two seconds. And you lose track of her?"

I shouldn't have worried about Martha. Dempsey's diatribe was like a wave breaking over a rock.

"You can't even make it as a paranoid!"

She thrust the notebook into a pocket and got up to leave.

"Hold it," I told her. "We're not done yet."

I would have been happy to see her walk out the door, except that I owed Brenda Gorn. I saw her lips begin to form the delivery of "Fuck you!" Then she thought better of it and let herself fall back into the chair.

"All right, Doctor. Convince me."

But I didn't have time to bring Dempsey up to speed.

"There was a gap," I suggested to Martha, trying to pick up the loose end. "You're pretty good at this, tracking people. You do it all day, every day, so you know exactly where the gap was: the gap between the girl—let's just call her that—leaving your sight as she turned off the path, and your looking back out of the corner of your eye and finding her gone."

"She did a loop around behind me, on the grass. Always the same. She disappeared at the furthest point of that loop."

"Where the loop came closest to Eastern Boulevard on the other side of the park? Is that right?"

"That would be correct."

She was right there with me, connecting the dots. I knew this because her eyes weren't staring, but tracking back and forth on short saccades that are typical of multimodal thinking.

"So it's possible," I suggested, "that the girl was picked up by one of the vehicles that were parked on that stretch of Eastern Boulevard."

"Correct."

"It's not a long stretch of road, because she wasn't out of your sight for long."

"No more than four vehicles."

"And which one would she have gotten into?"

"The van."

"How would you know?"

"Because of the space where it had been."

"Had you seen it before?"

"A couple of times."

"How would you know you'd seen that particular van before?"

"Because I keep track of the surveillance vehicles by their license plates."

1:00 P.M.

I was squeezed in the back of the state police cruiser between Brenda Gorn and Detective Dempsey. There wasn't any point in fighting the centrifugal forces as we took corners at high speed, tires squealing, siren wailing, blue lights flashing, and it made for an intimate ride as our bodies pressed against each other, now one way, then thrown the other.

When Dempsey's cell phone chirped somewhere deep between us, we struggled apart in order to avoid unnecessary contact as she retrieved it.

"Detective Dempsey," she said, clipped and harsh, as if to deter the caller; then, checking, with sudden gentleness, "No, nothing as yet."

I recognized the voice of Sasha McNeely, overflowing with anxiety in a rush of words I couldn't make out.

"I'll let you know as soon as we have anything. Anything. Anything at all." She had nothing to give Danielle's mother, but she listened patiently for the pleading voice to run down, nodding with eyes closed in inward concentration, speaking the words a mother might use to soothe a frightened child. "I promise," she said, almost whispering. "I promise."

When she opened her eyes at the end of the call, her face had a stricken look. With a decisive snap, she closed the phone, and when she turned to slide it into her pocket, she gave me a savage glance, warning me to make no use of the vulnerability I had witnessed.

All the while, the grizzled lieutenant in the front seat yelled orders into a handset, marshaling a SWAT team, sealing the neighboring streets, summoning a forensics unit. It sounded grim. If we found Danielle alive we'd need a professional to take care of her. Hence Abby in the following car.

I was something of an afterthought, too.

"I don't want you to say anything," Brenda had cautioned me as we flashed by other cars on the highway.

Dempsey had turned to glare out the window with an intent, hungry expression that took in no detail of the passing landscape. She was readying herself for the interrogation of the driver of the van, a forced entry more stealthy than the SWAT team's, but every bit as ruthless.

"Don't even introduce yourself," Brenda said.

Dempsey muttered something under her breath about fifth wheels.

"If you've got something to say, Detective," Brenda told her, "let's hear it out loud."

"This is a police investigation," she said, eyes front, as if she were addressing the back of the lieutenant's head. "With respect, I just don't think we need him."

"We wouldn't have this license plate if it weren't for Dr. Lucas."

"If it is a license plate."

"As of now it's the best lead we've got."

"Unless it turns out to be a bunch of numbers the bag lady pulled out of the air. If this is some crazy bullshit—" She paused as we were squeezed against her as the car hurtled around the exit ramp at eighty. Her body was tight and unyielding against my arm. "If this is some crazy bullshit the good doctor's manipulated out of his patient and we're wasting time on a wild-goose chase, while Danielle . . ."

Even the battle-hardened Detective Dempsey didn't want to specify what might be happening to Danielle at this moment. Pointedly, Brenda turned to look back to see if the cruiser carrying Abby was still behind us. Abby embodied our hope that Danielle would be found alive. Damaged, yes: we could accept that. As long as she were alive.

"Let's focus on what we've got."

Martha had given us the description of eight vehicles parked along the side of the park where Danielle had disappeared. Four had not been moved before the police arrived. Of the remainder, one was an open-top Jeep: not a likely vehicle for an abduction, but the police were tracking it down. One was a small sedan registered to a woman who lived nearby and had already been eliminated. Detective Wolpert, Dempsey's partner, was investigating the other sedan. Which left us with the most likely prospect: the van.

"It's registered to Arthur Hodges," Brenda said, reading from the fax sheet in her hand. "And Molly Hodges. He's fifty-nine. Molly's three years older. They have handicapped plates on account of Molly."

I was already spinning out possible scenarios based on these fragments.

"Molly's clean," Brenda went on. "Arthur has a misdemeanor on his CORI printout from fifteen years ago. An open and gross."

My heart leapt, but I said nothing. This was our man. He had to be.

"Nothing in fifteen years?" Dempsey asked.

"He was caught once," I said. "That's all it takes to tell us what he is."

"Open and gross could be anything," Dempsey said. "You could get an open and gross for pissing in the street. Open and gross doesn't mean he's a pervert."

"We'll find out what the offense was," Brenda said. "Can you get on that, Jim?" she asked the lieutenant in the front seat.

"It's just the tip of the iceberg," I insisted. "Your average pedophile assaults over a hundred victims during his career. You only catch them on one or two. People can lie low for decades after their first arrest. They learn from the experience. They get smarter. They take their stuff abroad. They go on vacations to places where no one cares."

"Anyway," Brenda said, "the open and gross was dismissed."

The lieutenant turned to hand Brenda another sheet of paper that had just printed out. We had slowed somewhat to thread our way through suburban traffic. I noticed the driver had turned the siren off to avoid giving warning of our approach. We passed a small shopping mall and edged our way through a red light.

"Arthur's a retired engineer. Molly's his wife. She's crippled with arthritis. The van's equipped with a wheelchair lift. Their house is paid off. No civil suits. Good credit rating. No children."

We turned off the main road and entered a maze of

streets with ranches and garrisons each standing on the minimum quarter-acre. The neighborhood was well kept up, with neat lawns, foundation plantings trimmed, few trees, and hoops above garage doors. When we came to Pond Meadow Drive, the driver turned off the flashing lights and we slowed to the speed limit.

As we cleared the development, the road deteriorated and we passed wooded lots with homes of an older vintage set back from the street. It was a secluded neighborhood of houses with detached garages, spaced out of earshot and out of sight from one another.

At the next corner we pulled up alongside an unmarked van and the lieutenant exchanged some words with the leader of the SWAT team. Opposite, the canine unit handler emerged from an SUV with his dog. A helicopter clattered a half-mile away. It could have been monitoring traffic on Route 128, except that rush hour was long gone.

"You got all your paperwork, Brenda?" the lieutenant asked.

"Let's go," she said.

The SWAT team van took off. We surged around the corner behind them and raced down the gravel driveway, but even before we had pulled up in front of the Hodges' house a dozen figures in black, helmeted and goggled, were surrounding the comfortable ranch with its attached garage, poised with machine pistols and shotguns at entrances and windows. There was no van in the driveway.

Brenda was out of the car before it had fully stopped. I had to run to catch up with her. When we reached the front door, half of the SWAT team had disappeared to the sides and back for simultaneous entry.

The lieutenant nodded to Brenda. "Good to go."

With all this firepower assembled, it seemed incongruous that she'd ring the doorbell. The officer standing next to the door shifted his grip on the sledgehammer expectantly. The officer with the shotgun heard something and stepped back. A dead bolt was drawn back, another lock clicked open, and the door opened a foot.

"Police," Brenda announced.

The door opened slowly to reveal a grandfatherly, bewildered man who looked past Brenda at the vehicles jamming his driveway, at the dog, at the black-suited paramilitary hefting a sledgehammer, at me, finally focusing on Brenda standing in front of him.

"Arthur Hodges?" Brenda demanded.

"What is this?" he asked fearfully. He had more questions, but Brenda cut him off.

"Are you Arthur Francis Hodges?"

"Yes. But—"

"This is a search warrant."

She thrust the paper at his chest so forcefully that he took a step back. The two burly SWAT team officers pressed through the gap in the door, and he was unable to get out of their way quickly enough as they brushed him aside.

All portals to the Hodges home opened at once. I saw shapes moving rapidly from the back door; two crossed the hall; the garage door flew open; at the rear, the steel bulkhead doors clattered open. I paused before crossing the threshold behind Dempsey and Brenda to see that a maroon van sat in the garage. It was not a family kind of van, more like a modified delivery van, with double doors opening at the side for the wheelchair lift, and no windows except at the front. As I turned to enter the house, two officers from forensics hefting tool kits ran up the driveway heading for the vehicle.

I closed the front door against the summer heat. Inside, the house was in tumult with the noise of doors being thrust open and furniture being shifted that came from every corner of the structure.

The air-conditioning was turned up high, and there was a clean smell of pine deodorant. The home was spotless. The oak floor of the hall reflected like a mirror. At the end of the hall I could see into the kitchen, where an officer crouched to examine the vegetable drawers of the refrigerator: above, neat rows of ketchup, pickles, and two kinds of milk were lined up, eggs neatly slotted in the door's top row. Everything in its place, and tucked away.

And not a lot of things. The furniture was sparse. Nothing—no newspaper, for example—was lying around. One disparate element was on the kitchen floor: a bucket of water with a sponge. Someone had been cleaning.

At any moment during the first ten seconds since we'd entered the Hodges house I hoped to hear someone call—from the back bedroom, the cellar, the garage— "We've got her!" But there was only the garble of radios, the curt exchanges of orders given and acknowledged.

I turned right off the hall into the living room. A woman's touch was evident here, different from the hall and kitchen, which were designed according to a more austere functionality. Lace drapes veiled the windows that looked onto the front yard. Both the couch and the upholstered rocking chair—the kind that swings back and forth without moving on the floor—were hemmed like dresses and filled with embroidered cushions. A sampler on the wall read MOTHER KNOWS BEST. There were other homey maxims, too, held by a straw doll on the wall; on the mantel a china clown sadly embraced a faithful dog; a miniature broom had another uplifting message attached. The whole effect was of a sentimentalized, faux-country look. Only a stern Oriental mask on the wall over the TV, carved from jungle hardwood, lent a discordant note.

As I entered, Arthur Hodges turned off the TV, and in the sudden silence, all eyes turned to me.

"And who is this one?" asked the lady in the wheelchair.

Molly Hodges was happy to see me. She grinned in childlike pleasure, and I could detect only the most minimal sign of unease—a slight asymmetry in the draw of her lips, less crinkling of the lower eyelids than would be expected from the expanse of her smile—and these could easily be overlooked. She was brightly made up and her hair newly permed in tight Shirley Temple curls. Like many people with a long-standing, dwindling illness, she looked preserved, as though, sheltered from the stresses of earning a living, she had fewer miles on her than the rest of us.

The hands that rested on the arms of the wheelchair showed the deformity of arthritis: knuckles like knots of trees, fingers deflected laterally. She pressed down to raise herself to shift to a more comfortable position, and the smile momentarily disappeared, to reappear even more brightly once the pain of her movement dissolved. We were visitors, important visitors, and she exhibited a shallow pleasure in our company that was at odds with the purpose of our sudden appearance.

I didn't answer her question in the hope that Dempsey, who would be happy to keep me out of it, would fudge it. I hadn't expected to be part of the process.

"Dr. Lucas is our consultant," Brenda said.

"What kind of doctor, if you don't mind my asking?" Arthur Hodges inquired.

"A physician," I said.

"A real doctor." Molly exhaled in deep satisfaction. Here was a man capable of truly appreciating her in all her medical complexity.

For Arthur, I added, "A psychiatrist."

"He's the profiler," Arthur Hodges said. "Am I right?" He winked at me in a mock-conspiratorial way, as if we two would keep some unacknowledged implication from his invalid wife. "We watch all that stuff on Court TV."

"Kind of," I admitted, with the same complicit smile.

Dempsey hadn't explained why we were here. As far as Arthur knew, we could have been searching for a drug dealer's stash of cocaine. But cops didn't take profilers along on drug busts.

And he'd scarcely glanced at the search warrant.

But this wasn't where the action was. We were filling time. We were corralling the suspects in their living room while the cops went through the house. We were waiting for the triumphant cry of discovery.

But it was difficult to imagine a less likely pair of suspects than these two. I was beginning to get a queasy feeling. Brenda avoided my eye. I ran over the interview with Martha to see if I'd followed her to the point we'd arrived at, or whether I'd led her.

Arthur wanted to talk. He was a big, comfortable man in a green polo shirt with an insignia, a pair of gold clubs, over the left breast. He was slightly overweight and balding, and his out-of-style glasses gave him the appearance of a kindly owl. If he had committed a crime, he was the kind of fellow you'd have difficulty picking out of a lineup. First, because you'd have difficulty remembering him. Second, because he didn't look like anybody's idea of a pedophile. Especially one who'd abduct an eight-year-old girl. He didn't look capable of hurting people, much less murdering a child. Not that his appearance made the slightest difference to me. I'd seen men who looked just like Arthur, after sentencing.

But Brenda was uneasy. Appearances did count. Her eyes passed around that comfy living room and took in the fussy décor and the case of glass tchotchkes—I noticed a Thai dancing figure among the porcelain figures—the lace and the frills. And here was poor, dear Molly in the wheelchair who couldn't hurt a fly. Had she been his accomplice, with those excruciating fingers gripping the van's handicap controls, ready to burn rubber for a quick getaway?

Dempsey didn't have her usual bite, either. She asked Arthur, "Did you drive your vehicle today?"

The more often a suspect repeats a lie, the better he gets at telling it. The first time he tells the lie, he may not have been able to foresee the implications, to calculate possible contradictions with what the interrogators already know, or to decide on the emotional shading and gestural display that should accompany the words. The first time, he's simultaneously both creating and performing. But from then on, he only has to speak the lines that he's rehearsed. He's seen how questioners react to his lie. He lies more fluently, more confidently.

That's why interrogators want to interview a suspect before he has a chance to practice. That's why a virgin lie, a lie that's about to be told for the first time, is so precious.

With Dempsey's first question, I pretended not to hear Molly's distracting attempts to engage me around her medical history.

I focused on Arthur's face, his hands, his posture, his feet, for the telltale signs. He had to know a witness had put his vehicle in the vicinity of Doosy's, or we wouldn't be here talking to him. But even if he answered this first question truthfully, if he was our man, he'd feel like he was lying to us, because now the heat was on him and this was when he had to begin to deceive.

Arthur's hand went to his face. It wasn't the masking gesture typical of liars, in which the whole palm with aligned fingers wipes the upper lip and mouth and sweeps off the chin. But it was enough: the head twisted down and to the right as the left thumb came up and swept the outside of the nostril in a downward motion. It was scarcely more than a touch. But it punctuated the answer to what should have been a simple question. "Yes" or "No" were too short to need punctuation.

"Did I drive my vehicle today?" Arthur asked himself aloud.

Liars repeat the question they've been asked because they're overloaded and they need more time. When it comes to the interrogation, the big one, they think they're ready and they're not: when it comes time to nail the virgin lie to the wall, they get performance anxiety.

"As a matter of fact, yes. I did drive my vehicle today."

And because of his stage fright, the answer came out stiff and formal. Not the colloquial, "Yes, I did." Or even the simple—and perfectly adequate—"Yes." Instead, the filler: "As a matter of fact," followed by the stilted "I did," as if he were already on the witness stand. "The witness stoutly denied . . ."

But when cops burst into your home and shoot questions at you, innocent people get stage fright, too.

From the other side of the wall—the bedroom—came the sound of a heavy object falling to the floor.

"Oh, my!" Molly wailed. "Arthur, can't you do something?"

"They have the judge's order, Moll."

"At least see what that was that went over."

"We're talking about the van in the garage, right?" Dempsey asked. She was covering all the bases, but she was finicky, and this would interrupt the flow of questioning.

"Right," Arthur replied.

The single syllable came drawn out and smooth, slightly breathy, patronizing. He, too, sensed the interrogator's anxiety, and it made him calm. Arthur was doing more than answering a question; Arthur wanted to show how calm he was. And not just that: the little smile on his lips was to show how calm he was compared to Dempsey, the hard-bitten state cop. I was beginning to sense another side of Arthur: he had a competitive edge, the kind of man who, if he got the upper hand, liked to rub it in.

"Where did you drive it today?"

He hesitated half a second. It couldn't be the hesitation of a liar forced to improvise on the spot, because if Arthur had abducted Danielle, he'd have rehearsed this answer twenty times. The pause was the tee under the golf ball: Arthur was going to knock the cover off the detective's questions. I saw a smug smile below cold eyes.

He said, "We went for a ride, Molly and me."

"Together?"

"Didn't I just say that?"

"You went for a drive together?"

His lips compressed in irritation, then relaxed. He sighed to show how tolerant he could be, making a show of submission to the detective. "Right. Together."

This was his alibi, the ace of trumps that should have whisked him clean out of the investigation, but he had to see that it wasn't going over with Dempsey. Her tough stare never softened.

"Where?" she demanded.

He turned to his wife. Little, crippled, heroic Molly was the alibi. A tough witness to shake. Brenda was sizing her up now. She would not relish the gruesome work of breaking her as she sat before the jury in her wheelchair. And going up against spunky Molly was Martha, memorizer of surveillance vehicles, certified crazy.

"Where did we go, Moll?" Arthur spoke in the tone of voice that people use when they're cueing a child to perform a cute trick.

Molly drew herself up in the wheelchair. "We like to go to East Cambridge. That's where we both grew up. We went to school together, you know, Arthur and me." She gave us a fond smile, with a coquettish glance in my direction. "We were high school sweethearts."

"The old neighborhood," Arthur said. "We've done well—"

"Yes, we have," Molly confirmed.

"But we still like to revisit—"

"Where did you go in East Cambridge?"

It was okay if Molly interrupted Arthur, because she was part of the script, and so it wasn't really an interruption, but Arthur didn't like being cut off by a female cop. He gave Dempsey an uneasy smile.

"All over the place," he said.

"We stopped for coffee at Doosy's," Molly offered helpfully, and stopped short on a glance from Arthur.

I supposed this piece of information was to have made its debut further along in the script. Molly could be gabby, evidently.

Dempsey took this shortcut in stride. "What time were you at Doosy's?" she asked.

"Heck, I don't know." Arthur spread his hands in a gesture of frustrated helpfulness. "Who keeps track of these things? We're retired. I am, anyway—"

"Approximately. About what time did you visit Doosy's donut shop?"

Arthur turned to consult his wife. "What do you say, Molly? Nine? Nine-thirty?"

"We've been going to Doosy's for forty years," Molly said. "It's a local tradition."

"What time would you say you visited Doosy's today, ma'am?"

"Well, I don't really know. You see, I rely so much on Arthur. What time do you think we were there, Arthur?"

"I'd have to say nine, nine-thirty. Does that square with the time you have, Officer?"

Dempsey was jotting in her notebook. She asked, without looking up, "Where did you park when you went for coffee at Doosy's?"

"You see?" Arthur looked around the group for someone to bear witness. For some reason, he chose me as a likely sympathetic audience. "She doesn't give away a thing. You ask a question and I give you an answer. I ask a question and I get a question back."

"We'll answer your questions in due course," Dempsey said.

"That's okay. I know how you people think."

"How's that?"

"How's what?"

"What you just said."

Arthur smiled in polite embarrassment, not understanding what was going wrong. "What did I just say?" He looked to me again, but found no answer in my face. He shrugged to let it go.

Dempsey, anyway, was only listening to Arthur with one ear; with the other she followed the other cops as they went about their noisy search, anticipating the dreadful moment when they suddenly fell silent.

"Hey—what's this about, anyway?" Arthur asked.

He might have just started to wake up to his predicament. A man waking up to his possible predicament. The search warrant had been flapping in his hand for several minutes.

He looked from one to the other of us. When no one made a move to answer his question, he gave a nervous laugh that came out like a cough. It was proficient. Either Arthur was guilty of nothing more than being parked in the wrong place at the wrong time, or he was very good indeed.

"You come in my house, turn it upside down—what are you looking for? It's just me and my wife here. What do you want?"

"We're looking for a girl named Danielle McNeely."

"Well—" Molly made a chuckling sound, half incredulity and half protest. "There's no one here by that name!"

I saw Arthur's gaze go over my shoulder in the direction of the garage from where there came the high-pitched sound of forensics vacuuming the van. Inaudible, unless you listened carefully.

"Maybe not, ma'am. But we have to be sure," Brenda told her.

But Arthur's thoughts were with the van. "What are they doing in there?" He nodded, indicating the garage.

"They're checking the vehicle," Dempsey informed him. "It's all there in your hand, in the warrant."

"But they're not, like, going to dismantle it, are they?"

"Not my van!" Molly said, raising her splayed fingers in distress.

"We're totally dependent on that van," Arthur said. "I wouldn't want you to think that any judge's order gives you the right to take our van apart."

"They're not about to do that," Dempsey said gently, softening for the first time. "We just have to check it out. That's all."

"Why don't we all sit down and have a cup of tea?" Molly suggested brightly. "Arthur, why don't you make some tea for our guests."

"Thank you, no." Dempsey consulted her notebook. "So where did you park?"

"Do you know Dracone Park?" Arthur asked.

"I'm familiar with it."

In his long-winded way, Arthur told us how he had parked in a location that matched Martha's description.

"But, you know, you still haven't told us what this is all about." He held up his hand to quickly cut us off. "And if you can't, just say so. We understand."

"Ongoing police investigations," Molly said smugly. "We know all about that."

Dempsey handed off for Brenda, the lawyer, to decide how much to tell them.

I had thought that Molly was merely providing her husband with an alibi. But what if she had been in the van with him at Dracone Park? What if Molly and Arthur were in it together? I'd seen it before: the perpetrator and the enabler. And some of the enablers had been, on the face of it, pretty unlikely. These were women who'd kept themselves in the dark as to what exactly they were helping their men do. They possessed the strange ability to stop thought short of the crucial implication, to prevent the mind's twitch that connects the dots.

"A little girl's missing," Brenda said, "and we have reason to believe you can help us in our investigations."

Dempsey's eyes were fixed on Arthur's face. But as Brenda told them about the case, I watched Molly's expression.

"She's eight years old," Brenda said, turning to Molly.

"Oh, my!"

It was a sigh more than an exclamation. Molly was, she implied, a person well acquainted with pain and loss, and offered up the quiet, full words of the silent sufferer. Arthur nodded with pursed lips. He could do no better than to chorus his wife, the perfect front.

"So young!" Molly said. Then, as was her habit of mind when confronted by nastiness, she was struck by a happier thought. "Maybe she's playing at a friend's."

"We've excluded that possibility."

"Maybe she's lost . . ." She suddenly found her happy ending. "She's lost! That's what it is. She'll turn up in her own good time!"

"She's been abducted," Brenda said firmly.

Molly was puzzled. "Abducted?" The word left a bad taste in her mouth. She frowned as if concentrating, as if trying to summon the implications of the term.

"Kidnapped," Arthur supplied.

"Oh, dear!"

She appeared to remain troubled by the notion, even slightly confused. Her head was tilted down, but I could see her eyes, and contrary to the look of a confused person, they scanned rapidly back and forth: Molly was thinking hard. She wasn't stumped by "abducted"; she was updating in the light of anomalous information. The quick eye movements were the equivalent of the green light that indicates the computer's hard drive is active. Molly was searching memory, processing, comparing, resolving conflicts. Whatever Arthur had done, Molly didn't know. She may have been willing to give him an alibi, but she wasn't part of it.

Arthur had practiced long for this moment—his whole

lifetime, perhaps. He avoided eye contact with everyone else by focusing on his wife. He had no need to mask by touching his face, and he kept his thumbs hooked into the front of his belt. He remained still. I was discouraged by how quickly he was adapting to the role of suspect.

"But," Molly tried weakly, "how can you be sure?"

She was stalling. Whatever arrangement she'd had with Arthur—if she'd had any formal agreement—she didn't know what she'd do now that the stakes had been revealed. She looked to me, the doctor who could assuage her pain, not to one of the two women who could answer her question. I saw fear in her eyes.

No one answered her question. It wasn't in the prosecutor's interest to tell what her witnesses had seen. The detective didn't want to show her hand. The silence sat like a weight, compressing the air in the room.

She appealed once more to me. "Can't you tell me, Doctor?"

"I wish I could," I told her, smiling my regrets.

Arthur, of course, came to her rescue. "They can't, Molly. You know that. It's prosecutorial privilege. They can't reveal their sources."

"No," Molly said, as if talking to herself. She shifted carefully in her wheelchair, and a grimace of pain crossed her face and was gone in an instant. "Course not."

Eventually Dempsey said, "We're doing a vehicle check."

"That's why you're looking at the van," Arthur said, but no one responded to the implied question.

"But why us?" Molly asked.

"Your van was placed at the scene of the abduction this morning."

"Placed?"

Once more, I saw fear in her eyes, quickly veiled by pain as she shifted in her seat. I wondered if pain induced by movement was a deliberate device she used to hide her emotional expressions.

"Well," Arthur said, "we were there. Dracone Park. If that's the area Danielle disappeared from." He turned to his wife. "It's okay, Moll. It's all routine. They have to check us out. Nothing to be alarmed about." He appealed to us to back him up, to save this sick woman from the anxiety that it really wasn't necessary for her to endure. "Right, guys?"

I saw Brenda exchange a look with the detective: they were of one, unsettled, unconvinced mind. Mild, comfortable Arthur and immobile Molly made a very unlikely pair of child abductors.

"This is a picture of Danielle," Dempsey said.

She handed Arthur the sheet of paper with Danielle's blown-up school picture. He studied it carefully, frowning, shaking his head. "Lovely girl," he said, handing it back to the detective rather than passing it to his wife. "Too bad."

Dempsey started to give the picture to Molly, but when she didn't reach for it, she came around to Molly's side so that she could hold it for her. Molly was slightly turned away and I didn't think the others were in a position to see that she barely glanced at it. During the several seconds that Dempsey held the paper before her, her eyes were mostly turned down, away from the girl's smiling face, toward the bottom left-hand corner of the paper.

"Did you see anyone like this, Mrs. Hodges?"

Instead of answering, Molly shook her head.

"She's eight years old. She was wearing a T-shirt, pink, with a bear on it, and denim pants, and pink and white sneakers."

Molly shook her head at each item on the list. "No," she said quietly, "we didn't see anyone." She was about to elaborate on not seeing anyone, but Arthur spoke.

"I wish we had." He waited for a further question, but no one asked one. "I wish we could have been more helpful."

Dempsey asked Molly, "What time did you return here?"

"Time . . ." Molly opened her hands to show time, like sand, running through them. "It's not something I attend to much."

"It would be ten-thirty, eleven," Arthur said. "Could have been eleven-fifteen."

"Would any of your neighbors have noticed you coming back from Cambridge? The people in the house across the street, maybe?"

A look passed between husband and wife.

"I think not," Arthur said slowly, with a show of reluctance. "She's a single mom."

"Divorced," Molly put in. "Her kids are with their dad—"

"While she straightens her life out."

Arthur made an expansive gesture of live and let live.

"She's in a program," Molly whispered conspiratorially.

"Anyway," Arthur said to change the topic. "There's nobody home, if you know what I mean."

"Did you go out again today?"

"No. I was working on the van."

"What were you doing?"

Arthur was in his element. The engine was misfiring, he told us, and he noticed he'd been losing power on hills. He made eye contact with everyone in the room in turn, even Molly, as if he were making a presentation.

So he changed the spark plugs. But that didn't do it. So he noodled around with the air filter.

He was gabby, usually a disaster for a liar, but here he was on safe ground. Sure, it would have been quicker to take it to a garage and have a computer diagnose the problem. "But I'm an engineer by trade, you know, and I miss that stuff."

"What kind?"

The hands he waved in front of him were pristine, even down to the nails.

"A chemical engineer. I used to do a lot of work on plants making synthetic materials from hydrocarbons in India, Thailand, Indonesia, that kind of thing."

"You changed the spark plugs."

"Then I cleaned the van."

Brenda, Dempsey, and I scrupulously avoided eye contact.

Dempsey paused to gauge the precise angle of her question, to tune her voice to just the right nuance of casual menace. "Why did you do that?"

"Arthur's meticulous," Molly said. "If you knew him, it would be obvious to you."

"I clean the van inside and out once a week."

"Every week," Molly said, nodding her head for emphasis. "Every week that van gets a cleaning from top to bottom. And I mean, a cleaning!" She smiled proudly to each one of us in turn. "Arthur's a fanatic."

1:45 P.M.

We reconvened in the ops van parked at the curb outside the Hodges' home. The front of the cargo compartment was filled with communications equipment, which crackled into life at odd moments. The rest of the space was taken up with five swivel seats around a narrow table. The air-conditioning was blasting.

"All right," Brenda said when the three of us were assembled. "What have we got?"

The claustrophobic space felt like a pressure cooker in which emotion was intensified to a point close to explosion. It wasn't difficult to guess how Dempsey felt. Scowling, she had stomped out of the house without a word to either of us. Now she sat hunched forward over the table, hands clasped before her.

"What we've got," she said, "is a wild-goose chase."

"It doesn't look too good," Brenda agreed.

"Right. It doesn't look too good," Dempsey agreed sarcastically. "So the sooner we get back on track, the better."

"Wait a minute," I said. "You believe this guy?"

"Yes," Dempsey said in the same tone. "Unless forensics found a body in the van."

"Hold on," I protested. "There are half a dozen behavioral indicators that say he's a liar."

"Oh, please!"

Brenda, at least, appeared willing to hear me out. She held up her hand for Dempsey to stay quiet.

"He has an alibi, Paul," she said kindly, as though breaking bad news about Santa.

Dempsey was less kind. "Doctor—how can I explain this to you?—this isn't one of those touchy-feeling things that maybe kind of is and maybe kind of isn't. It doesn't matter how you see it."

"But didn't you see the way he had everything pat, ready to go?" I asked. "He was waiting for us."

Their professional, impassive faces stared back at me, unconvinced, unsympathetic even, to this line of evidence. Seeing was believing, but they weren't willing even to look. And believing was seeing: you had to be already halfway there to notice what I saw.

"We're wasting time," Dempsey prompted Brenda, as though reminding her of a forgotten appointment.

"Paul," Brenda began hesitantly, "I appreciate your help, I really do, but this is a whole different kind of workup, if you will—"

The passenger door opened and the forensics tech climbed in.

"The van's clean," she said.

"How clean is 'clean'?" Dempsey demanded.

"Very clean. Like, pristine."

"There you go," I said.

Dempsey's face was screwed up in annoyance. "There you go, *what*?" She was close to losing it. She wanted to lose it.

"He cleaned the van," I said. It seemed obvious enough to me. "He scrubbed it down."

"Right," Dempsey agreed. "He's a neatnik. Did you see that house he lives in? It's pristine, too. So what? Cleanliness is a crime?"

"Okay. But this is a guy who cleans his van on the day a girl's abducted."

"Okay, we'll pull them all in. All those guys who cleaned their vans today."

"But this guy cleans his van on the day he changes the spark plugs and the air filter. That's messy stuff."

"So he cleans first, then does the tuneup."

"I don't know," Brenda said. She was trying to let me down lightly. Maybe she was regretting calling me in on the case. "It makes sense from a psychological point of view, what you're saying. But we can't go on that. What we need is hard evidence. Something a jury can relate to."

"What else?" Dempsey asked the forensics tech. "Give me something. What else have you got?"

"Nothing."

"But you can't know that until you have your samples analyzed," Brenda said.

The tech looked uneasily to Dempsey for support. She was young, eager, and efficient, and it seemed that the DA wasn't liking what she heard. "We don't have any samples," she said. "There wasn't anything. Nothing we could bag, anyway. No clothes, no hairs, no paper, no stains."

"No coffee spills?" I asked, thinking of Danielle's errand.

"We looked for those," the tech said coldly, as if to say, "Don't tell me how to do my job."

She continued her report to the detective. "We vacuumed. Maybe we'll get some hair in the bag that we didn't see. But there's nothing big."

"That's good, then," I said. "No torn clothing. No blood."

"Maybe," Brenda said. "Even if he did it, he's not going to kill her in his own van."

"What about fingerprints?" Dempsey asked.

"We don't have anything much there, either. Just two sets of adult prints. We'll check them against the owners."

"What did he use to clean the van with?" I asked the forensics tech.

"Looks like a bleach solution." She answered to Dempsey, as if she was the one who'd asked the question.

I looked from one to the other for a reaction. I was tired of setting myself up for Dempsey to shoot me down. Eventually, I asked, "That doesn't strike you as odd?"

"How so, Paul?" Brenda asked. She was patient, but she couldn't entirely exclude the effort it cost her. I could see in her eyes that she thought I'd dragged her down a dead end.

"Bleach denatures protein," I told them. "Bleach breaks down biological material and body fluids so they're unrecognizable. Bleach degrades DNA. It's very good for all these things. But it's not your first choice as a cleaner, except to clean your toilet."

My hygiene lecture wasn't going over well. The forensics tech stared at me with a puzzled frown. Dempsey professed boredom. She didn't need to push—my credibility was toppling all by itself.

"You wouldn't clean your van with bleach. You'd use soap. But you'd use bleach if you wanted to cover your tracks. That's why—and we're dealing with a neatnik here, an expert cleaner—that's why it strikes me as odd."

They said nothing. They were done with me, even Brenda, but I went on anyway.

"Another thing," I said. "There was no computer in the house. Everybody has a computer. Everybody's hooked up to the Internet."

Still no response. They were waiting me out.

"The guy's an engineer," I insisted. "And he doesn't have a computer in his home? Doesn't that strike you as peculiar?"

"Doctor, I'll tell you what strikes *me* as peculiar. I think it's peculiar we get a license plate number from a lady that's certifiably crazy and on the say-so of your patient—"

"She's not my patient."

"On the say-so of this schizo bag lady, we shoot all the way out to Waltham—helicopter, SWAT team, the works. Meanwhile, a little girl who's been kidnapped is still being held as a prisoner somewhere and it's ninety degrees and a hundred percent humidity, and we don't know if she has anything to drink, and we're here psychoanalyzing some respectable citizen with a solid alibi. Now, that's what strikes me as peculiar. In fact, I think it's fucking nuts!"

This time, Brenda did nothing to restrain her.

"Do you mind if I take a look inside the van?" I asked the technician.

She deferred to Dempsey.

"What are you going to do in there, Doctor? Channeling?"

"I don't know. I want to get a feel for Mr. Hodges."

"Move on," Dempsey said. "It's a dead end."

"But do you mind if I check out the vehicle? It's nothing to you, right? What I do?"

"What do you say?" she asked Brenda. "Do we have any urgent need for Dr. Lucas right now?"

"You follow up with the other leads we discussed,"

Brenda told her. "He and his wife can come back with me."

When I left the ops van I saw that the other police vehicles were pulling out. The assault team was long gone, and the clatter of the helicopter no longer filled the sky above.

The overhead door to the Hodges' garage was open, and the last of the forensics team emerged carrying toolboxes. I found Abby drinking iced tea in one of the cruisers.

When I opened the door she read the disappointment in my face. She climbed out and we strolled up the driveway, passing the iced tea back and forth between us. It tasted like nectar, the cool astringency washing away the aggravation that I'd accumulated in the van with Detective Dempsey.

"Nothing at all?" she asked.

"He has an alibi."

"Who?"

"His wife says he was with her all day."

"Well, we know that doesn't mean much." Abby had a glint in her eyes as she proffered me the waxed-paper cup of iced tea. "I'll give you an alibi any time you need it."

"And I'd do the same for you."

As our eyes met, Abby smiled. She didn't have to explain the joke: an expert on deception, I was not only pathologically honest but a hopelessly incompetent liar. It was a moment of unspoken understanding that we enjoyed too seldom.

"Let's hope it never comes to that," she said, "or we'll both be in big trouble."

"I'll drink to that."

Small moments like these gave me hope that we

might salvage our relationship. For a while, it seemed that the crisis of the murder investigation had brought us closer as we faced a common danger, but then we'd sunk into a routine in which we only saw each other at the end of the day. Then, exhausted, almost too tired to talk, we sat down to an improvised dinner. The agency took up much of Abby's time. I'd gotten precious research money to begin a new project on changes in brain blood flow during lying. The weekend became a time to catch up on paperwork.

These were excuses, of course. Our busyness disguised the hollow center of our marriage. This was the space our son, Adrian, had filled—that he'd overflowed. A child's death leaves a wound that never heals—we knew that—but our loss was harder because we couldn't comfort each other. Abby was dealing with it in therapy. It seemed interminable. She couldn't share with me how much we both missed Adrian—nothing more than the occasional, unelaborated remark— precisely because this was what she was talking about in therapy. As her emotional life moved off limits, Abby's interior world grew more and more opaque to me. In moments of stark candor, I wondered if I really knew her at all.

Suddenly, standing in the driveway, Abby said, "I want to do something for his birthday."

"I do, too," I said.

In six days it would be Adrian's fourth birthday, and this was the first we were talking of it.

"I just don't know how to do it."

"I know," I said. "Is it like a birthday party? Or a memorial?"

"I don't want it to be either. I was thinking we could plant something. A tree, maybe."

"Yes," I agreed doubtfully. I was afraid to put a foot wrong.

"You don't think so?"

"Yes, it's certainly an idea. A good idea. I just think we should consider all the things we could do to celebrate his life."

It was impossible to suffer the emotions that welled up while we stood in the driveway of a suspected child abductor, and yet the moment was too rare to pass up.

"But you don't like the idea of the tree?" Her tone had sharpened.

She waited me out.

"I don't know," I said. "What if it died?"

We looked away, breaking contact. This place was contaminated. Arthur would already have noted our sharing of the iced tea. I wanted to pull Abby back, but I couldn't take her hand in view of those lace-draped windows.

"What did you think of Hodges?" she asked.

"He's lying. He got shifty around stuff that shouldn't have bothered a man who'd spent the morning cruising around the old neighborhood with his wife. The problem is, the signs are subtle."

"Brenda didn't buy it?"

"She's under a lot of pressure. The cops have to come up with a suspect."

We'd come to the garage and stepped inside. We circled the van in opposite directions, stealthily, as if it might be a sleeping elephant. I didn't know what I was looking for. It was a perfectly ordinary van, a dark red, nondescript van of the type that countless small businesses used—florists to make deliveries, workshops on wheels for plumbers and electricians—except that there was no logo on the side, no white vinyl pipe containers, no racks for ladders. And no windows except up front. Usual and customary in a business vehicle, but odd in a family van. Beneath the sliding side door, the body of the vehicle had been cut away to accommodate the shiny steel floor of a wheelchair lift. Had he posed in this opening in one of his wife's wheelchairs, I wondered, asking for help from the helpful girl carrying the coffee? "Here, honey, let me hold those while you . . ." Was that how he'd lured her into the darkness of the windowless van?

"Help yourself," said a voice behind me.

I didn't know how long Arthur Hodges had been watching us from the back of the garage. I knew he hadn't been there when we'd entered. He stood on the top of the stairs from the kitchen. He'd opened the door silently, then taken a step, then closed the door. It gave me a creepy feeling that he'd closed the door. He was smiling, enjoying the moment of power over us.

"Go ahead," he invited me, gesturing toward the van. "Everyone else has."

When I hesitated, he came down the three stairs to my level to point out the features.

"This hoist can handle three hundred pounds," he told me. He chuckled. "Not that Molly needs that kind of muscle. She comes in at a hundred and ten. Not an ounce more than she weighed on her wedding day."

I was staring at the blank wall of the van's side, and Arthur answered a question that hadn't been asked.

"No windows, you see, because Molly's agoraphobic. Matter of fact, if she had it her way, she'd never leave the house. But she has to, to go to doctors' appointments and so on. That's why I put in the sound insulation. So now she doesn't have to see the big outside world, and she doesn't have to hear it." He pressed a remote I hadn't

seen in his hand and the door swung out and back, and
the deck of the wheelchair hoist descended. "Check it
out," he said proudly. "It's like a cocoon inside there."

Although Abby had come into view a couple of seconds before, Arthur pretended he hadn't noticed her until now.

"And who's this lovely young lady?" he asked. "This
is your assistant?"

"This is Abby Lucas, who's the director of New Beginnings, the agency the missing girl is from."

"Danielle," Abby supplied.

But Arthur might not have heard. He waggled a questioning finger from Abby to me and back again, inviting
me to fill the gap. "And . . ."

Reluctantly, I volunteered, "I'm her husband."

"Same name. But you never can tell. I've been caught
out before, jumping to conclusions." He laughed. "Hey,
you could be his daughter, right?" He laughed some
more. "Am I right?"

"I don't think so," Abby said.

"Lucky guy," he told me.

When the child abductor took Abby's hand, when he
made contact, skin to skin, with my wife, I felt an urge
to kill him.

"Go ahead, hop in the cocoon," he told Abby. "Try
it out."

Aren't cocoons what spiders hole up in?" Abby
asked once we were safely in the back of the
cruiser. She shuddered beside me.

Brenda sat morosely on the other side of Abby, head
down, staring at the back of the seat before her. Arthur
Hodges hadn't been the quick break in the case that she
needed. She said, "There's a lot of creepy guys out there.
We have to find the right one."

"What else have you got?" I asked her.

"Nothing specific. We have police officers going
house to house, working out from the park a block at a
time." She made a gesture, it could have been of futility.
"Any known associates. The usual things."

This wasn't like Brenda. She was a fighter. Arthur
had really taken the wind out of her sails. No wonder he
was so pleased when he encountered us in the garage.
He'd done a snow job on the DA, and the forensics team
had left with nothing but a vacuum bag of dust.

"What about Paul's analysis of the interview?" Abby
asked. "Don't you think that gives us something?"

Brenda paused to choose her words carefully. "I have

the greatest respect for Paul's work. I mean that sincerely. For close-in work, when we're pretty sure we've got the guy who did it, no one's better. This is different, though. We can't go on intuition," Brenda sighed. "It just doesn't work."

"But what about your own experience?" she asked. "I only spent two minutes with the guy and I have the strongest feeling he's the one."

"We can't arrest someone on creepy feelings."

"But you felt the same way about him, too?"

"Sure. So what? I have to be back at my office for a press conference at two-thirty. A girl is missing. Every TV station in New England will be there with a camcorder and a reporter shouting out questions. I can't stand up in front of them and tell them about my creepy feelings. I need a suspect."

I didn't envy her predicament. The press would be cautious and supportive today. Tomorrow, they'd be more aggressive. The next day, they'd be out for blood.

"If it's all the same to you," I suggested, "I think it would be worthwhile talking to Martha again."

"Sure." Brenda shrugged. Her mind had moved on to other matters, things that might make a difference. "Can't hurt." Already, she was rehearsing the press conference.

The police didn't want Martha disappearing into the anonymous crowd of homeless people sleeping under the bridges of Storrow Drive, or riding a bus to San Francisco, or getting admitted to some hospital that they didn't know about—just in case, against Detective Dempsey's better instincts, she turned out to have information that was material to their investigation. So they'd arranged to have her committed for observation to the Harvard teaching hospital, the New England Methodist, where I was on staff.

The psychiatric unit at the Methodist was on the eighth floor of the Cavanaugh Pavilion. As I waited for the nurse to buzz open the door, I admired the spectacular view of Boston, the water of the harbor glinting through gaps between high-rises of the financial district. The unit was a far cry from the Sanders Institute. For the most part, the patients at the Methodist were depressed elderly ladies and students from local colleges who'd made suicide attempts—hardly a clientele likely to bust out or stage a riot.

I stopped at the nursing station and leaned over the counter to ask Rose Schiff, the nurse manager, where I'd find Martha Kinnard. I was hoping to do an end run around the red tape.

"She's in the dayroom," Rose told me. She was going to let it go, but then thought better of it. "You know," she said, "you might want to check first with her attending."

"Who is that?"

"Dr. O'Donnell."

She watched my face as my heart sank.

"Good luck," Rose murmured as I turned to go.

It was common knowledge that Judy O'Donnell and I didn't get along, though we put on a courteous, professional front when we encountered each other. Not that Judy would admit, even to her most intimate confidant, that she harbored mean thoughts. Judy was sweetness and light, which made it all the more aggravating to dislike her. But in academe, where truth is widely believed to be relative to one's point of view, nothing creates animus so much as being proved blatantly, publicly wrong. And Judy's error was as big as it gets. Her Pollyanna assessment of a mutual patient resulted in three people almost getting killed. I had been one of them.

Judy, however, was irrepressible. Sure, she'd slipped off the television screens for a few months; she wasn't sought by news show producers for a quote on the latest spree killing; but she soon reinvented herself as the practitioner of alternative treatments, the reasoned and scientific advocate of a nebulous spirituality, wellness, and healing. She was right for the part: eyes twinkling with kindly sincerity behind wire-framed glasses, Judy was an almost archetypal figure, someone who resembled the person you might have imagined your grandmother to be in her mid-thirties.

I approached her office with a sense of dread, not because of old history, but because I expected Judy to put every obstacle in the way of my interview. All from the most lofty of principles. Judy, a stickler for the minutest ethical nuance, never herself seemed to encounter such moral impediments. Judy always had the ethical wind at her back.

"Come!" she called when I knocked, without bothering to check the window of her door. "Paul!"

She gave me a smile of excellent quality, as if pleasantly surprised, and waved me to a seat.

"So? What brings you here?"

"I think you know, Judy."

"No, really."

"I came to see Martha Kinnard."

"Martha?" She questioned her memory for an instant. Martha, she implied, was not at the top of her list of priorities. "Of course. But I didn't know she was your patient."

Judy hadn't lost her touch. She'd put me in a nice bind. If I admitted Martha wasn't my patient, for what purpose could I conceivably want to interview her? How would my visit to her here, in a hospital, be therapeutic?

If I said she was, then I owed my allegiance to Martha, not to the police.

"She's not."

"Okay." Judy spread her hands to indicate the gap that needed to be filled with explanation. She leaned forward slightly with an intent look of expectancy.

"You probably know about the girl who's disappeared?"

"Danielle McNeely. Yes."

She settled back. I'd named the stakes. I'd defined the hold she had over me if she really wanted to screw me over. And because everything was confidential, it could never be traced back to her.

"I've been in the ER all morning. That's all anyone's talking about."

"Martha was at the park where Danielle was abducted."

"That must have been very traumatic for her."

"It was even more traumatic for Danielle."

"But you don't know that."

"We may never get a chance to ask her."

"You're not Martha's doctor. So what exactly is your business with her?"

"I want to ask her a few questions."

" 'Nothing but the facts, ma'am'?"

"She could help us find Danielle."

"Which is what we all want."

"All right, then." I shifted as though getting ready to go. When Judy made no reciprocal move, I had to ask, "You don't have any problem, then?"

"On the contrary, I'm very uncomfortable with you seeing her."

"I just want to ask her a few questions, Judy. Where's the harm in that?"

"You sound like a cop."

"Okay, I sound like a cop. We agree. I'm just going to get on with my business. We had a discussion. The discussion was inconclusive. I left your office. You don't know whether I got on the elevator, or what I did."

"I'm not going to look the other way. That's not the way I do things."

I sighed in recognition that this was the truth. "Right."

I paused, concentrating on breathing regularly, and tried to clear my head of the old anger that flooded back. Maybe she wasn't intent on stopping me. If I was lucky, perhaps all she wanted was to torment me for a few minutes.

"Are you going to report back to the police?" she asked.

"Yes. Of course. We have to find the girl."

"But you're not a cop, Paul. You're a psychiatrist."

"I don't care what I am. I just want to get this done."

"I care what you are, though."

"Thank you, Judy."

"You can't switch sides."

"We're not on opposite sides, for Chrissake! We're together on this. We want to save the girl. I have a certain expertise that, right now, the police need. I want to help them. The fact that I'm a doctor is totally irrelevant."

"But if you interview Martha as a patient—and you are a psychiatrist, you are a physician on the staff of this hospital—then what she tells you is confidential."

"Not if she releases me from that."

"How is she going to do that?"

"She's going to say, 'Dr. Lucas, you can talk to the cops.'"

"But that's the problem, isn't it?"

"No, Judy. The problem is that some pedophile somewhere in this city has hold of a little girl named Danielle.
That is the problem."

"The problem is that Martha isn't competent to give
consent."

"Jesus!"

"She's deluded—as you well know."

I imagined Judy kidnapped in a soundproofed van. I
imagined her driven long through the night and de-
posited, bound and disoriented, in a Southern state.

"And she's specifically deluded about law enforcement," Judy was saying. "So it's impossible for her to
give reasoned consent to waive her confidentiality privilege."

"There's got to be a way to cut me some slack."

"You know the procedure. You know what you have
to do. If it's so urgent, get a judge's order."

"Hang around the courthouse, wait for the clerk, wait
on the judge in chambers, argue the need for immediate
action, have Martha hauled down to the courthouse? I
don't have the luxury of doing it by the book."

"I know it's inconvenient."

"I don't have the time."

"A principle's at stake here."

"And there's a bigger principle. This isn't just about
one patient and her rights. There are two people involved. You have to include the bigger picture."

"No, you're wrong there. I don't have to consider society, or the greatest good of the greatest number. I have
a duty to protect my patient."

"Who gave you the privilege to shut yourself up in an
ethical Switzerland and tell the rest of the world to go to
hell?"

"It's not my privilege. The privilege belongs to my patient."

"This is a matter of life and death. We have to cut corners."

"Once you let expediency take over you don't know where it's going to end up."

"It ends here. I have to take care of this piece of business, then it's over."

"You can't trample people's rights. They're precious."

"Judy, I'm not a secret policeman."

"How do you know?"

"This is about a little girl. This isn't political."

"What's political? You think you know. Today, you think you know."

"That's right. Today, I know."

"It's a slippery slope, Paul."

I stretched my head back, eyes closed, and sighed in frustration.

"Then you be the judge," I said. "You sit in with me while I interview Martha. You stop me if I get out of line."

She started the spreading gesture of reluctant refusal, but I put a stop to it.

"You owe me," I told her curtly.

"What?"

"You almost got me killed. You almost got my wife killed. Now you owe me. I'm calling in the marker."

"I don't believe this."

"Believe it."

"What do you think this is? This isn't the Sanders Institute. We don't do things here that you do in prison. We don't have markers. This is the civilized world. We don't keep score here."

I let her talk and sat unmoved, without protest.

She was soon talked out, and when, in the silence, I still didn't answer her, she asked me, "Well?"

"I want you to make amends for what you did," I said. "It's primitive, but it's a very simple ethical notion. You know I'm right. All the argument in the world can't change that."

She was going to come back at me, but changed her mind and looked down.

"I think there's room for compromise," she said.

I waited her out.

She said, "I'll let you interview her, provided I sit in. I'll be the sole judge of what's okay and what's not. If I determine you've crossed the line, you'll move on. Agreed?"

The prospect of Judy refereeing my interview with Martha was about as appealing as having Dempsey sit in, but I knew this was my only shot. The trouble was that the interview I anticipated would close the gap between Martha's delusional world and my own, an interview so compromised that Judy would immediately rule it out of bounds.

"Okay," I lied.

Judy was figuring out angles. "I don't think I want the interview here in this office," she said. "Give me a couple of minutes to set it up."

After Judy left, I mulled stratagems that might neutralize her once we began the interview. Dempsey had defined herself as the enemy; Judy was too astute for that. I needed her out of the room, pure and simple. All I needed was fifteen minutes alone with Martha. In the best of all possible worlds, there'd be an admission and Judy would be called down to the ER.

On an impulse, without a plan formed in my head, I

called the ER and asked to speak to the psychiatry resident on call. It was Waller. I had some vague idea of asking how busy they were, but when I found out Ken Waller was the resident, I felt free to improvise. Waller was in superficial ways an exemplary psychiatrist in training, but he had no intrinsic interest in people; Ken Waller was really interested in molecules and was squandering a psychiatric residency so that he could eventually cash in with Big Pharma.

"Ken? Paul Lucas."

"Hey, what's up?"

"Wanted to give you a heads-up on a possible admission coming your way."

"What's the name?" he asked.

"Well . . ." I hesitated.

"What's the name of the admission?" He was already irritated that I wasn't pumping information to him at his preferred processing speed.

"That's the thing."

"I don't get it." He made this sound like a reflection on me.

"The thing is, this admission can't come in under her real name."

"I see." I was slowing him. This was outside the box; therefore the computational possibilities were infinite.

"This was one of those calls from a friend of a friend. She's actually a borderline from hell."

"The friend, or the patient?"

"The potential patient. She overdoses every six months. Cuts herself sometimes. Gets hospitalized. Usually this is in Los Angeles. Or New York. But right now she's in Boston. Hence the call. You probably know who I'm talking about."

He started to say a name, but I cut him off. "No. This

has to remain anonymous. That's the whole point of my calling you. And this call, by the way, is off the record."

"Sure." He was excited. A celebrity. He'd take a thorough history. It was party chitchat to die for. "Of course."

The best liars maneuver you into telling your own lie. Who better to do this than you yourself? They sketch an outline, and you fill in the blanks. I felt myself warming to this unaccustomed work.

"When she hits the ER, you'll recognize her—and don't take any crap from her just because she's a celeb, okay? The fact that you were humming one of her songs in the shower this morning means nothing to us. Okay?"

"Cool."

"Strictly business."

I heard Judy's voice in the corridor outside the office.

"Admit her under Jane Doe," I advised. "We do this all the time."

"Right."

"And just to cover yourself, you might want to have the attending on call down there when you-know-who arrives."

2:45 P.M.

I went looking for Judy and almost bumped into her as I stepped out of her office.

"We're in the group room," she said. "She's waiting for us."

Now that I'd sent out my decoy, I wanted to get the interview started quickly.

"The group room gives Martha plenty of space," I said as we walked briskly down the corridor. "She won't feel crowded. Plus a big room is harder to bug."

Judy gave me a questioning look. But at that moment, her beeper went off.

She broke step to check the message. "Shoot!"

I watched her calculating whether she could ignore it—a call from the ER, surely not—then whether she could delay it. Finally, she succumbed.

She swerved into the nursing station and grabbed a phone. Judy was one of those people who have the irritating habit of looking you full in the face as they hold a conversation with someone at the other end of the telephone, so either you are in some way part of a conversation you can't hear, or your face is a kind of wallpaper.

"Ken? I'm right in the middle of something." She gave me an eye roll of frustration. "What've you got?" She emitted a series of curt yeses as she acknowledged the high-speed stream of information Ken was emitting. Then she broke eye contact with me and the yeses slowed.

"Really?"

A smile of surprise and soft incredulity began at the corners of her mouth. Her eyes scanned back and forth as Judy appraised possibilities, generated implications. She was going for it.

"You're sure?" she asked. "Holy shit!"

She glanced at me to check if she'd revealed too much of her excitement. Satisfied that she had this celebrity to herself, she turned to hide her expression from me and dropped her voice.

"I'll get started," I told her.

She turned back to me, hand covering the mouthpiece of the phone, pulled in two directions.

"I'll be there in a minute," she said.

She had the phone back to her ear. It wasn't clear whether she was talking to me or to Ken.

Martha spotted me through the window in the door of the group room, but even before I'd touched the door handle, her eyes had shifted to the carpeting in front of her feet. She sat rigidly, knees together, arms folded tightly across her chest. I saw that no one had managed to persuade her out of the several layers of clothing she wore, though it made more sense in the coolness of the hospital's air-conditioning.

The space was circled by chairs from the patients' community meeting that had recently broken up. Martha sat at twelve o'clock from the door. I closed the door and paused to introduce myself, but Martha didn't acknowledge me. I chose a seat two away from her so that we both faced in the same direction, watching the door and those who passed outside in the hallway.

It was quiet in the group room. I heard the distant hum of the air-conditioning fan, the occasional voice that carried from the nursing station. A young man stopped in front of the door and peered curiously through the window. To my surprise, Martha waved him away. There was a certain authority in her gesture, and he at once disappeared from view.

"I thought you'd be back," Martha said.

"Yes," I agreed, though I didn't know her reasons.

"I've been thinking about the girl."

I wasn't about to mention her name, but Martha employed the same abrupt gesture to cut me off that she'd used with effect on the would-be intruder. This wasn't a time for me to talk, anyway. Martha had her own agenda.

She stared intently before her. "I've been thinking about the way she disappeared," she said.

"I'd like to hear what you think," I said quietly.

"I think they're closing in on me."

She spoke as if enunciating a truth that we already recognized, that merely needed stating so that the preceding argument could be seen to follow from it.

"What did you see that concerns you?"

She never looked at me. She stared intently ahead and described in wondrous detail an intricate machine. I would have called it a city park, Corporal Eddy Dracone Park, but soon I was lost in the mechanism that Martha laid out. The cogs in the machine, which she referred to as "elements," were the regulars, zombie figures who in predictable, quotidian ways crossed the triangle of grass and blacktop, or cruised the roads that bordered it, or parked. Everything—everyone—was connected. All moved according to strict rules. There was no free will, much less whimsy or caprice, in the behavior of these robots. To call the coordinated actions a conspiracy would have been to trivialize her predicament. In Martha's vision, Corporal Eddy Dracone Park had become a malignant clockwork toy.

And then there were those who entered the field once, strangers who might or might not be part of the design. Who might be mere "noise," but who could also be new introductions presaging a reprogramming of the mechanism itself. Last of all, and most ominous of all, were departures by the regular elements from their customary trajectories.

"That's what bothers me about the girl element," she told me.

"She disappeared."

"She'd never done that before. She'd always been perfectly regular. Her behavior was suspicious but predictable."

"The van, parked close to where she disappeared?"

She repeated the license plate number from memory. "That may have been around before. But I can't be sure." She was doubled over with the effort of memory, hands clasping her head in distress. "I can't be sure!" She rocked forward and back in the chair with violent thrusts, as if her thoughts were stuck far back in her head, like ketchup that needed a smack at the bottom of the bottle, and had to be jarred loose. She was anguished by her inability to reach a conclusion. "I can't be sure."

"It isn't possible to track everything," I said. "We're not machines. It's beyond our human capacities."

"That's not it. I used to be able to think and now I can't." She turned to address me for the first time. "I used to have a good mind!"

"Part of the problem is, you've been distracted. So much of your time is taken up with monitoring your surroundings, maintaining safety. It's not what your mind was made for."

She was trying to read me. Maybe she was trying to determine whether I was a robot. Or worse, a fully human man who was lying to her. She realized she couldn't do it—she wasn't able to read trustworthiness from people's faces—and gave up and looked away.

I would have liked to continue working Martha gradually toward the abduction, but I couldn't count on the interview continuing much longer. At any moment, Judy would realize she'd been had and would come storming off the elevator. Martha had chosen a seat that put her in line of sight with the indicator lights above the elevator, allowing her early warning of approaching visitors, and by sitting by her I'd afforded myself the same view.

"What about the other elements?" I asked her. "Were any of them acting strangely?"

"The one who tried to get me to eat donuts didn't smoke his cigarettes."

"He offered you donuts?"

"I didn't want them anyway. I wasn't about to eat his filthy donuts."

"He wanted something."

"Of course. He wanted me out of the park. I'm bad for business. That's what he said." She scoffed at the transparency of his excuse. "They think everyone's a fool."

I thought she'd disturbed some neighborhood drug

dealer. Except that bribing with donuts wasn't their method of dealing with people who got in the way. "What kind of business was he in?"

"He's from the donut shop. Doosy's."

"He's the manager of Doosy's?"

"No. He just works there. He's a young kid."

"That is strange. Someone who works in the donut shop offers you donuts to go somewhere else?"

I found I'd assumed the same stance as Martha: leaning forward, elbows on thighs, hands clasped before me, staring ahead. When I turned to her I found her watching me with new interest. I was catching on.

"When was this?"

"A week ago."

"Where did he want you to go?"

"He didn't care. He just wanted me to eat his donuts. 'Take these,' he said, 'and go someplace else. You're bad for business.' "

I didn't want her to get sidetracked into what transformations the donuts were to work on her body, and I went on quickly. "And then today, this same element changed his routine."

"He goes on break after the morning rush. Everyone gets their coffee and donuts on the way to work, and then it quiets down, and this element goes on break. If it's not raining, he goes to the same seat in the park and smokes two cigarettes."

"But not today."

"I think they're going to replace him. I think they know, after he tried to palm the donuts off on me, that I'm on to him, because he never smoked his cigarettes and he never came back from break. Maybe that's what happened with the girl, too. Maybe she's being replaced."

3:00 P.M.

As I hurried past the nursing station on my way out, Rose called to me, "Dr. O'Donnell asked if you'd wait a moment so she could speak to you."

"Rose, I wish I had a moment."

"She's on her way up from the ER."

Rose was giving me fair warning to stay away from the elevators. "Ask her to call me on my cell," I said as the first security door buzzed open for me.

I took the stairs to the fifth floor, then cut across through an orthopedic floor to another bank of elevators, and from there to the parking garage.

It took several tries before I could raise Brenda Gorn on the phone.

"I don't have a whole lot to tell you since we last talked," she said.

"No, I've got something for you."

I described what Martha had said—editing out the paranoia—about the man from Doosy's.

"We asked everyone there if they noticed anything unusual," Brenda said.

"But the cops might not have talked to this guy if he hadn't come back from break."

"Do you have a name for him?"

"No. But you can figure out who he is by the time he takes his cigarette breaks. He's a creature of habit."

"Paul, do me a favor, will you?"

"Sure."

"It's better if you pass this on directly to Detective Dempsey. Then nothing gets lost in transmission."

"She's not going to want to hear it from me."

"I'll ask her to call you. Where are you going to be?"

"I'm heading back to New Beginnings. Abby's taking this pretty hard."

"That's where Carol is."

It took me a moment to remember that this was Detective Dempsey's first name. "All right," I sighed.

The police seemed to have taken over Abby's agency. Instead of Nan, the usual receptionist, a cop demanded some ID from me when I tried to come in the door. The social workers weren't going to get much work done today, and Abby had made several of the offices available to detectives so that they would have a quiet place to interview people. I found her in the lobby and took her aside.

"Do you think this guy taking a cigarette break could be something?" she asked. Her face was tense and drawn.

"It's something," I said. "It's a line of investigation. If he wasn't involved, he was in a good position to see something. Then again, maybe he was involved. He changed his routine. Why did he do that?"

"But do you think that means something?" Her eyes fastened with new hope on my face.

I said, "Martha thinks it was unusual."

Abby nodded sadly.

"No," I said. "Her paranoia works for us. Nothing moves on that patch of dirt without her noticing. The woman's like a hawk."

I wasn't making any headway in my attempt to raise her spirits. She smiled fondly at my gallant effort and brushed my cheek with her fingertips, but it was a moment that had no future in that public place.

"Detective Dempsey's at the donut shop," the cop on the door told me. "She wants you to meet her there."

"Lunch," I promised Abby. "We'll have a late lunch together."

The police had come up with nothing, and now the only thing that looked remotely like a lead was information I'd produced from a witness Dempsey had discarded. The last person she wanted to be one-upped by was the cop killer.

When I crossed the park I saw Dempsey and Wolpert talking to a young man. Whatever Brenda had said to her in the phone call about the importance of hearing from me directly didn't seem to have made much impression, because they'd evidently started without me.

Even so, they appeared to be doing no more than going through the motions. Wolpert didn't look interested in the witness. He turned away to scrutinize a man who'd stopped on the other side of the street, then scanned the cars stopped at the red light, then turned back, head slightly to one side in an attitude of forbearance, to the man they were interviewing.

Wolpert was a big man with a chubby, appealing face, about ten years younger than his partner. He wore chinos and a long-sleeved white shirt with the cuffs turned up to his elbows and stood with his jacket slung over one shoulder hooked on the end of a finger. When you met Wolpert, he seemed like a decent man, the kind of guy you might confide in if you weren't careful.

Dempsey had her back to me, but as Detective Wolpert glanced around he saw me coming and gave her a warning toss of his head. She was expecting me, and she wasn't going to show that my arrival was important enough for her to break off the interview.

I slowed so that I could get a good look at the person they were questioning. He was a gangling young man whom I initially took to be twenty years old, but as I came closer I could see from his face that he was older than that—twenty-seven or twenty-eight, maybe. His emotional immaturity, grasped from a distance, had thrown me off: he had the forward lean, the hungry eye contact, and the exaggerated hand gestures of someone who recognized his difficulty in holding others' attention. He was excited, restless on his feet, distracted by irrelevant motion in his vicinity. As I closed in on them, I could see that he was overly responsive and too eager to please the detectives. Even before I heard him speak, I knew that he'd be impulsive, that his emotions would tend to overshoot, that he'd react first and think later.

He had long, unkempt dark hair and glasses and was dressed in the striped shirt and dark pants of the donut shop uniform. As I joined them I noted a few of the neurological soft signs I'd expected. No single sign was telling in itself, but collectively they hinted at a subtle perturbation of brain development: a couple of facial tics that he largely succeeded in melding with the spontaneous emotional expression of his features; an occasional stammer; nervous laughter that threatened to run away with him; the obliteration of the earlobe's loop, so that the bottom of the ear was joined obliquely to the neck.

Wolpert had been one of my interrogators on the Francone case, and he gave me a silent, sardonic bow. He'd shifted so that his arms were crossed over his jacket, and he made no move to extend his hand.

"This is David Feldman," Dempsey said reluctantly, without bothering to turn to me.

"Dave," he corrected her and shook my hand vigorously.

He went one beat too long, and I noticed an infinitesimal delay in his release of my hand, confirmation of immature frontal lobe function. I was encouraged. He'd be vulnerable in interrogation. There was no reason why Dave wouldn't turn out to be a perfectly adequate liar— he wasn't in any way retarded, and his general intelligence was in the normal range—but he'd have trouble withholding a response when he should remain silent. Given the right provocation, he'd blurt.

He was pleased with the attention he was getting. He looked even more excited when he heard me introduced as "Doctor." He pointed at me as if he'd made a cunning assessment. "You're the one who does the DNA testing," he said, as though I'd been undercover and he'd that moment unmasked me.

When he didn't get the endorsement he expected, he said, pointing again, "You're the—you're the profiler!"

"Kind of," I conceded. I was coming to accept this characterization as a rough approximation of a role I was none too clear on myself.

He gazed at me in admiration. I was the real deal. Suddenly Dave found himself in the middle of a TV cop show, and this was his scene. He was The Witness. Later, there might be other roles for him. And he might not be averse to these—Prime Suspect, Perp, Defendant. I'd seen other limited men in high-profile cases allow themselves to be carried by this narrative momentum, to surrender to a destiny of sorts.

"So when was that?" Dempsey asked him with some irritation, repeating the question that my arrival had displaced. "When did you go on break?"

Dave was very interested in me. He'd rather have been asking me questions than answering Dempsey's, and it took him an effort to reorient to her agenda. He was an uncoordinated, slightly goofy, twenty-eight-year-old kid.

"I don't know," he said. He smiled. He was coy, spinning out the time during which we'd lavish our attention on him.

"Think about it," Wolpert said quietly, evenly.

"Well . . ."

Dave considered. Of course he knew the answer. He always took his cigarette break at the same time. Martha had said so, and that was good enough for me. I wondered, then, why he was playing with us. Maybe he was a lonely guy who simply craved the importance we conferred on him. But serial killers liked the attention of the police, too. They inserted themselves into investigations. They turned up when bodies were discovered. They got their photos taken among bystanders at crime scenes. They couldn't leave well enough alone.

As Wolpert and Dempsey questioned him without much enthusiasm, I looked for signs of anxiety. If Dave was connected to the crime, he should have been worried that the detectives had returned to interview him. But it was difficult to assess, because Dave was in motion a lot of the time, shifting his feet, kicking at the blacktop of the path. He brought his hands up to his face often, touching his nose, picking at his cheek. He had a characteristic mannerism that I thought bore watching

as a marker: As his middle finger closed on the bridge
of his glasses to hoist them farther up his nose, the center of his face contracted, wrinkling his nose and retracting his upper lip in a ticlike snarl.

Like a lot of anxious people, Dave gave more information than was asked for, but he could also have been
more talkative because he was enjoying himself. He was
anxious, I concluded, but he was also excited, and I
didn't like that.

"What's the usual break you take?" Wolpert was asking him.

"Fifteen minutes. That's officially. Usually I stretch it
to twenty. No one says anything. So long as I don't push
it to twenty-five. I'm reliable. I show up first thing in the
morning to open on account of I live near here, and the
manager appreciates that."

"And this morning? How long did you take today?"

He glanced in my direction as if to check whether I'd
caught something. "I had to take care of some personal
business." Then the finger came up to hoist the glasses;
the nose wrinkled and the upper lip curled.

"Okay," Wolpert continued pleasantly, patiently. "You
took care of your personal business. So what time did
you get back to work at the shop?"

"That would be about quarter of ten."

"That's almost an hour, Dave," Dempsey said.

There was the slightest edge of menace in her voice,
and Dave's posture stiffened. His feet stopped moving
and he stood stock-still. He was waiting for the big question that he knew would have to come sooner or later. His
face was calm. His hands stayed down. He was prepared.

"So . . ." She waited, letting the pressure build, lips
pursed, a negligent backhand gesture to indicate the expanse of possibilities. "Where did you go?"

I watched him carefully and made no attempt to conceal it. He glanced at me, and I could tell he didn't like the scrutiny. But I had to see every little twitch in his face. If Dave was implicated, this was the first time he'd been put in the position of having to lie to us. Whatever he told us now, he'd be married to this virgin lie for the rest of his life. If he was implicated.

He was slow in answering. He seemed to want to talk; his lips opened, but the words were jammed up in some neurological gridlock, and his nondominant hemisphere, the stronger half, took over. He reached out a hand, fingers grasping disjointedly at air, a place-keeping, message-to-follow gesture. For someone who isn't a professional interviewer, it was only a delay of two seconds. In my lab, we measure the crook of an eyebrow, a blink, a change in gaze, in milliseconds, and two thousand milliseconds might just as well be two thousand years.

"I went home."

Then came the finger hoist and the tic.

If you weren't looking for it, the mannerism was just noise, just another burst of behavioral static lost among the heavy output of gestures and fidgeting that emanated from Dave in a continuous stream.

I thought I had a working theory now of how the finger hoist and facial tic worked. The mannerism wasn't a marker for anxiety. The important thing was that it came after anxiety. He was anxious before the lie; then Dave lied; then came the release of anxiety. The tic discharged tension like a capacitor discharging the buildup of an electric charge.

Maybe he had gone home. Then, in a flat, literal sense, the answer was true. But if he'd done other things before going home, if he'd abducted the girl, then this partial answer that hid the truth was as deceptive as if he had lied, and his brain and his body would respond as if he'd lied. I was suspicious that there had been an awful lot of neurological grinding of gears for such a sparse output. But on the other hand, just because someone's deceptive when he's asked a question by the cops doesn't mean he's nervous about the crime they're investigating. That may not be his secret at all. Maybe Dave had other things to hide. Maybe he'd had a date with someone's wife. Maybe he'd scored some coke. Maybe he'd gone home to check out some porn on the Internet.

"Where is that, Dave?" Wolpert asked kindly. "Near here, you said?"

"A couple of blocks over." He pointed. "Everett Avenue."

We all turned to look in the direction of the invisible Everett Avenue. It seemed as though we were turning to verify what Dave had told us, because he corrected himself.

"Three." He looked to see what was on my face. "Three blocks."

Cops pay attention when someone changes his story. If he lied to us about this small, insignificant detail, they think, then he'd lie about the crime. I don't buy that myself, but I could see that the detectives' interest had ratcheted up a notch.

"Two, three." Wolpert smoothed away this wrinkle, but in doing so drew more attention to it. "A couple of blocks." As far as he was concerned, he seemed to imply, it wasn't a big deal. "Who's there, at home?"

"My mother."

"That's nice. You come back to a home-cooked meal at the end of the day."

"Yeah."

"Who else?"

"No one. That's it."

"Just you and your mom?"

He nodded. Dave didn't trust his voice. He swallowed hard. His throat was dry, and his prominent Adam's apple rose and seemed to stick before descending.

"And that's why you had to go home unexpectedly during your break?"

"It wasn't unexpected. Sometimes, if things are slow, I take my break and lunch at the same time. Bob, the manager, doesn't mind. It works better for him, because he has a full crew the rest of the day."

"Your mother home during the day?"

"Yeah." He smiled. He'd reached the point he'd been waiting for, the solid step in the welter of questions, the thing he really knew. The rest came out in a rush. "She was right there in the den. She saw me come in. She'll tell you."

It was more than the detectives had asked for, which they duly noted. But there wasn't any further they could go on this line of questioning, and they had to accept his alibi at face value for now.

"So you walked over—where? Across the park? In that direction?"

Dempsey pointed over his shoulder, straight across the park to the spot behind the bench where Martha had sat. But Dave wouldn't turn to look. He didn't actually flinch when Dempsey pointed, but his head tilted as if he expected to be smacked.

"You're not looking, Dave."

"I don't have to. I know where you mean."

"Okay. Which way did you walk home, then?"

Dave gestured limply toward the corner nearest New

Beginnings. It made sense if he was heading for Everett Avenue. If he'd taken that route he'd have walked along the path right in front of Martha Kinnard.

"What did you see?"

"I didn't see nothing."

"You had your eyes shut when you walked home? You weren't looking when you stepped off the curb?"

"I didn't mean that."

"Okay. You saw something, then."

"I saw where I was going. But not . . ."

They waited for him to fall into the hole that had that instant opened before him. But they should have been more patient.

"But not what?" Dempsey asked. And she should have left the prompt to Wolpert, the softer touch. "What was it you didn't see, Dave?"

"You're getting me confused," he said, buying time.

Wolpert gave it to him. "All right, then."

If this had been my interview, I'd have nailed down the precise route he'd taken across the park, then asked if he'd passed anyone on the benches. But even if they knew what Martha had said, Dempsey had ruled her out as a credible witness. I kept my mouth shut.

"There wasn't anything I didn't see. I didn't see nothing. Anything."

"We're not trying to give you a hard time, Dave," Wolpert offered. "You have to understand we're up against it here. A girl's been kidnapped, and we have to find her. I expect you can understand the pressure we're under to find her?"

Dave bobbed his head, relieved to have the pressure off, pleased the cops were asking for his help. "Sure. Yeah." The finger came up to the glasses, the tension discharged. "Ask me anything you want."

"See, the time you took your break is the time that Danielle disappeared. That doesn't make you a suspect. Not necessarily. But if you're not involved, I'm sure you want to give us your full cooperation. Which is why we're asking for anything you might have noticed as you went from here, across the park, to the road there, and across the road. Anything at all." He paused. "Do you remember any of the vehicles that were parked along that side of the road?"

"Not really."

"Not one?"

"Well, maybe one."

Wolpert shifted his jacket and held his pen poised over a spiral notebook. "Okay."

"It was a sedan. Kind of greenish-gray. A Ford. Compact. I don't know the model."

"That's okay," Wolpert reassured him. He could have asked Dave how he knew it was a Ford if he didn't know the model, but he'd play along for now. "Where was it parked?"

Dave hesitated. He seemed about to indicate a point in the middle of the police yellow ribbon, then shifted to the left.

"Over there?" Wolpert asked, puzzled. "You're sure?"

Dempsey gave Wolpert a raised-eyebrow sign that she'd had enough.

"I think."

"Only, you were headed in this direction." Wolpert pointed to the right to the corner nearest New Beginnings, ninety degrees and a hundred feet from the spot Dave had indicated.

Dave signaled his inability to explain with a shrug, as if this precluded further inquiry. It seemed to be a well-practiced gesture.

"So was there something unusual about this Ford compact that attracted your attention?"

"I'm trying to help you out," Dave said sullenly. "Okay? I'm doing my best."

They wrapped up the interview. It seemed I'd sent them down another dead end, except that after they'd thanked Dave for his cooperation they asked him to stay put.

"What? Right here?"

"Is that a problem?" Dempsey asked him.

"Am I under arrest?"

"Are you going someplace?"

"No."

"Then you're not under arrest."

"If I want to—"

"See that unmarked police car with the two plain-clothes state police detectives sitting inside it?"

Dempsey pointed down the street to a sedan parked fifty feet away. Dave, sulking but tractable, said nothing. I wondered if he was disappointed not to be placed under arrest.

"If you move from this place right here, those detectives will inform me, and I will personally come after you."

Her phone chirped, and she flipped it open and checked the caller's number before answering. From the grimace she made, I figured it had to be Sasha McNeely, and from what I knew of Sasha, Dempsey was going to be tortured by these calls for the rest of the day. She walked away so that we wouldn't hear. She had no progress to report, no news, no leads, nothing to give this mother but simple human kindness. In a job that requires toughness, kindness exacts a price, and the detective hunched over her phone as if making headway against a cruel wind.

When she was done, finally, Dempsey and Wolpert left

to return to Doosy's to interview the manager and corroborate the chronology of Dave's story. Dave lingered restlessly, kicking the ground with the toe of his sneaker.

Shyly, he asked, "Can I, like, ask you questions?"

I drew myself up to refuse, then, as if permitting some
official barrier to break down, relented. "Sure."

He smiled. "So. Doctor. What do you think?"

I didn't have to ask him what the topic was. He was
the moth, and I, the profiler, held the flame. Dave wanted
to fly through the flame and out the other side.

I prepared him with a sidelong conspiratorial glance.
"You mean, from the profiling perspective?"

He gave me a wolfish grin. "Yeah!"

We stood side by side watching the detectives cross
the road. At the pedestrian crossing, they stepped out
seemingly oblivious to traffic, except when Dempsey
cast a sharp glance at the driver of a panel truck who
looked like he might not yield to them.

"Off the record?"

"Shit!" Dave exclaimed appreciatively. "You're really going to tell me?"

On the other side of the street, as Dempsey was about
to enter Doosy's, Wolpert turned to look back and, noticing that I was still in conversation with their witness,
touched Dempsey's arm for her to wait. But she entered
Doosy's without responding, leaving him alone on the
sidewalk. He didn't like me talking to Dave alone, and for
a moment it looked as if he was going to start back across
the street. But then he followed his partner into the shop.

I turned to survey the park with the donut shop behind
us, as Danielle must have seen it when she began her return to New Beginnings. Dave, I was pleased to see,
copied my movements at once.

"As a profiler," I said, "the first question you have to

ask yourself is whether this was an organized or a disorganized crime."

"A blitz job," Dave said. He was very excited, and although I didn't turn to make eye contact with him but remained fixated on the park in front of us, he gazed at me with an intensity and depth of scrutiny that made me feel more and more strongly that he was involved.

"Right," I said. "A blitz job suggests someone did the crime on the spur of the moment. No plan. No preparation. Probably doesn't know the victim. Just happened along. Acted on impulse. Versus organized."

I figured Dave already knew all this. He was a crime groupie. He knew how an organized serial killer conducted himself. I wanted him to fill in the blanks, but he was nodding, urging me to say more.

"Which one do you think?" he asked.

"Well, I don't think we have a serial killer here," I said.

He looked disappointed. "He could be," he protested.

I was interested in his use of "he." Where I'd been careful to keep all the participants as abstract as possible, Dave had personalized the perpetrator.

"I think," I said carefully, "that if a serial killer was operating in Massachusetts, we'd know about it."

"This could be his first one."

"It could."

"Everyone has to start somewhere." He laughed at his own joke, a throaty chortle that was like snorting.

He was right, though. I'd seen half a dozen men come through the Sanders Institute as they angled for an insanity plea; they were failed serial killers, murderers who hadn't made it past their first kill.

"So which do you think he is?" Dave insisted. "Organized or disorganized?"

"You tell me."

He gave me a suspicious glance that was gone so quickly I couldn't be sure what I'd seen. It would have been easy to underrate Dave. He didn't have the temperament for violent crime, but he was no goofball. I didn't meet his eye but looked over the park again, as if I'd already forgotten him.

My manner seemed to satisfy him that I wasn't setting a trap. He asked, "How would I know?"

He wanted to tell me. He wanted to show off. I made him wait. I shrugged. "I don't know," I said absently. "Maybe you watch this stuff on TV."

I changed stance and made the closing-up expression that signals a person's intention to end the conversation. I wanted to hurry him, to use the immaturity of his nervous system—the lack of impulse control, the abrupt onset of emotion, and the difficulty in modulating it once aroused—against him.

Out of the corner of my eye I saw his right hand come up in an involuntary staying gesture.

"I'll tell you what I think," he said in a rush. Then, almost humbly, "For what it's worth."

I turned to him with a social smile, tolerant, polite. "Okay," I said, careful to exclude any suggestion I was patronizing him. "What's your opinion?"

"Organized," he said, as I'd hoped he would. "Definitely organized."

"Could be." I nodded as though considering what he'd said, another prelude to breaking contact. "Maybe."

I was in the act of turning when he said, "I'll tell you why."

I turned back to him and stood with my arms folded, attentive but very gently confrontational, testing him. "Okay," I said, "let me hear your theory."

"He had to know her."

"A lot of people did."

"Right. Everybody knew Danielle. She used to come in the shop all the time. Every morning like clockwork."

I was disturbed by the past tense but let it go. "Nine o'clock."

"Nine-fifteen."

"It was a regular part of your day."

"Of course."

"She came in at nine-fifteen, and then . . . what?"

"She'd step up to the counter, and I'd get her order and then I'd give it her."

"Always the same?"

"She always said the same thing."

He'd used the past tense three times now, and if I'd been at Sanders, I'd have taken this moment to bring it to his attention, except that Dave had a wistful smile on his lips and a faraway, nostalgic look in his eyes, and I decided I'd go wherever he was.

"What was it Danielle said?" I murmured softly, enough, I hoped, to nudge the recollection into speech.

"Oh, I don't know." He was slightly embarrassed, pleasantly so, as though I were teasing him about a girl-friend he wasn't ready to acknowledge. He shook his head shyly to fend me off. "Something like, 'Hey, Dave, what's up?' "

"She always said the same thing."

"It was . . . it was . . ." He wasn't stupid. It was just that he didn't have the words handy to express himself. But he knew what he felt. He knew because it was famil-iar. And it was familiar because whenever he thought about Danielle, the feeling came over him.

I took the shortcut. "She liked you," I said.

I wasn't about to ask him if he liked Danielle. I al-ready knew that. And from the dreamy look that came over his face, I had a strong feeling now that Dave had had a hand in her kidnapping.

"A lovely girl," I suggested, hoping for more.

"She's . . . ," he began, and stopped. I wondered what kind of incriminating remark he'd been about to make. "She's a beautiful person." It all lay close beneath the surface, the love—or whatever he called it—that made Dave tick.

"Trusting."

"She'd go out of her way to help someone."

"That's what she was doing when she disappeared."

"She helped the social workers."

A mischievous part of me would have liked to ask him if Danielle took it upon herself to help people in wheelchairs, just so that I could see his reaction. To the trained observer there's no such thing as "No comment." People answer the question whether they like it or not, with words or without. But I rejected the impulse. The trouble with ambush questions is that they tend to end the interview. This was a police investigation, and it wasn't for me to stir things up.

"She had a way about her," he said.

"You said, 'She had a way about her,' as though Danielle isn't around anymore. She's not dead, is she?"

"No!"

He'd answered impulsively, without thinking. On his face, for an unguarded instant, was a look of horror. I wondered how far down the road he'd gone in his imagination, playing at serial killer. Because if he'd taken her, he would have to kill Danielle. There wasn't any other way to get away with it. If he helped in her release, if he told the police exactly where she was, if he hadn't molested her, he might make a deal with Brenda. That was his only hope.

Then, a moment later, recollecting himself, he said what he should have said. "How should I know?"

"We want her back unharmed," I told him, as if this were something he might not know.

He wouldn't look at me. "Yes," he said. "Course we do."

"If there's anything else you can think of," I suggested. "Anything."

"I was on break," he said, with a stubbornness that interested me.

"You went home," I said, a statement, not a question. "That's why you were gone so long."

He was getting antsy, and this interested me more. "Personal business," he said, as if the words prevented entry to the subject.

"Your mother was home?"

"Look—" He was balking.

"I'm not a cop," I reminded him.

He stared at me questioningly, wondering whether to ask me what this had to do with profiling, but he was a submissive person, a follower. "Right," he agreed doubtfully.

"How is your mother?"

A distressed, confused look came over his face, and his eyes flickered back and forth. "Not good. Matter of fact, she's quite poorly."

I let the words weigh on us, giving him the chance to flesh them out. "I'm sorry," I said at last, with the emphasis reserved for terminal illness.

"Yeah." He looked away. He shrugged, acknowledging the raw deal they'd been dealt, as if to say, "But what can you do?"

I decided to push further, taking the risk that he might flare up and walk away. There were no walls, no door, to hold him. I said softly, "How sick is she, Dave?"

His eyes came to mine in a flash of anger. Not at the intrusion, but at the pain I caused him in bringing his mother's condition freshly and starkly to mind.

"She's got . . ." The Adam's apple climbed his neck as Dave swallowed on nothing. I heard the faint smack of his dry tongue against the roof of his mouth. He was scared. He spoke the single word as though it were a confession: "Cancer." He hung his head to hide his face from me.

"What kind?"

"Pancreas, the doctor said."

"He talked to you about it?"

"Yeah."

The doctor had brought him into the office to tell him his mother would be dead inside six months. Three, maybe, if the diagnosis had been delayed.

I let him hear me sigh. "That's a tough one," I said.

"Tell me about it."

He glanced up to check my sincerity, and I gave him a wry smile of sympathy. He was hungry for contact. Dave wasn't made of the stuff of serial killers. That talk had been bravado, his private fantasy. Dave wasn't a killer— not by intent, anyway. If he was implicated in Danielle's disappearance, he was a different kind of pedophile, an inadequate man in need of love, the unconditional positive regard that only children are capable of. I didn't see him as a child-snatcher, unless he'd been caught up in something whose implications he didn't fully understand. Unless he'd been used by someone else with darker and more sadistic motives.

"You check in on her pretty often."

He nodded jerkily, the prospect of being alone in the world without his mother strong enough to disrupt this simple movement. "She's out of it a lot of the time."

"That would be the painkillers."

"Right."

"They confuse people. Especially when they're sick."

He could have made any number of responses to this. If he'd been in the clear, he might have directed anger at the drug companies or the doctor who gave his mother medications that messed her up. But Dave's concern was to keep his alibi viable.

He said quickly, "That's only sometimes. Most of the time she's with it. She knows where she is. She knows what time it is."

Which was the most important thing to know: when Dave arrived home, when he left. She wouldn't want to admit that she was confused. For people who are sick, one day is pretty much like the last one, and with a little repetition Dave's mother would "remember" where he'd been during that crucial time period.

"Sure," I agreed.

Behind him, a plainclothes officer got out of the car parked fifty feet away and walked briskly toward Doosy's. He had a piece of paper in his hand, a print-out for Dempsey.

"Anyway, what's this got to do with profiling?"

"It's what we call screening."

I made a quarter-turn and looked across the park. Dave turned, too, so that for a moment we both gazed at the point on the other side where Danielle had been abducted. But Dave couldn't look at that spot for long. He wanted to leave. I heard his foot scrape on the blacktop again.

"What's screening?" he asked.

"It's when you ask someone questions to see if he fits the profile."

"Do I?"

From his tone of anxious excitement, it was clear that

Dave wasn't sure whether he sought the safety of being ruled out, or the notoriety of being awarded the status of suspect. The radio stations were issuing bulletins. Local TV stations were interrupting regular coverage with updates. Everyone with nothing pressing to do was following the story. And here was Dave, someone I guessed had been an outcast in high school, who was written off in the neighborhood as a jerk, now—maybe—at the center of this Big Thing. I thought of the old paranoia joke: Better to be wanted by the FBI than not to be wanted at all.

I turned so that we stood face to face less than three feet apart and looked into his eyes. He was afraid of his mother dying, but this, the investigation, the crime, the consequences, didn't scare him.

I was distracted by Dempsey, Wolpert, and the cop with the printout exiting Doosy's and charging into the road, hands held high to stop cars.

"Do I?"

He turned at the squeal of tires behind him as Dempsey, with agility I wouldn't have credited her with, pivoted with one hand flat on the hood of the sedan that had almost run her over.

"You already know the answer to that," I said.

3:40 P.M.

We gathered in the small conference room at New Beginnings: Brenda, another lawyer from the DA's office, Dempsey, Wolpert, other detectives, and a few of the uniformed brass. Another physician, a Dr. Kerensky from the medical examiner's office, sat beside Brenda at the head of the table; he had erected a tripod with a whiteboard behind Brenda and looked like he was prepared to give a presentation.

We sat around the brown Formica conference table in our shirtsleeves and blouses in the sweltering heat. A floor fan scanned the room, but its breeze dissipated before it got very far. Brenda fanned herself with the printout that the detective had rushed to Dempsey in the donut shop. Dempsey hadn't deigned to tell me what it was. She'd invited Dave Feldman to accompany them to New Beginnings for some more questions, and when he looked like he might balk, she told him she'd already cleared it with his boss, and she made it sound like he didn't have a choice.

The attorney from the DA's office, a young man who

looked like this was his first job out of law school, wrote "David Feldman" in red marker at the top of the dry board and underlined it. He dutifully added the main points of Brenda's summary as we went along.

"Let's put together what we've got," Brenda said. "David Feldman, twenty-eight years old, employed three years at Doosy's, mostly reliable, sometimes takes longer breaks than scheduled, but the manager says he's an okay employee. No problems with customers or other staff. Serves the victim regularly. Makes a point of it, sometimes jumping in when another employee takes her order. Which he knows before she opens her mouth. Knows her by name. They banter back and forth. Could be construed as flirty—that's my interpretation, not the manager's. And he knows where Danielle lives."

She waved the paper teasingly in front of us. "Mr. Feldman has an arrest record. Not a conviction, mind you—the case was dismissed—but an arrest for indecent assault and battery on a child. Young girl three years older than Danielle on her way home from school. Feldman followed her, called her by name, knew which class she was in at school, knew her address, knew her route home, fondled her breast areas, tried to kiss her, girl struggled, passing motorist pulled over, Feldman took off. Could have plea-bargained the charge down to lewd and lascivious, but Feldman played hardball. The motorist couldn't pick him out of the lineup. The mother didn't want to put the girl through a trial and told the DA the victim wouldn't testify.

"The MO isn't impulsive. With this first girl, he did his homework. He picked his spot. He's known Danielle for a year. He's been patient, as he was with the other victim. But the other side of his MO is that he doesn't put anything together that's going to give him a shot at evading detection. With the first girl, he talked to her a couple of times. Asked her out on a date. She told her girlfriends but never mentioned the creepy guy to her mother. The fact that he doesn't figure out how he's going to get away with the crime is a plus for us."

"He has an alibi," Detective Dempsey said wearily, as if everything Brenda had said was beside the point.

"Check it out," Brenda told her brusquely.

I caught Brenda's eye and she nodded for me to speak.

"The alibi is his mother. She's pretty sick, heavily medicated, probably confused. She may not be credible."

"Let's pay her a visit," Brenda told Dempsey. "Let's test this alibi."

She called on other police officers who reported on cars that had been parked near the scene. Some of these had been identified by the license plate numbers that Martha Kinnard had provided, but no one acknowledged this. None of the owners of these vehicles had seen anything suspicious, and although some of these people hadn't been able to clear themselves from consideration, neither did they arouse suspicion because of a past criminal history.

Other detectives had questioned any male adults who might have had recent contact with Danielle: family, fathers of playmates, neighbors. Others were still involved in tracking down known pedophiles in the area. The net had been thrown wide, and it was an impressive effort, but it hadn't provided the police with leads.

Many of the people in the room had worried, preoccupied expressions. They leant forward attentively, eager to take the fight to the enemy, but they needed something to run with, and they weren't hearing anything to give them a direction.

"Some of you already know Dr. Kerensky, from the medical examiner's office," Brenda said. "We don't need a push to do our jobs. We all know time's of the essence. But I want you to hear what he's got so that we're all clear on what we're up against. After this presentation, he's going to brief the media, and that could help bring forward any witnesses that were wavering before."

Dr. Kerensky was a man in his mid-thirties with precisely parted hair and rimless glasses. He'd taken off his jacket as a concession to the temperature in the small conference room, but in his starched white shirt and tie he seemed immune to the heat. He stood when introduced, but didn't smile. He had a stack of charts on paperboards leaning against his chair, and he brought them up and turned at once to place them in view, making minute adjustments so that they sat to his satisfaction symmetrically on the tripod.

He looked over his audience and nodded here and there to detectives he must have known from murder trials where he'd been the state's expert.

"Brenda's asked me to estimate how long we've got before the victim expires from dehydration or heat prostration," he began.

People shifted uncomfortably in their chairs. We were hot and sticky, but everyone had a cold drink. Everyone felt a ripple of the fan every six seconds, however faint. No one dared imagine what it might be like at this moment for Danielle.

"The first chart," Dr. Kerensky said, "shows the loss of water from a clothed body of the victim's known weight—we calculate her surface area from body weight, that's really the metric we're most interested in, but body weight—"

He caught himself. It was easier to diverge into the

minutiae of calculations than to think about heat, ago-
nizing thirst, delirium.

"Given the victim's known body weight and an ambi-
ent temperature of ninety degrees—pretty much what
we have in this room—she'll lose about a hundred and
twenty milliliters of fluid an hour. In other words, if
she's in a room like this one, she needs to drink one of
those sodas sitting in front of you every three hours to
stay hydrated. That's just to keep up."

He swept off the first chart to reveal a second.

"If she's bound or in other ways covered so that air
can't circulate around her limbs and torso, you can see
here that she's going to have difficultly dissipating
heat."

He scanned his audience to see if we were following
this.

"You're going to release this to the media?" Dempsey
asked.

"Yes," Brenda said. "We want whoever's holding her,
whoever might have some idea where she is, to know
exactly what the stakes are."

"Question," Wolpert said. "What's the red line on the
first chart?"

"This one here at the bottom? This is the point at
which fluid loss is no longer compatible with life."

The room fell silent. No one moved.

Dr. Kerensky hurried on. "What we don't know is
whether the victim is able to put back the fluid she's
losing."

Collectively, we calculated the likelihood that Danielle
was being cared for in even the most minimal way. Dave
was here with us. Arthur would assume he was under
surveillance; he couldn't risk a trip to her hiding place
to give Danielle a soda every couple of hours. I wondered

what the chances were that they had a confederate who was minding Danielle.

Wolpert voiced our thoughts. "If someone's got her in a house—in a cellar or tied up in an attic or someplace—then they'll make sure she gets enough to drink. She's valuable to them. That person's placed himself at risk to get her and he's going to protect his investment. So I don't see why we need to look at these charts."

"What if she's tied up in a van somewhere? Or in the trunk of a car?" Dempsey put in. "And what if that vehicle's parked at a mall, baking in the sun? What if they don't want to go anywhere near her till they're sure they're in the clear and no one's watching them?"

Dr. Kerensky had a chart for that and he put it up on the tripod. "This is what happens when you raise the temperature. To—here—" he tapped the spot "—one hundred and twenty degrees. About what you'd expect in a van in a parking lot. Or here, one hundred and five, about what you'd expect to find in a self-storage locker."

He stood back to contemplate the chart. Whereas the previous graphs had shown a line gently trending downward, this one dove steeply toward the red line, the line of death.

The chart was purely mathematical. Nothing could have been scrubbed so clean of emotion, and yet the effect was grisly. I found myself wondering how Dr. Kerensky had come by the data, and thought, ungenerously, of the "scientific" experiments of Dr. Mengele, of subjects suspended in freezing brine to discover how long it took them to die. I had to remind myself that Kerensky was the messenger, the deliverer of truth.

Each of us, in his or her own way, constructed the logic of our investigation. I thought of the syllogisms of my undergrad philosophy class. People who take a large risk to acquire something value that thing. People seek to preserve what they value. Therefore, Danielle was being given water.

But there was another syllogism. People who value their own lives seek to stay away from danger. Danielle was dangerous to be around. Therefore, Danielle was not being given water.

And a third. The kidnappers valued their safety more than they valued Danielle. The closer the investigation moved to the kidnappers, the more we threatened their safety. Therefore, the more successful we were in discovering the perpetrators, the more likely they were to let Danielle trend down toward the red line.

"Bottom line, Doc?" Wolpert asked.

"Best-case scenario? She'll last into tomorrow. Worst-case?" He turned to his chart, tracing the near vertical component to its meeting with the red line. "She'll die this evening."

"Maybe," Brenda said, "we won't show the press that chart."

She had picked a CD out of its jewel case and gotten up to place it in the player at the other end of the table. "They do have this."

I was taken aback at first to see Abby on the screen. She sat on a low stool in what appeared to be a studio with a blue backdrop with the East Cambridge police insignia. She wore a blouse and an embroidered vest that placed the recording in the spring of this year.

Brenda said, "This is a video the city police made as part of their missing child prevention program. Parents can bring in their kids, have them videoed, get their fingerprints on file." She turned to me. "It's policy at New Beginnings for all new clients to register their kids in the program."

On the screen, Abby leaned forward, hands between her knees, toward a nervous young girl who fidgeted three feet in front of her.

Danielle was a slender eight-year-old with straight brown hair held back at the sides by pink barrettes and bangs that she periodically brushed aside when they fell over her eyes. She wore jeans and sneakers with pink laces and a T-shirt with a picture of the Grand Canyon on it.

Danielle's eyes were fixed on Abby's face as she awaited her cue.

"Would you tell us your name?"

"Danielle McNeely." The words came out joined as one, with an Irish lilt. Not her mother's accent. A grandmother, perhaps, from the Old Country.

"Where do you live, Danielle?"

"Twenty-seven Francis Street, East Cambridge."

It wasn't so difficult after all. They would be questions she could answer. She gave a big sigh of relief. Abby smiled at her and the girl reflected her expression like a mirror, mesmerized, delighted to be the center of Abby's attention.

She was an appealing child, engaging, open-faced, easy to read, and intrinsically happy. Her effect on the people sitting around the table was immediate: the more you liked Danielle, the greater the pain and helpless anger of those who hunted her abductors. Wolpert shot a violent, inscrutable look toward Dempsey, but she had turned away to hide what she was feeling.

Abby told Danielle, "Okay, now turn and face the camera," and Danielle rotated like a toy soldier, head tilted down so that the shy smile also contained an element of mischief.

She glanced aside to Abby for affirmation, and Abby told her, "Now turn so you face me."

She stood to attention before Abby, more confident now, ready to take part in the game she saw evolving.

"Very good," Abby said, putting on a pretend military gruffness to play along with Danielle.

Here was a maternal Abby I hadn't seen since we lost our son. In a moment, she'd dispelled the anxiety in the situation: they were safe; better yet, they'd have fun. It was clear that the girl adored her and that Abby loved the girl. There was a wealth of implicit understanding in their glances. Abby had only to touch her arm to draw Danielle closer.

"Now, tell me, Danielle, what do you do in an emergency?"

"Call 911."

"Correct."

Danielle compressed her lips to overcome a slight case of giggles. Abby, hamming, gave her a look of stern warning.

"And what's an emergency?"

"Like, someone having a heart attack?"

"Right."

"Or a dog gets hit by a car."

"Yes."

"Or if a house is on fire."

Abby put the young performer through her tricks. They'd almost forgotten the camera, absorbed in their private joke that lay in exaggerating their roles, riffing with the ease of long familiarity.

It was only thirty seconds of video, a mundane, routine police project, but its effect was more wrenching than all of Dr. Kerensky's graphs.

"That's going to be playing on a lot of stations," Brenda said. "She's a sweetheart. It comes straight across. If there's anyone with anything to do with this abduction who's having second thoughts, this has got to shake them loose."

After everyone had received his or her assignment, the meeting broke up. Dempsey, Brenda, and I went back to Abby's office to call Dave's mother.

Brenda switched the phone to conference call, and the three of us huddled around Abby's desk as the phone rang in the Feldman home.

It seemed to ring forever.

"Forget it," Dempsey said. "We're wasting time."

Brenda held up her hand. "We need her," she said. "We want her to let us in without a search warrant."

I was about to say that it might take a sick person some time to react to a ringing phone when Linda Feldman picked up.

"Mrs. Feldman?" Brenda asked.

"Yes?" With her mouth almost pressed against the phone, her slight, breathy voice was hardly more than a sigh.

"This is Assistant District Attorney Gorn."

We waited while Linda Feldman assimilated this as best she could. Perhaps, having previously suffered episodes of delirium from her painkilling medications, she was wondering if she was hallucinating again. In the end, she played it safe, assuming a noncommittal tone, until Brenda could establish her ontological status.

"Oh, yes?"

"I'd like to talk to you."

"All right."

"I'd like to come over and talk to you directly."

"I'm kind of tired right now. Maybe if you could . . ."

"It's about the girl who's missing. Danielle McNeely."

"I know. I saw it on TV."

"You could help us."

"I wish I could. I'm so sick. I can hardly help my-self."

She was starting to taper off, the volume of her voice dwindling, the words separating from one another. You could almost hear her attention wander.

"If we could just come over. Ask you a few questions."

"All right," she surrendered.

"Will you be able to let us in, Mrs. Feldman?"

"Come in the back door. It's not locked."

The uniformed police had kept the press out of the lobby, but there were several print reporters and three camera crews waiting on the steps outside, and as soon as they saw movement they leapt to attention and mobbed Brenda as she came through the door.

I hung back at the bottom of the stairs. I'd been the subject of interest of these crews during the Francone murder investigation, and I knew that though they'd brought hundreds of faces into focus since they framed mine, they'd recognize me. I didn't want Brenda to be distracted by having to explain my presence, so I waited for her and the detectives to absorb the media onslaught, and then, with their attention distracted, I slipped out the front door unnoticed and set off in the direction of the Feldman apartment.

The police cruiser carrying Brenda and Dempsey caught up with me a block from Everett Avenue, and I slid in beside Brenda in the backseat.

"This is going to be tricky," she said. "That's why I'm coming along. We don't have enough for a search warrant to turn the place over and we don't need a search warrant to look for Danielle. The problem is, we can only look in places where Danielle could be. Anything in direct line of sight's fair game—lying on the table in plain view—but we can't search for incriminating evidence in drawers, or under mattresses, or what have you. For that we have to get her to waive her Fourth Amendment rights."

"She sounded pretty shaky."

"That's why you're along."

"To see if she's competent to waive her rights?"

"I don't give a damn whether she understands what she's doing. The law says she doesn't have to. I just want you to get her to do it. We need 'yes.' "

Brenda was clipped and tense, closer to the edge of anger than I'd ever seen her before. If she said that was what the law was, then I believed her. She went by the book, and I'd only known her to break the rules once—for me.

Dr. Kerensky's charts had unnerved us. We felt we knew Danielle. She had touched us. The photos Sasha McNeely had pressed on me were burning a hole in my pocket. Brenda would keep to the letter of the law, but no more than that. If she wanted me to manipulate Dave's mother into allowing us to turn the house over for signs of Danielle, I'd do it for her.

I said, "We want to get access to his computer. We want to see what Web sites he visits."

"David Feldman's stuff is a gray area. If the computer belongs to him, then his mother can't give us permission to go over its hard drive. If we did that, a court could throw out any evidence we found."

"Let's get real," Dempsey snapped. "We want to see anything that'll lead us to Danielle. We don't have to say we found something. Once we've got the son of a bitch in custody we can come back with a search warrant and 'find' it all over again."

The investigation was sliding off center. We wanted the girl. Screw the trial. We wanted to get the perpetrators so we could find the girl, and if, later, we had an opportunity to bring them to justice, then we'd make do with what we had.

We pulled up in front of 203 Everett Avenue, a three-family clad in vinyl siding that directly abutted the street. Three steps led up to a common entrance with busted mailboxes. The Feldmans had the first floor. We circled round to the back as instructed, Dempsey stooping to peer into grimy basement windows, and walked up half a dozen steps to an uneven back porch.

We'd already been given permission to enter her home, and Brenda didn't want to give Mrs. Feldman an occasion for second thoughts. She opened the door slowly, and we stepped inside the kitchen.

"Hello," she called.

A cat that had perched precariously atop a pile of dirty dishes beside the sink regarded us suspiciously, then, in a sudden loss of confidence, leapt to the floor and swerved gracefully through the open door to disappear into the gloom of a hallway. It was a filthy kitchen, and the smell of decaying food made us grimace. On the table was an ashtray overflowing with butts; an empty beer bottle lay on its side. The plates, from supper, perhaps, had been licked clean by the cat, with the exception of small mounds of mashed potato that remained untouched.

We listened. We hoped against hope that this would be easy: Danielle would spit out the gag and call out above, below us, for help. But all we heard were voices coming from a television in a nearby room.

"Mrs. Feldman," Brenda called.

We heard a voice, but couldn't make out words, then

shuffling in the hallway from the direction in which the cat had departed.

"Who's there?" a woman's voice came, challenging and afraid. Her voice was hoarse and dry.

"Assistant District Attorney Gorn, Mrs. Feldman. Brenda. I'm the one you spoke to on the phone."

As she shuffled closer to the light in the kitchen, we saw first the pale pink housecoat that, in spite of the heat of the day, she held tight about her narrow frame. Her face was tired and thin, with the sallow complexion of the chronically ill. Except that she hadn't been sick long enough to be chronic. The cancer was wasting her quickly. She held one hand extended in front of her like a blind person, not trusting her balance, prepared for surprises. Her eyes, unfocused, stared ahead and had difficulty finding us.

"I was in bed," she said, looking us over without surprise or curiosity.

It wasn't clear, from the vague scan of her eyes, whether she understood who we were. Some weeks ago she'd given up the attempt to color her hair, and the gray roots formed a stripe at the edge of her hand as she smoothed the wiry, wayward strands.

"I didn't have time," she said, "or I'd have got myself ready for you."

"That's okay," Brenda told her. "No need to get yourself all fixed up on our account."

"No."

"I've brought some police officers with me. We're looking for that girl who disappeared."

"Danielle."

"Yes. Danielle McNeely. This is your apartment? You rent it. Is that right, Mrs. Feldman?"

"Yes."

"How many rooms do you have?"

She looked dazed. "Well . . ." She turned uncertainly and waved her hand. "All back there."

"Just this floor?"

"Yes."

"And the cellar? Does that go with your apartment, or is that separate?"

"That's not us. That's the landlord's. He stores stuff there."

Her attention wandered, and Brenda saw that she'd have to stick to short, easy questions and keep them coming at a brisk rate if she was going to get Linda to stay on track.

"How many people live here, Mrs. Feldman?"

"Just me and my son."

"That would be David?"

This question broke through the lethargy, and it seemed that for the first time Linda put the three things together: a missing girl; her son with the record of sexual assault; cops in the house.

"What's this about?" she wanted to know.

"It's routine," Brenda said. "We're checking possible leads. Your house is near where Danielle disappeared. We're checking the neighborhood."

"Oh."

"Do you mind if we look around?"

"You don't have a cigarette, do you?"

We looked from one to the other, but there were no smokers among us. We were aware how immensely this small thing would improve our standing with her.

"Sorry," Brenda said, with real regret. Then, a sudden thought: "But before we leave, we'll go down to the store on the corner and bring some back for you."

"Thanks," Mrs. Feldman said without conviction. She had few expectations that promises would be fulfilled.

"What brand?" Dempsey asked.

But Linda had already given up on the topic. "What?" she asked.

"What brand do you smoke?"

"Marlboro Lights." She looked at Dempsey as if reappraising her character.

"As soon as my partner gets here, I'll send him down to the corner store for a pack of Marlboro Lights."

"Your partner?" She was bewildered. "Who are you again?"

"My name's Carol. I'm a detective in the state police."

"Right." She was oriented once more. "You're looking for the little girl."

"Right."

She lowered herself slowly to one of the chairs at the dining table. "Is this about my Dave?" She addressed Dempsey, whom, she had decided, possessed the most credibility.

"It's one of the leads we have to follow up on."

"I wish I had a cigarette."

"Right now, we're following up on every lead so we can rule people out who don't belong in the investigation."

"This is on account of what happened before."

"Yes."

She stared at a spot away from us, thinking hard. "I don't know," she said, almost to herself.

"If we could take a look around," Brenda suggested.

"Oh," Linda said with something like a laugh, at a proposal that was too preposterous to entertain seriously. "She's not here, you know."

"If we could take a look around," Dempsey told her, "then that would give us the possibility of ruling Dave out of the investigation."

"I don't know," Linda said.

She was torn in her loyalties, between a wretched son, but a son nevertheless, and a little girl she didn't know who'd never done anyone any harm.

"We have to find the little girl," Dempsey said. "The doctors say that in this heat we don't have much time."

She turned her head suddenly at the mention of doctors. "Is she sick, then?" She looked from one face to the next. "They didn't say that."

"If we don't find her soon," Dempsey said very quietly, almost whispering, in a tone of grief that seemed genuine, "she's going to die."

In desperation, Linda flicked aside butts in the ashtray, looking for one that might yet yield a couple of puffs.

Dempsey took the chair across the table from her. The rest of us did our best to fade into the woodwork. She had Linda's attention.

"We know what Dave did before. It was a while ago. He hasn't done anything since then to bring himself to our attention. But you know we have to follow up on anyone who's been in this kind of trouble."

"He hasn't done anything."

"Did you see him this morning?"

"Well, I don't know. I think I did. I'm sure I did. But he hasn't done anything."

"That's what I expect to find."

"Nothing."

"Then you've got nothing to hide. Isn't that right?"

She wavered. The trouble was, she didn't know whether there was anything she had to hide.

"Will you let us look around? See if there's anything that ties him to this case? And if there's nothing, then we can cross Dave off our list."

Linda stared down at a long cigarette burn on the plastic tabletop. She circumnavigated it with her fingertip, as if it were a diagram of the problem she didn't want to enter. She understood the dilemma. The first arm, the one in which Dave was clear of the crime and there was nothing in the apartment for the cops to find, was clear enough. It was the other arm, the possibility that Dave was involved, that there was something here that would tie him to the girl, something she didn't know anything about, that was causing the difficulty.

The moment presented a quandary for the interviewer, too. It was a tough call, but Dempsey decided to move boldly ahead, to name the arm of the dilemma where the true conflict of loyalties lay: the son—possibly a bad son—versus the unknown, innocent girl.

Dempsey said, completing Linda's unspoken thought, "And if Dave is involved—God forbid—then you want us to talk to him as quickly as possible. We have to find that little girl before this becomes a murder case."

"I know he isn't involved."

"All right, then." She waited two beats. "But just in case."

Linda glanced sideways suddenly, as if someone had called her name or a movement out of the corner of her eye had caught her attention, though there was no one standing in the direction in which she looked. It was a look I'd seen many times in patients who were hallucinating.

"I just took my medication," she said by way of explanation. She made a sweeping gesture with the flat of her hand that started at her eyes, her unreliable eyes, up her brow, and then over and down one side of her unruly hair. "It's hard to think."

"Think about this, Linda," Dempsey persisted. "If he did it—if—then he doesn't deserve your protection."

She sighed in recognition. "I know."

"If he's hurt that little girl—"

Linda looked up abruptly into Dempsey's face, shocked, as if Dempsey were giving her fact, not hypothesis. "He hasn't, has he?" she asked.

"This is the way it is, Linda: If Dave's hurt Danielle, then he has no call on you."

"But he hasn't. So far as I know." She turned to look at us, appealing for reassurance, then back to Dempsey. "Are you telling me something different?"

For the first time, Dempsey began to understand how confused Linda was, and she hesitated. She turned halfway in my direction, but she wasn't about to yield to me.

"No," Dempsey said. "We don't know. We have to find out."

Linda nodded her head, distracted again, glancing quickly sideways. I saw her lips move silently.

Wolpert arrived, squeezing his large frame into the tiny kitchen, but Linda didn't seem to notice.

"Which is Dave's room?" Brenda asked. "Would you show us while Detective Wolpert goes to the corner store to fetch some cigarettes?"

"Marlboros," Linda said, addressing me.

"You got it," Wolpert said.

But Linda had already forgotten the agenda and didn't get up from the table.

"Can you show us around?" Brenda prompted her. "Down here?" Brenda started down the corridor.

"It's a mess."

She was struggling to rise from her chair, and I moved in behind her and gave her my arm for balance.

Dempsey was impatient and had already reached the end of the corridor and was standing at the front door that led to the hallway of the apartment building. Brenda, too, had gone ahead, and now came back for us.

The corridor was just wide enough for me to support Linda at her side. As we came to the diagonal of the staircase that rose from the front hallway to the apartments above, we passed a door that led down to the basement, which was padlocked.

"Is this yours?" Brenda asked, holding the padlock.

Linda shook her head. "The landlord's."

We stopped at the first door on the left. The sound of the TV, voices of a man and a woman arguing, came loudly against the hum of a small air conditioner.

"The den," Linda said. "My room."

The drapes were drawn against the daylight, and the only illumination came from a small lamp on the bedside table.

"My son got me that TV," she said.

"Does he pay rent?" Brenda asked.

"No. He doesn't make enough for that. He buys some of the groceries and that's about it."

"Can we see Dave's room?" Brenda said, barely concealing her impatience. "Which one is his room?"

"The parlor. He sleeps on the couch there. I'm warning you, though, it's a mess."

Dempsey paused at the threshold to the parlor and with a professional eye calculated the man-hours it would take to sort and catalogue items to be retained as evidence, surveyed the stacks of magazines, towers of videotapes and discs, a pile of dirty laundry on the floor against the wall, a bulging closet with a door that couldn't close, and scattered cartons from fast-food outlets. Dave's sheets still covered the couch. An enormous, old-fashioned television in a self-contained console held pride of place against one wall, with a VCR and a DVD player stacked on top of it, and a recliner chair set before it. In the far corner, an armchair was strewn with discarded clothes. In another corner, discreetly turned so that any casual intruder would not immediately catch a glimpse of the screen, sat the computer.

Even at the doorway, we smelled the stale odor of Dave's clothes, like a presence.

"Only," Linda was saying, "he doesn't watch much TV now. It's the Internet. Everything's the Internet. He's up all night on that thing." She gestured toward the computer.

"Do you use it much?" Brenda asked.

"Not as much as I used to."

"But you do, from time to time?"

"I used to buy things on eBay."

"On this computer here?"

"Yes."

"So it's yours as much as Dave's?"

"I bought it."

"And you use it."

"When I can get on it."

"Because your son's using it all the time."

"Him and his friend."

"Who's that?"

"An older man. They have this hobby of e-mailing people all over the world. They're trying to get an e-mail from someone in every country in the world."

"And they do that here, on this computer?"

"John has some technical problem with his own, so they use this one."

"His name is John?"

"I don't know his last name."

"Could you describe him for us, Linda?"

And even from Linda's sparse, fragmented description, we had no difficulty recognizing Arthur Hodges.

After she gave us permission to search, Wolpert came back with the cigarettes.

All I'm asking you to do is raise one finger," Brenda insisted. "Or scratch your nose. Or pull on your ear."

"I don't like it," I told her.

"You wouldn't have to say a word."

"I'm not a cop," I protested. "I'm a physician. I have certain obligations . . . taboos." Even as I spoke, my own words sounded wishy-washy and self-serving.

"In a situation like this, we all have to do what we can."

"It's just that I'm not comfortable with this role as a kind of adjunct police interrogator."

"Who said comfortable? No one's asking you to get comfortable. This isn't the kind of mix where you can cherry-pick your point of entry. Here we are, Paul. Deal with it."

I was stung by the edge to her voice: anger, mixed with the earliest tinge of contempt. A girl's life hung in the balance, and I was quibbling over some obscure corner of my precious integrity.

"All right," I said.

She let out a breath she'd been holding back, and her shoulders came down as the muscles around her neck relaxed. "Thanks, Paul," she said, conciliatory. "I didn't mean to stick it to you."

"Sure you did." I waved away her protest. "But that's okay."

"Everybody on this case is screwed real tight."

"I know." I wondered what the effect would be on Abby if we didn't find Danielle. She was counting on me, too.

Dempsey and Wolpert waited for us in Abby's office. They sat side by side in the chairs that Abby used for couples therapy, and as we entered the room, they abruptly broke off what seemed to be a heated disagreement.

"Okay," Brenda said. "Detective Dempsey will lead this interrogation. Detective Wolpert will assist. I'm going to make sure the interview is open and aboveboard. Other than that, I'm not going to say anything. Neither is Dr. Lucas. He's here as an advisor."

Dempsey looked at me suspiciously. "Does he know something I don't know?"

"Dr. Lucas has agreed to help this investigation by sharing his expertise on lie detection."

I guessed from the compression of her lips that Dempsey would have liked to make some choice remark, but she held back.

"A lot of the time it won't be clear-cut," I said. "When I am confident that he's flat-out lying, I'll point my pen up."

Dempsey didn't like it. I suspected, anyway, that she never intended, once the interview began, to look my way.

Wolpert was disengaged. He sat hunched forward,

preoccupied with his own thoughts. Both of the detectives, it was clear, wanted to get a crack at Dave Feldman now that he'd been tied to Arthur Hodges. We were certain we had the culprits. But there was a desperate quality to our certainty. It had to be these guys.

Arthur was under surveillance; half a dozen of their colleagues were now going door to door questioning Arthur's neighbors, locating any possible witnesses who might break his alibi or give some clue to where he had gone that morning after he had abducted Danielle. But here in this room was where the action was, with the weaker, more vulnerable of the pair. It was all about breaking Dave.

"A couple of suggestions," I offered.

Wolpert was on his way to the door to fetch Dave and he kept on going, because whatever I was going to say didn't matter to him. Even Brenda gave the impression that I was speaking out of turn. I didn't care. They were going to screw up this interview, and I wouldn't let them.

"There's one of him. There's going to be four of us," I said. "To me, that's two too many."

"Suits me," Dempsey said.

Brenda hesitated.

"Four educated, professional people sitting here facing him," I said, "all staring at him. He's going to clam up."

"Okay," Brenda said. "I'll give my spiel at the beginning, then leave. Sergeant Wolpert can leave after he drops Dave off. If he starts talking, if he wants to make a statement, we'll be outside."

"Your spiel," I said, holding her from leaving. She turned, with her hand on the door handle. "I think you should praise him for cooperating with the police. I think that will mean something to him."

Dempsey scoffed. "Right!"

"Why not thank him? He's going to help us. We believe he's going to help us, or we wouldn't bother talking to him. He's here voluntarily, isn't that right?"

"That's what I'm going to tell him," Brenda said.

"A lot of perpetrators like Dave—lonely, no status—are otherwise law-abiding citizens. More than law-abiding, except for their one big thing. Dave's the kind of guy who respects authority, especially people he perceives as powerful. He wants your approval. What does it cost to give him what he wants? If it makes things go our way?"

"Okay, we'll give him a badge."

"Sure, he's a perpetrator. He knows that. But that self-awareness can slip to second place when there's something else he wants. It only has to happen for a moment. Then he'll remember he's a perpetrator and that all we want to do is burn him. But if he forgets it for a few seconds, he gives us an opening."

"I'm going to tell him he can leave anytime he wants," Brenda said, deflecting the topic.

"We don't have to tell him anything," Dempsey said. She was responding to me, still resentful of my presence.

"No," Brenda said. "I don't have to tell him. But I'm going to. I want everything explicit. When we come to trial, I don't want any opening for defense counsel to get his statements thrown out."

We sat silently in the office while Wolpert went to fetch Dave, Brenda staring abstractedly at the files laid out on Abby's desk, touching them at their corners to line them up without awareness.

We were engaged in two separate efforts. There was finding Danielle. And there was collecting the evidence that would convict the perpetrators at trial. If it came to it, I knew Dempsey and Wolpert would do what it took to save the girl. To get to the girl, they would cut corners in obtaining evidence. If suspects' rights were infringed, if as a result they ran the risk that statements the perpetrators made could be thrown out of court, so be it. Once they got the girl, they'd do their best to convict her abductors. Even Brenda, the stickler, would bend rules to save Danielle. I knew I would, in her position. And more and more, I was in their position. I was lining up with law and order.

She must have thought over what I'd said, because when Wolpert returned with the suspect, she was quite fulsome in her thanks for his cooperation, her apologies that he'd had to wait so long, solicitude that he'd had a cold drink.

By the time Brenda excused herself, leaving Dave to Dempsey and me, he was quite softened up.

And he was enjoying himself, almost. He sat forward on his chair, alert, attentive, and fixated on Dempsey like a bird dog. He really wanted to help this cop get her man. I marveled at the human capacity to erect walls between the different aspects of ourselves, blinkering ourselves to such an extent that we neglect the most basic loyalty of all, to the whole.

I remained silent, as we'd agreed. I concentrated on gathering observations that would give me a baseline on Dave. I wanted to know how he behaved when he wasn't stressed: how much he shifted in his seat, how often he stammered, the range of quiver in his voice. I wanted to know, when he had no reason to lie, how often he touched his face. I'd track what went before each tic that accompanied the finger hoist of his glasses.

He sweated in the close office, as I did. Dempsey

continued to fan herself with a file that she picked up from Abby's desk, but a different, fatter file than the one she'd used previously.

"I don't want you to tell me anything that isn't true," she warned him.

Dave frowned and nodded with sudden jerks of the head, as if the thought of someone misleading the police irritated him. Perhaps it did. In the next few minutes, he'd lie to Dempsey, but that thought was contained in another watertight compartment of his mind.

He wasn't shifting in his seat. His hands stayed down on the arms of the chair. He blinked a lot, but otherwise there wasn't much to see in his face. At this point in the interrogation Dave was a good liar, not because he was skilled in deceit, but because he believed what he said. Right now, he was sincerely helpful.

"You understand what I'm telling you?"

Dave nodded again and added, "Yeah."

The syllable he spoke emerged hoarse and raspy from his dry throat. But then, he was helping a detective solve a major case. Maybe a murder case. Anyone in that position was allowed a little stage fright. I struggled to keep an open mind, to see the evidence before me without bias. A sympathetic nervous system in overdrive didn't make someone guilty.

"If I ask you a question and you don't know the answer, just say so."

"You got it."

"It's okay not to know."

"I know."

"What I don't want . . ."

She paused as if he might be ready to supply the answer himself, and Dave did say, "Yes," nodding his head in agreement, as if he did know the rest of her sentence.

"What I don't want is lies."

He shifted. Dave rocked back in the chair. His right hand came up off the armrest as if he wanted to shield himself from a descending blow, and then he became self-conscious and lowered it again. He was changing gears, out of the cooperative mode, back to Dave the suspect.

I expected that Dave, the man with no allies, the fringe member of any group that would have him, the scapegoat, often lied out of weakness. And because he wasn't very good at planning and computing consequences, it was most likely he'd use a scatter approach, throwing off lies like seeds from a flower pod, with the expectation that in producing many, a few would take. He'd have little investment in any single lie—if it worked, so much the better—so that the act of lying itself didn't make him anxious. Dempsey recognized this.

He started to protest, but she cut him off.

"No!" she ordered, stopping him dead at the first syllable.

She waited a couple of beats, as you do when you tell a dog to stay, to make sure he obeys, before you relent and let him come to you.

"If you reach a point when you don't want to tell me the truth, just say nothing. Okay?"

Dave hesitated, not knowing whether he was to speak. "Yes," he said.

"You don't have to tell me anything you don't want to. So you don't have to lie to me. You don't have any reason to lie to me. So don't." She fanned herself with the thick folder, regarding him. "I can't stand liars," she said with sudden harshness, looking away.

"Me neither."

"All right, then."

She stared at him silently, increasing the pressure of

silence. Dave looked to me for relief, but by then my eyes were already deflected to something I might have written on the pad of paper on my knee. He shifted uncomfortably and cleared his throat. Still, Dempsey held him in her gaze.

Finally Dave raised his hands, palms up, in a gesture of helplessness. "So what do you want to know?" he asked her.

"I want to know where Danielle is."

Dave's mouth gaped, but before he could utter a sound, Dempsey's accusing finger shot out and she yelled, "No!"

She could have slapped him in the face and gotten less effect. He opened his mouth, censored what he was about to say, started again, blinked twice, licked his lips, swallowed with difficulty.

"I'm not asking you a question," Dempsey said menacingly. "So there's no cause for you to lie to me."

"I wouldn't. I wasn't."

"I'm talking to you. You're not talking to me. I'm talking to you."

"I know. It's just—"

"You know why?"

"Why what?"

"Why I'm talking."

"No."

"Because I already know everything. Except that one thing. Where Danielle is."

Dave touched his nose, blinked, sniffed, prepared to lie. I pointed my pen up, but Dempsey was in her element. She didn't need me.

"I don't know what it is you know," he said. "I mean, about me. There's nothing to know about me. Not with Danielle."

"We've had a chat with your friend Arthur," she said.

Dave looked blank. "I don't have no—"

"That's his real name. Arthur Hodges. When he's with you, he goes by the name John."

She described Arthur. She described the van.

The van bothered him. His nose twitched as if it might elevate the glasses unassisted.

"I don't know anything about that," he said. "I never saw his van."

His middle finger came up, his face ticced, I pointed my pen straight up, but Dempsey wasn't looking.

She held up Abby's chart that she'd been fanning herself with all the time she'd been talking, then tossed it casually onto the desk so that it slid in Dave's direction.

I hadn't expected her to turn the corner so quickly. I kept my eyes on Dave. He had made an abrupt inspiration at the mention of "John," a tiny gulp of air that broke the rhythm of his previous respiratory rate, and I saw him straighten as the axial muscles of his back stiffened, but apart from the tic, he hadn't leaked much. He might have been prepared for the possibility that his connection to Arthur would become known, but even the revelation that Arthur had lied to him about his name hadn't shaken him.

I wondered if Dempsey, in the urgency of finding Danielle, wasn't cutting too many corners. If she played her best card—the Arthur connection—straight off, in the hope of bulldozing him into a confession, and Dave didn't cave, she'd strengthen him.

Dave looked at the folder for a long time. He must have been calculating how much the police knew of what he and Arthur had been up to. Or he was innocent of the abduction and guilty only of sharing his pedophile interests with Arthur? If he hadn't had any involvement in Danielle's abduction but was frightened the police would uncover some other illegal activity, this would throw the interrogation off-kilter.

"I know John." He corrected himself quickly. "Okay. Arthur." He glanced up, and the demeanor of downtrodden meekness had disappeared. "So what? Is that a crime?"

It was his first act of defiance, and it made me uneasy. He was on familiar ground, I thought. They'd expected the abduction to be so quick and smooth that they wouldn't be seen. But if one of them was snagged by the police investigation, this was their fallback position. He and Arthur had rehearsed this eventuality. Dave knew what to expect. He knew what he'd say to Dempsey's next move.

Dempsey backed away. "Did you know that everything on a computer hard drive stays on that drive forever?"

Dave shrugged indifference. His hands stayed away from his face. He sat solidly, almost comfortably slouched on the hard wooden chair. His glasses looked like they needed an assist, but he ignored them. Dempsey had lost momentum. He didn't care what was on that hard drive. If the police discovered that he'd visited Russian hardcore child porn sites, he was prepared to accept what was coming.

Dave surveyed the room with studied nonchalance. It was an exaggerated pose, but he made his point.

"We had a long talk with Arthur," Dempsey said.

But she couldn't get a rise from him. Dave looked moodily at the floor.

She said, "Arthur told us it was your idea."

I thought this was a mistake. If your bluff fails, you don't up the stakes, you back away and come again from another angle.

"What?" he asked. This was the moment Arthur had warned him about.

"Don't play dumb," Dempsey said.

"What's the idea you're talking about?"

Dempsey seemed to lose it. She picked the bogus folder up and slapped it on the desk. "Kidnapping Danielle McNeely. That's what I'm talking about. I'm talking about a young girl who used to come to you for coffee who's going to die of heatstroke if we don't find her soon."

She leaned forward across the desk and glared at him. Dave turned his head away, but he wasn't scared by her outburst. I figured Dave was used to this. A lot of people in his life had tried to bully Dave. The light streaming in through the window caught the sheen of sweat on his forehead, but we were all sweating. He wasn't flustered. He wasn't about to bolt. He studied Dempsey out of the corner of his eye.

"What are you saying, then?"

"I'm telling you Arthur's putting it all on you. That's what."

"Putting what on me?"

"You want me to spell it out?"

Dave had switched their roles. Dempsey found herself in the position of giving out information. She was giving and getting nothing back. This was beyond Dave's capacity for low cunning, I thought. Arthur had coached him.

"Do you?" she challenged him.

Dave shrugged. The indifference he depicted was close to real. "If you want."

"Arthur said it was your idea to kidnap Danielle."

"It's a free country." He paused to show that however Dempsey thought she was turning it on, he experienced no duress. He was comfortable. "Arthur can say whatever he wants."

"Even if he puts you in it?"

"You're full of it."

Dempsey laid her hand flat on the file, as in times gone by a witness would lay her hand on the Bible to take the oath. "It's all here."

Dave stared at the file. He wanted to call her on it. I thought he was deciding whether to ask to see it, but it was unlikely Arthur had scripted this eventuality for him, and I felt sure he would have warned Dave not to improvise.

I saw a flicker of doubt cross his face, but it was dispelled in a blink. Then the muscles around his face and forehead softened, and a smile of something that in another person in another context would have been serenity took possession of his face. It was going to be okay. All he had to do was stick to the script. Stay confident. Give them nothing.

"You've got nothing," he said.

"We've got the hard drive from your computer."

Again, a blink, a slight tightening of the eyebrows in anxiety, another blink, a deep inspiration, and it was gone. Sure, there was stuff on the disk he didn't want to become general knowledge. It might even be illegal. But nothing that would get him a life sentence.

"That's my property. You can't take it without a search warrant." He gave us both a complacent smile. "It's tainted evidence. That's what you've got."

"One, it's not your computer. It belongs to your mother."

"She's sick."

"Not as sick as you are."

He turned his face away. "You can say what you

like." When his perversion was linked to his mother, he could feel a smidgen of shame.

"And two, we didn't need a warrant because she gave us permission to search the apartment. Your mom wants us to find Danielle. She'll give you up, if that's what it takes to find Danielle."

"Okay. So you got the computer."

"If there's any child porn on it, even if you think you deleted it, I want you to be absolutely certain that we'll find it."

"Good luck," he said. And as an afterthought, "Enjoy."

I didn't turn my head to look at Dempsey—I didn't want to signal Dave that he'd scored a hit—but I saw out of the corner of my eye that she tapped the point of her pen several times in a stabbing motion at the pad in front of her.

"I know you did it." Her voice was strangled with anger. "You little fuck."

He didn't protest. Dempsey was leaning forward, ready to cut off any denial, but Dave stared at her impassively. He was used to abuse, I thought. He was the kind of kid who was teased throughout the school years. The other kids sensed something off, a degree of incoordination, a mild speech impediment, tics, and they went for Dave like a brood of hens pecking at the chicken with a patch of discolored feathers.

"Why haven't you charged me, then?" he asked.

This was the endgame that he and Arthur had foreseen. The only unexpected factor was Martha Kinnard remembering the license plate of Arthur's van. But for that, the police would have nothing, and Dave and Arthur would have had all the time in the world to stash Danielle in a place of their choosing. The only difference was that the police investigation had developed faster than they'd planned. The difference was that Danielle was in limbo.

I thought of the grandfatherly Arthur, the father figure Dave yearned for—I was guessing—the two of them united by a common hobby. I wondered how the two of them had discovered each other.

"If you think I did it?" Dave repeated. "Why haven't you?"

Dempsey sat silently.

"You haven't even given me my Miranda."

The door opened and Wolpert came in. He didn't explain this sudden entry, but went straight to the other side of the desk where his partner sat and leaned over behind her so that he could whisper a few words into the ear farthest from the suspect.

Dempsey immediately got up and left the room.

Wolpert took her place at the desk. He sat silently without looking at either Dave or me. I felt like he was standing guard over both of us.

Dave, of course, couldn't take the silence for long. "Hey," he said.

He made a shrugging gesture of incomprehension with his hands held palms-up, but got no response from either of us. He made it again, more emphatically, but Wolpert still didn't respond.

"Would someone please tell me what's going on?"

Wolpert pursed his lips as he selected what words he would speak. "There've been developments," he said. He seemed to consider the import of his own words, eyes downcast, a frown of concentration pulling his eyebrows together.

"I don't understand," Dave said.

"That's correct," Wolpert told him.

We waited.

"This is fucking crazy!" Dave burst out.

Wolpert considered him with a dispassionate, clinical gaze.

"If this is one of your whacked-out games . . ."

Wolpert broke off eye contact. He was drawn into himself, insulated from us.

Dempsey burst into the room without warning. She walked briskly to a point six feet from where Dave sat and stared down at him as though she hadn't seen him in quite this way before, as though recognizing him for the first time.

Then she turned away. Wolpert had stood up, but she shook her head that she didn't want her seat back and looked around for a spare chair, which she placed to one side of the desk. She was closer to Dave. She faced him obliquely. Her face was hidden by the bright sunlight that came in through the window behind her.

"All right," she said. "Let's take this from the beginning."

"Excuse me. Can you just tell me what this is all about?"

"I'm asking the questions."

"What if I don't want to answer?"

"Try me."

They sat eye to eye, Dave with his head turned awkwardly to confront the detective, squinting into the sunlight in his attempt to read her face.

If this had been a ploy, it was working beautifully. But I didn't think it was.

Dave couldn't hold his gaze into the glare of the sun, and soon he looked away. It was the act of submission Dempsey required.

"How long have you known Danielle McNeely?"

"You mean, the girl who's been abducted?"

Whatever had come Dempsey's way, she had gained back the initiative and she could, if she wanted, afford to wait him out. After a couple of seconds, she'd made her point, and she said, without rancor or bravado, simply, "Yes."

Dave was restless again, a good sign. He was repeating her questions, too. "How long?" he asked himself. "I don't know. About a year. Could be more. Who knows?"

"One year, about."

"Yeah, give or take . . ."

"Yes?"

"Nothing."

"When was the first time you saw her?"

"I already told you. I don't—"

"The occasion. Where were you? What were you doing? Why was she there?"

"At the coffee shop. You already know that."

"No, I don't. Things have changed. Let's assume I don't know anything anymore."

He was going to protest but thought better of it. Really what he wanted was information. The cops had something on him, and he didn't know what it was.

He shook his head, unable to satisfy her. "I don't remember the first time." He hoisted his glasses and grimaced, but I didn't bother to signal the lie. "I've served hundreds of customers. I can't be expected to remember every one."

"But you got to know her."

"By sight, sure. She was a regular. She—"

"More than that. You knew her name."

"Yeah." He spread his hands, at a loss. "So what? Everyone did. You're going to pull everyone in who knew Danielle's name?"

He was starting to wriggle free from the grasp of her

questions, and Dempsey pulled him back. "How did *you* know Danielle's name?"

He repeated the helpless, uncomprehending gesture. When he answered, his words had the inflection of a question. "I asked her."

"You asked her what her name was?"

It was the first time Dave had put a foot wrong. He recognized it at once. It was a minor error, but he did his best to correct it at once. "Or someone told me—I don't know."

"But you just told me you asked Danielle what her name was. You just said that."

The liar's dilemma: after an error, do you "correct" it—but in doing so change your story and thereby give the appearance of inconsistency? Or do you tough it out?

"I said it, but—"

"All right, then." Dempsey rammed her question into the gap. "Where were you when you asked her what her name was? In the park? Or in the coffee shop?"

Dave plumped for the lesser of the two evils. "In the coffee shop."

"And what did you say to her? 'Hey, little girl, what's your name?' "

"No."

Dempsey put on the accent of a degenerate hillbilly. " 'Hey, Luscious, what do they call you 'round these here parts?' "

"It wasn't like that. You make it sound sick."

She was corralling him, herding him toward the truth as the lesser evil. She couldn't entirely suppress the rage in her voice. I felt it myself.

Dempsey goaded him. "What, then?" She loved this part of her work.

"I told her my name first. I said, 'Hi, I'm Dave.' And

I held out my hand, and we shook hands, and she told me her name was Danielle."

Dempsey was silent for a moment. After the quick-fire rhythm of her previous questioning, the pause came as a shock. She sat back, straight in her chair. She took a deep breath, and when she let it out, her words came as a husky whisper.

"You touched her."

He was caught with his mouth open, caught in the act of speaking, but without the presence of mind even to tell the most elemental lie. Because it was the truth.

Wolpert's bass came like a wrathful god from behind a cloud. "You touched her!"

Dave tried again to speak, but still words would not come, and I thought there was a chance that Dempsey might have broken him. Dave teetered on the edge.

He said, "I touched her," like a confession.

That's how we all wanted to hear it.

"Okay," Dempsey said, as if she might even understand such a thing. Then, in a neutral tone, "How did you touch her?"

It was a leap, "How?" instead of "Where?" But she showed she was right there with him, because Dave didn't have any difficulty with it.

He wasn't looking at us but instead his eyes were fixed at a point on Abby's rug to the side and four feet in front of him while what he saw was in his mind's eye. "I took her hand real gentle," he said, his voice softened in the spell of reverie. "Because she was only a young girl and her hands were small."

"Did you touch both her hands?"

"No." He looked up quickly, reminded of her presence. "Only the one."

"Did you touch her today?"

"No."

"Did you touch any other part of her?"

He wasn't put out by the question. He said, "No," without the need to defend himself against her implications.

"I know you care about her, Dave," Dempsey told him. "That's why I know you want to help us find her."

"She's a sweet girl."

"That's why you want to help us find Danielle before anything really bad happens to her."

"Yes."

"We have to know everything," Wolpert said, not unkindly.

Dave nodded agreement. "I know that."

"Where else have you seen Danielle? Across the street, in the park?"

"Yes."

"Would you meet her there?"

"If I was on break, sometimes I'd run into her."

"And you talked."

"She was a friendly girl."

"A lonely girl, as you probably discovered."

"Yes, she was."

"She didn't get much attention at home. I suppose you knew that."

"I did . . . I guessed it."

"That was all she wanted, really. A bit of attention."

"She was friendly."

"She lived nearby."

"Yes—if I remember rightly."

"Twenty-seven Francis Street. A couple of blocks."

"Could be."

"Did you ever go to her house?"

"No."

"How did you get Danielle's T-shirt?"

He woke up now, scrutinizing each person in the room in turn, as if to see which one of us had lured him into this trap.

"You had her T-shirt," Dempsey prompted him.

"I've had enough of this bullshit."

"Our dog found a T-shirt under the floorboards of the closet in your bedroom. The T-shirt belonged to Danielle. We know that because Mrs. McNeely identified it."

Dave stood up. He said, "I want a lawyer."

The T-shirt doesn't tie him directly to the crime," Brenda was saying. "This wasn't what Danielle was wearing today. It's the one with the picture of the Grand Canyon that Danielle was wearing in the video. Mrs. McNeely says it went missing a month ago."

"It shows motive," Dempsey said.

"I agree," Brenda said. "I'm with you. But it's a stretch."

"I say we arrest him."

"If we arrest him now," Brenda said, "if we lock him up, then that's it. He goes nowhere."

"That's the point," Dempsey said. "We want him where we control him." Her hands made a gathering gesture, but it could equally have been a slow, powerful squeezing motion.

"That's the advantage of arresting him. The probable cause grounds are a bit flimsy. We could just about do it."

"What's not to like about it?"

"Because we want him, but we want Danielle more."

"So we let him loose—and he's going to lead us to the girl?"

"Perhaps."

"He's not that stupid."

Brenda turned to me.

"He might be," I said.

The four people in the room were silent as if considering. But it was a silent standoff. Dempsey wanted me to stay out of the debate. I had no right to speak, no standing whatsoever.

"He cares about the girl," I said. "His partner might want her dead, but Dave doesn't."

"Oh, this sick fuck cares about his victim?" Dempsey asked. "He cares about her so much he rapes her and kills her?"

"We don't know he's raped her," Brenda said quietly. "We don't know if he's killed her."

But Dempsey was on a tear. "Maybe . . ." She spluttered in her fury. "If he cares so much about Danielle . . . maybe when he gets done with his sentence he can become a social worker!"

"Or a psychiatrist," Wolpert added.

"Okay," Brenda said, indicating a truce. "Let's think about what we've got. We have a history of indecent assault. We've got a T-shirt that ties him to the victim. A T-shirt he stole from the victim. We've got opportunity—he was in the vicinity. We've got means—he has a connection to Hodges and the van. He was on speaking terms with Danielle. He could have lured her into the van."

"He touched her hand," Wolpert said. "He admitted he touched her."

"And that will go over with the jury," Brenda said. "But it's like the T-shirt: It's frosting. It's not the cake.

What we need is something substantial that ties him to the victim's abduction."

We knew she meant Danielle herself. Or the body of Danielle.

"We have to work on the assumption they've stashed her somewhere. We have to act on the hope that they've got Danielle locked up. Even if it's one chance in a hundred—which it isn't, it's better than that—it's the only assumption that makes sense. Feldman can lead us there."

"Or," Dempsey said, "he can tell us where she is."

"Once he's under arrest, he'll have a lawyer sitting right beside him." Brenda's tone was cold, threatening. "We arrest him, he gets a lawyer, and he clams up."

Dempsey shrugged. "Even lawyers sleep."

Brenda paused, as if the implications of what the detective said were rolling balls that had to come to rest. When she spoke, the words were clipped and severe. "I hope you're not suggesting what I think you're suggesting."

"I'm not suggesting anything. Just stating the facts."

"If you step out of line with this suspect . . . If you put a hand on him, I'll come down on you."

"You've got your job."

"I'm warning you."

"We've got ours."

They stood, eye to eye, as Brenda's cell phone rang, a series of chords whose tongue-in-cheek melodrama sounded ludicrously out of place. It rang three times before Brenda turned aside, flipped it open to identify the caller, then answered.

She mostly listened, frowning, without taking her eyes from the detectives. Finally she asked, "Has the mother identified her?"

My heart sank. For an instant, Dempsey's face was squeezed tight in a grimace of anguish. Then she turned violently away and cursed under her breath. While Brenda listened and nodded, I began to rehearse how I'd break the news of Danielle's death to Abby. I was flooded with memories of the time I'd spent sitting beside the hospital bed where Abby was recovering from emergency surgery after the accident. While she was still groggy from the effects of anesthesia and pain medication, I had held her hand and indulged in the luxury of unrestrained sobbing, at a loss for words I could possibly use to tell her Adrian was dead.

"I know you're sure," Brenda told her caller. "But I want to be certain. Yes. That's why I want the mother to ID her."

Brenda slapped her phone shut. She was like a sleep-walker who, waking, is unaware of the effect her behavior has had on those around her.

"That was the computer lab," she said. She looked from Dempsey, to me, to Wolpert, puzzled by the expressions on our faces. Then catching up with us, "The computer lab, not the morgue. Sorry. They've decrypted the hard drive on Feldman's computer. They have a list of the child porn Web sites Feldman and his buddy visited. They have pictures of kids. Some of them are of Danielle. But I want her mother to confirm that's who it is."

"Are they nude pictures?" I asked, thinking of the effect on the fragile woman who'd appealed to me in the lobby downstairs.

"The pictures of the other kids are nudes. The ones of Danielle are candids. They look like they've been shot from a distance."

"From a van," I said.

"Could be from a van. Others weren't lined up, or Danielle isn't centered. Maybe taken by someone who had to conceal the camera and couldn't look through the viewfinder."

"They didn't try to hide the pictures?" I asked.

"They tried. They used commercial software to erase the hard drive, but our recovery software is better. We have a pretty complete history of where they went on the Web and the sites they visited."

"Can we tell when they tried to erase the hard drive?"

"It was last night. Twelve hours before Danielle went missing."

"So they had a schedule," I said. "They did a cleanup before they snatched Danielle. They kicked over the traces. They had a day and a time when they would go into action."

"So what are you saying?" Dempsey asked. "That we're up against master criminals?" She looked to Wolpert, the other professional.

"It tells us this was an organized crime. It wasn't an impulsive, spur-of-the-moment snatch, which is good."

"How's that?"

"Because they have a purpose for Danielle. They know what they want to do with her."

"And that's good?"

"It's good because if it's an organized crime they have a place to take her to. They prepared. Maybe there's water there or food. Maybe it's a cellar with an air conditioner. I don't know. But if it's planned, they're not rushed. They don't have to do their thing and kill her and move on."

Dempsey said, "They didn't do such a good cleanup if they left the girl's T-shirt behind. Or maybe that was part of the plan?"

"That was a mistake," I said. "And it tells us something about Dave Feldman."

"Okay," Brenda said. "Spin it out for us."

"The T-shirt should have been gone along with everything else, but Dave isn't disciplined. I'm assuming Arthur is the planner. Dave goes along but he doesn't entirely follow orders. There's a potential split we can exploit."

"We have to have them in custody first," Dempsey said.

"The other thing is that in spite of the risk, Dave held on to the T-shirt. It was a stupid risk. It shows he has an emotional attachment to the girl. He risks being caught on account of the T-shirt, but he keeps it anyway."

"They all do," Dempsey said dismissively.

"This isn't a trophy that some serial murderer keeps to evoke the victim. Dave took the T-shirt before Danielle became a victim. And once she became a victim he had access to any number of more desirable trophies. Clothes with the girl's scent on them."

Brenda frowned and looked away. She was already on edge and didn't need this spelled out.

"This isn't a trophy," I said. "This is a love token."

"Oh, please!" Dempsey said disgustedly.

Wolpert snorted in disbelief and shook his head as if to clear it of some foul odor. In their eyes, I could as well have been the sicko.

"We've got to use what we've got," I reminded them.

It was hard to get them back to focus on our objective. I said, speaking slowly to emphasize each word, "If Dave, in his own sick, perverted way, loves Danielle—" I held up my hand to forestall their protests. "And you can call it anything you want, but it's still going to come back to some kind of love, however repulsive you think that is—then that gives us an edge. If he loves her, that's leverage we can use in an interrogation. If all he wants is to use her for sex, he'll discard her when he's done. If that's all she is to him, as far as he's concerned, she's better off dead, because then she's not a witness he has to worry about. But if he loves her, he wants to possess her. He wants to keep her alive. He wants the same thing we want."

I seemed to have reached a stalemate with the detectives. They regarded me suspiciously, as though I invited them down the slippery slope: to explain is to understand; to understand, condone.

"I don't have a problem with that," Brenda said. "Feldman's the weak link. He's the one we want to work on."

"So . . ." Dempsey toyed with the implication. "We'll arrest him?" In her eyes was a hungry look, a yearning to cause pain.

"Yes," Brenda said. "Let's take him in."

I worry I'm a distraction," I told Brenda.

I'd stayed back in Abby's office to talk to her alone.

"Dempsey and Wolpert are good cops," she said. "They're not going to be thrown off-line because of you. They'll give you grief, but you can take it."

"I want to help in any way I can. If I can be useful, I'll stick around."

"Would you, Paul? Would you stay? I want to keep you in my back pocket. We need to have other interrogation styles besides the standard good cop/bad cop routine. We need everything we can get right now."

We'd caught the weather report on TV, and there was no relief from the heat on the way. Tonight would stay hot and sticky. Dr. Kerensky's red line was constantly in our minds. We knew that if they'd left Danielle in the trunk of a car, she'd be dead by now.

I asked, "You're going to put pressure on Dave Feldman?"

"As soon as he gets a lawyer. Whatever the detectives

said, we're doing this by the book. They were just letting off steam. You know that, right?"

I wasn't so sure, but I nodded agreement. "It could be all over once he gets a lawyer. A lawyer might tell him not to talk."

"I think it's going to work for us. Any lawyer's going to tell him he'll be looking at first-degree murder if we don't find Danielle soon. He needs to cut a deal fast. He's not going to hear that from us, but he might listen to someone who's appointed to defend him."

"You're not pulling Hodges in?"

"Not for now. We have him under surveillance."

"He won't go to Danielle. He's disciplined. He likes playing games with you people."

"Feldman's a better prospect. We're concentrating our efforts on him."

I called the people at the Sanders Institute to tell them I'd be out the next day and to arrange coverage for my patients.

Brenda pushed to get Dave Feldman arraigned so that he could get an attorney appointed and, she hoped, begin negotiations on a plea bargain. The court appointed Jerry Papandreas.

The name didn't mean anything to me, but Abby remembered him right away.

"He was the lawyer at the refinancing."

Her office had become the local command center, and she'd yielded it gracefully to the detectives, so we were sitting in one of the offices down the corridor that belonged to a social worker who was on vacation. Framed pictures of her kids sat on the desk and the file cabinet, a young girl and a boy of about four—the same age our own son, Adrian, would have been—smiling shyly into the camera.

Abby was arrested momentarily by the image, stopping absentmindedly in mid-paragraph, staring, then turning away as though the lapse had not occurred. There was no more than a superficial similarity between the boy in the photo and our dead son. Perhaps Abby was unaware, in her stream of consciousness, that she had paused to reflect, shake herself loose of the memory, and continue speaking.

She couldn't accept comfort from me, and that was a source of bitter sadness. I was afraid I was approaching the day when a declining sadness and a rising bitterness would meet—the affectionate equivalent of Dr. Kerensky's red line. And if the lines had already touched, it was something—like Abby noticing and not noticing the photograph of the little boy—that I kept from myself.

"You remember Jerry Papandreas," Abby said. For some reason she was scrutinizing my face as though I might be attempting to hide something. Or else I couldn't read her expression.

We'd remortgaged our home more than a year ago, and I struggled to bring a visual image to mind.

"The pudgy guy with all the pens," she prompted me.

Jerry came back to me in fragments. A fussy and fastidious manner. An anxious checking and rechecking of documents that went over and beyond the meticulous preparation any mortgage company could have required. I recalled a sheen of sweat on his forehead, in spite of the air-conditioned office. The face was coming back to me. A round face, dark hair thinning at the front. Fortyish. Jerry was dressed in a poorly chosen suit that he wore with the top two buttons of the jacket fastened, and a bulging, strained triangle of white shirt showed in the region of the navel, as though his current girth were a temporary aberration that would soon dissipate.

"Okay," I said. "Right."

"But Jerry's a real estate lawyer."

I shrugged. "It's the luck of the draw. The court-appointed lawyer could be anyone. Whoever the judge picks. No one wants to have his face on the news associated with a couple of pedophiles. Jerry happened to be in the wrong place at the wrong time. He's probably half-decent. I expect he does a bit of criminal work on the side."

"Drunk drivers are about as far as it goes for Jerry's criminal experience." Abby wasn't speculating about Jerry's practice. She spoke as though she had something to tell me. "Maybe a couple of assault and batteries and a handful of domestic abuse cases a year."

"You know him?" I asked.

"I see his wife."

"In Bristol?"

She looked away, and I knew that meant trouble. Her chin was raised in a defiant tilt.

Abby rented an office one afternoon a week in a psychiatric practice on Main Street in our town. Though she was devoted to her girls, she didn't want her work to consist entirely of troubled adolescents and the young women they turned into; she wanted to include people with brighter futures, middle-class men and women who had more substantial resources to draw on to pull them out of the difficulties that brought them to see her.

"You're seeing Jerry's wife in therapy?"

"I've been seeing her for about a year. They have problems."

"Should you be telling me this?"

"Probably not." She gave a "What the heck" wave of her hand. "But I'm going to tell you anyway."

Abby had mentioned Jerry's wife in what might have

seemed a casual aside. But a psychotherapist, especially an experienced one like Abby, guards her patients' secrets. We occasionally discussed our patients—a juicy murder over dinner, for example, or a troubling case that had gotten under the skin where one of us needed the other's help in gaining greater objectivity—but these were always people the other spouse didn't know. Even when we gossiped, we never included people we might come across in a different context. The boundary between the professional and the personal life protected us as well as the patients. So what Abby had just said was a betrayal of trust that shocked me.

"I don't think you should tell me."

"I want you to know."

"I don't want to know."

"There are things about Jerry you could use."

"Are you out of your mind?"

"No. I'm very rational. Right now, I'm very clear on what needs to be done."

"It's confidential. You're crossing the line."

For a moment, she stared, unseeing, at the shy boy in the photo.

"You think it's unethical?"

"You know it is."

"You think it's unethical to tell you about the problems Jerry Papandreas has in his marriage?"

"Yes, I do."

"You think it's unethical for me to tell you about the pictures Lena Papandreas stumbled onto when she went to use the computer and clicked on the wrong file?"

"It's unethical."

"You don't think it's unethical for men to snatch eight-year-old girls so they can force sex on them? That's unethical too, isn't it?"

"It's not the same thing."

"Give me a break!"

"I don't want to sound like—"

"Like a whiny social worker?"

"You know what I mean."

"I know exactly what you mean. That's the problem."

"What is this?"

"You don't know? Wake up, Paul! This is personal. This is about me and a little girl called Danielle. Who was—is—a spark of light and joy in this world, to everyone who ever came in contact with her."

"I know."

"No, you don't."

Her tone was cold, and when I looked up, her eyes upon me were cold, too, and unforgiving.

"Jerry has a thing for young girls."

"That's enough!"

"No, it's not. I haven't even started."

"I don't want to hear anymore."

"You don't. And I don't want to tell you. But I'm going to. And you're going to listen. Even though you don't want to. You're going to listen, because you have to. If you didn't want to hear, you could have gotten up any time you wanted and walked out of this office. You still could."

I sat still. I looked at the worn rug between my feet. She was right: I didn't want to leave. I told myself I was there for Abby.

I thought, *I'm immune to this. I can sanitize whatever she tells me and I won't use it. Let her talk. She needs to let off steam. I'll compartmentalize it and it'll be as if I forgot it.*

"Okay," I said briskly, as though summarizing a case history, "Jerry has a thing for young girls."

"Not as young as Danielle. Fifteen, sixteen. The girls are old enough for the attraction to be understandable, at least."

"But even if I wanted to, what would I use it for? What would I do with this . . . shit?"

"He doesn't know his wife found out about his little hobby."

"So I'm going to blackmail him? Is that the idea?"

"He won't know where the information comes from. You see? Maybe the police told you. They're all over the Internet now."

"And I threaten to tell his wife?"

"It's a weapon for you to use. You're a creative man. You'll think of something."

"This is sleazy."

"Afraid of getting your hands dirty?"

"I'm not afraid."

"Tell him to throw the case. Tell him to advise the reptile he's supposed to be representing that he has to tell the police where Danielle is. That's all we want. Isn't it? What else is there?"

It wasn't so much the amorality of what Abby was proposing that tipped me off-balance. I dealt with sociopaths and their rationalizations every working day. What flummoxed me was that I no longer recognized my wife. The champion of the rights of the downtrodden, a zealot for whom fairness and justice were sacred, had mutated into a harpy who would sacrifice any principle that interfered with the preservation of this one life.

"Picture this," she said. "A nude cheerleader, fifteen years old. Maybe sixteen. High-kicking. No panties. Wispy, blond pubic hair—"

"Okay!" I said, holding up my hand to cut her off.

"Here's the part you need to know. She's waving fluorescent pink pompoms in the air."

I'd heard plenty of dark secrets, but I'd never felt so dirtied. This was personal, and I couldn't exactly say how.

"This is the good part. The photo has a caption. The way Lena described it, it's like a banner unfurled along the top. It says, GO FORT WAYNE HIGH!"

"So when the cops are interrogating his client, all I have to do is whisper in Jerry's ear, 'Go Fort Wayne High!' and he'll know exactly what I'm talking about."

"You won't even need to whisper. That's the beauty of it. You can say it out loud, whoever's there. It's a code that only you and Jerry will understand."

"You know I'll never do that."

"You never know what you might do. You just don't know."

"That's what you have rules for. So you do know."

"If you don't, I will," Abby said.

We stared eye to eye in a standoff, and I had the feeling of alienation once more, the confusing impression that my wife had been replaced by a facsimile. I tried to look for the old Abby. I gazed into her blue eyes, and they looked back glacial and unyielding. I pulled back, looking at her sideways to get a change of perspective, my eyes scanning her hair, the set of her mouth, as if looking for an entry point on a map, one familiar element that would key in all the rest.

"You'd call Jerry up?" I asked.

"If you force me. If that's what I have to do. But if I have to do it, it won't work as well as if you do it."

"Are you done?"

"I'm going to tell you everything," she said. "Every sordid detail."

At that moment, I knew that if it came to it, if some theoretical, hypothetical matchup ever escaped into reality, if Danielle was on one side of the balance and I dangled from the other, Abby would sacrifice me.

It's a strange sensation, sitting across a table from someone who is totally unaware that you know his biggest secret. Secrets are my business, of course, but I'm careful to keep them segregated from my personal life. When I leave the Sanders Institute at the end of the day, they remain there, held back behind the heavy steel doors. My role as a forensic psychiatrist, too, ensures that secrets remain inert, confined within a definite purpose.

We were in a conference room at the East Cambridge police station, a scrupulously featureless room with windows providing a view of the empty parking lot. I sat beside Brenda on one side of the table with Wolpert and Dempsey. Jerry Papandreas sat on the other with his client, Dave Feldman, at the corner.

I resented Abby for infecting me with the knowledge of Jerry's secret, but at the same time I tingled with the secret power. I felt an old, childlike excitement at watching my adversary stumble about while I remained concealed within my hiding place. I mistrusted the edge of pleasure this gave me.

Jerry didn't have many papers to shuffle because for him the case was only an hour old. As we waited for him to retrieve a notepad from the recesses of his briefcase, it seemed to me that Abby's information gave the scene an air of unreality. In a bizarre inversion of the classic nude dream, Jerry went about his business entirely oblivious to the fact that he was psychologically naked.

Our eyes met, and his gaze lingered for a second on my face. I realized I'd been staring at him and looked away. Even though our previous contact had been fleeting, his wife was Abby's patient, and he would know who I was. The element of doubt written on his troubled, chubby face therefore had to do with whether I remembered him. And if I did, did our prior connection in any way create a conflict of interest for him?

The air-conditioning was having trouble keeping up, and Jerry was sweating. He certainly hadn't volunteered for this case. It would bring him nothing but trouble. He'd been in the wrong place at the wrong time, and now he'd do anything he could to wriggle out of it. If this turned out badly, if Danielle were found dead, Jerry knew the notoriety would stick to him. He'd be tagged with this case for the rest of his career. In the middle of an introduction, the other party would hesitate, a frown corrugating the forehead, the handshake slackening, and he'd ask, "Hey, weren't you the guy . . . ?" Jerry would correct him—perhaps he was already preparing his lighthearted chuckle—"The attorney. I was just the attorney."

Our connection wasn't enough to allow him to escape. If he went back to the court with an excuse that feeble, the judge would ream him out, and that would finish it, even if later he came up with circumstances that should have allowed him to recuse himself.

Next to Jerry, Dave Feldman was paying close attention to the preliminaries. His enjoyment of this early phase of his notoriety was evident. For now, he had what the police wanted, and everyone in the room treated him with meticulous respect. We seemed to defer to him, almost. Seated at the head of this conference table, he could have been the chairman of the board. Here people might play along with the fiction that he was innocent until proven guilty, but outside this room that tag was a mere technicality. Within days, I thought, he would have a rude awakening when he was remanded to jail and doused in excrement for the first time.

When it was my turn to be introduced by Brenda—as "our advisor," and without the "Dr."—I was careful to give Jerry no opening to mention our previous meeting, and shook hands with him without expression.

"Jerry," Brenda began, "you're comfortable having your client present at this conference?"

He looked startled, as though he hadn't considered the alternative. "Sure," he said, without conviction. "You're all right with that, aren't you, David?"

Dave nodded resolutely. "Oh, yeah." He wouldn't have missed this for the world. He was living in the midst of a TV forensics show and getting more famous by the minute.

"Because I want to be able to talk frankly," Brenda said.

"Okay with us," Jerry said. He was afraid, and took out a white cotton handkerchief and extended his chin to stretch the folds of skin so that he could mop the underside of his neck.

"There's no death penalty in Massachusetts," Dave offered before Brenda could speak.

It was something he'd learned, and he wanted to

show us he knew the score. It sounded like something Arthur might have told him: "There's no death penalty in Massachusetts, so don't let them put a scare into you with that old saw."

Jerry told him not to speak and reminded him of the Miranda warning. But this was his story, and Dave wasn't content to be a mere spectator.

"Well, there isn't," he insisted.

Wolpert's lips opened and he took in breath, preparing to speak, then thought better of it. Brenda had warned them. She had the detectives on a short leash.

Brenda examined the nails of her outstretched fingers as she paused for effect. "Technically speaking," she said, "there is no death penalty in Massachusetts. However, if we don't secure your client's cooperation in finding Danielle, if this young girl isn't found alive, I can promise you that the perpetrator will die in prison."

She let the ambiguity of dying in prison hang there for Dave's consideration: he could be killed a couple of months after the trial, his head caved in from repeated blows from a lock-in-a-sock, or he might fade out after fifty years of watching cartoons and three squares a day.

"Of course," Detective Dempsey said, "we'll do everything in our power to protect you in prison, but . . ." She shrugged and raised her hands, palms up, in a gesture of helplessness. Or it could have been indifference.

"They have special units for—" Dave began, but Jerry Papandreas cut him off.

"There's a waiting list for those spots," Dempsey said. "You have to get in line behind the priests."

Dave pouted moodily. "Anyway, I'm innocent."

He smiled, looking at each of us around the table in turn, as if his demeanor could be in any way convincing.

Wolpert started to say something but was silenced by a sharp glance from Brenda.

"We believe," Brenda said, "that the person who abducted Danielle McNeely did not act alone. He had an accomplice. The person who put this together, who planned it, who—we believe—initiated the crime, the instigator—we have him under surveillance. We can pull him in anytime we want."

I watched Dave as Brenda rounded out her bluff. He blinked when she told him she had Arthur, and the muscles below his lip contracted, pushing his lower lip forward in a sign of tension. He maintained his slouch, but he didn't sit so comfortably in his chair, and his pose of indifference was strained.

"The other person, the accomplice—we believe he isn't in so deep. He's in serious trouble—don't get me wrong—but we think we can work with him."

"Okay," Jerry said. "What do you have for us?" And he quickly added, "This is all hypothetical, of course."

"You can call it what you want," Brenda said. "It's not hypothetical to us."

"But, I mean, it's off the record?"

"I'll agree it's not admissible." Brenda surveyed the three witnesses, the two detectives and me, any of whom was capable of leaking to the press if things went bad. "If that'll satisfy you."

"Agreed."

"All right, then. It's not complicated: we want the girl."

"What are you offering?"

"It depends on the condition she's in."

Dave's lips moved and the muscles around his neck tightened slightly, drawing up his shoulders. He may have thought of himself as gentle, loving, even, but Arthur had control of Danielle now, and he had just realized that he couldn't be sure what Arthur, left to himself, without Dave's chivalrous restraint, would do to her. Perhaps he was starting to realize that he had never had control of this operation and that Arthur, from the very beginning, had set everything up the way he wanted.

Brenda spelled it out, driving the wedge deeper between the two suspects. "If Danielle's been raped," she said, and let the hypothetical hang over the table for two beats.

Dave kept his eyes down, but he couldn't prevent himself from squirming in his seat. He was angry. He wanted to speak. Maybe he wanted to denounce Arthur.

"If this little girl's been harmed," Brenda went on, "we'll ask the judge to run the sentences on and after—kidnap, rape of child, anything we can think of. For practical purposes, it'll be a life sentence. Life without parole. Natural life."

"You can't be sure the court will go along with that," Jerry offered uncertainly.

He knew he was out of his depth. A man's life was in his hands, and his fear was evident in his eyes, in the sheen of sweat on his face, in the fussy mannerisms of adjusting the pen so that it lined up alongside the spine of the black leather organizer open before him. I wondered if a faint echo from Fort Wayne High made him uneasy. He'd placed his client at the head of the table, distinct and apart, rather than have him sit in solidarity by his side.

It was the first time Brenda had put any heat on him in the negotiation, and it looked as if Jerry wasn't going to put up much resistance.

"It's the bad guy we want," Brenda said. "We want Danielle safe and sound, back with her family. We all

want that." She waited, but Jerry seemed slow to agree.
"I think we do."

"Sure. Of course."

"The other guy's going down forever."

"We don't have a problem with that, obviously."

Jerry, remembering his client, looked questioningly
to Dave. Maybe, when it came to it, Dave wouldn't want
to give Arthur up. He stared down morosely as he made
loops with the tip of his index finger on the veneer of
the conference table.

"Obviously," Dave said, and although we didn't exchange glances, it seemed that the four of us on the
other side of the table breathed a sigh as we turned this
corner in the negotiations.

This was exactly what we wanted, for Dave to reflect
on how his interests and Arthur's might now begin to di-
verge. Affable Arthur had befriended lonely, outcast
Dave, but mostly it had been an alliance of convenience.
Arthur had used Dave's computer. Arthur had used
Dave's connection with Danielle.

Then Dave added, "I've done nothing wrong."

"That could be true," Brenda agreed. "But even if, up
to this point, you've done nothing wrong, if you with-
hold evidence and this little girl dies, then you're an accessory to murder."

"Now, wait a minute," Jerry protested. "You can't lay
that kind of stuff on my client."

"You wanted him here. Did you want to change your
mind? Do you want us to talk without him?"

"No," Dave said. "I'm staying here."

"You know what 'accessory' is?" Brenda asked him.

"It means you're in it with him."

"It means you're in it with him all the way. Right up
to sentencing. It means even though you might not have

done certain things, you're part of it, so you get the same sentence. If this girl dies, even though you weren't the one who killed her, it means you could get life, because you're an accessory."

We watched for this to sink in. Dave thought about it, head down, eyes veiled. He had already known what an accessory was. Arthur had prepped him for this line of attack. Finally he pursed his lips and shrugged his shoulders in seeming indifference.

"So?" he asked.

He glanced up to see how we were taking this, and I caught a glint in his eyes I didn't like. Dave wasn't as afraid as he ought to have been. If anything, it was a look of triumph that he'd let escape. He knew something. Not having to do with where the girl was, but about strategy. We'd done what he expected, and he was ahead of us. He worked in a donut shop, but he was ahead of these cops and smart lawyers. He was looking down again, hidden from us, tracing loops of infinity on the table.

"So even though you're innocent, it won't make any difference if it turns out you knew something that could have saved this girl."

With his finger on the very edge of the table, Dave, eyes down, performed a delicate maneuver whose significance was known only to himself.

Brenda went on, "Right now, the other guy, the bad guy, has Danielle. Or he knows where she is. He controls her. He's out there, going about his business. But you're here. Even though you're here, if he's done something to her, it's on you. If you're an accessory, what he does, it's like you did it."

"Wait a minute," Jerry protested. He turned to his client. "That's not strictly true. You're not responsible for what the other guy does. How can you be?"

He would have said more, but Dave cut him off.

"Who says I even know this other guy?"

"We're not saying anything," Brenda reassured him. "We're not saying you did anything to Danielle."

"Then why's he under arrest?"

She held up her hand to forestall Jerry. "Right now, all we're saying is that you have a connection to a little girl who's disappeared."

"Why do you keep calling her a little girl?" Dave asked, irritable.

"What do you call her, then?"

He shrugged and turned away sulkily.

"She's a kid, isn't she?" Brenda persisted. "Danielle's a child?"

She waited a moment to see if he'd acknowledge Danielle's vulnerability, but when she got no response from Dave, she returned to the heart of the matter, the deal.

"If you give us information that allows us to find Danielle unharmed, we'll significantly reduce the charges you're looking at. The kidnapping charge will go away."

She paused a moment to get a read on him, but Dave kept his head down.

"Provided, of course," she went on, "that we have your full cooperation in prosecuting the other guy."

We waited to see some glimmer of response from Dave. He savored his power. He was not intelligent, but he was cunning enough to understand that as soon as he made his deal he'd shrink to nothing. The deal would only move him a step closer to prison.

He sat very still. Both hands were poised with the tips of his fingers on the edge of the dark wood of the conference table. His eyelids fluttered briefly once, suggesting the turmoil of excitement he held back. Twice the muscles beneath his lower lip contracted, turning down the corners of the mouth and clamping the lips shut to conceal an incipient smile.

Dave felt pleasure during this moment of silence while he held us hostage to his decision. Here he was looking at twenty years in prison—a lifetime if Danielle died—but his mind was insulated from this dire future; all he felt was this triumph of the present. He had us. For a lone moment in his life, he had power over the people who ran things.

When he spoke, he didn't look up, not trusting himself to conceal his feelings. "What are you offering?" he asked.

Brenda didn't want to tell him a number. Plea-bargaining isn't any different from buying a car: the first person to name his price loses. But more important, Brenda couldn't afford to scare him. One year, five years, ten years—these were just numbers to Jerry. But Brenda had to cushion Dave from the shock of real time—and she did have to put him away for real time. After the media frenzy and the manhunt, no one would stand for anything less, even if he delivered Danielle to us alive.

Dave had walked free until yesterday. He was a man for whom prison was a remote, abstract possibility. And now he wanted a number. He thought he did.

"You'll be out of prison while you're still a relatively young man."

He snorted. " 'Relatively young'? What kind of a deal is that?"

He sneered at the four of us facing him along the conference table. Dempsey's hand clenched in her lap. Wolpert stirred, twisted his neck as if stretching a pinched nerve. Brenda sat immobile, eyes fixed intently on her prey. Any one of us would have been happy to kill him in the most brutal manner.

We waited him out in silence, each immersed in his or her own violent fantasy. When he spoke, I was lost in the imagined action of swinging Dave's head, one of my hands with a firm grasp of the hair, into the hard, sharp edge of the table. I was deeply satisfied by the crunch as the more fragile nasal and facial bones caved in.

"I don't want to be sexually dangerous," he said.

Because of where we were coming from, we missed the point. Detective Dempsey had a contorted smile as she suppressed her desire to tell Dave how she would be willing to rid him for the rest of his life of any risk of sexual danger.

"If you want to deal with me, then you have to guarantee I won't be charged with something that could make me be committed as a sexually dangerous person."

Massachusetts law permits a person whom a court has pronounced sexually dangerous to be incarcerated for a day to life. This comes at the end of the prison sentence he has served for the sex crime he's committed. Provisions in the law mandate annual hearings to determine whether he is still sexually dangerous, and a few men who can show that their predatory mind-set has responded to therapy are released. But Dave was correct in surmising that if Danielle didn't come out of this alive, he'd be declared sexually dangerous and incarcerated for the rest of time.

This kind of knowledge was far beyond Dave's expertise. He and Arthur had discussed this worst-case scenario at length during those slow evenings over the computer. They'd gamed the fallback positions, the what-ifs of getting arrested. They'd rehearsed this. They'd played out their strategy as far as the plea-bargaining stage.

Brenda had a look of puzzled skepticism. She, too, was wondering where this had come from. This was a tricky issue for her. The purpose in designating someone sexually dangerous was to keep him on the radar screen, especially if he ever made it back to the community.

But Dave was looking up now, attentive and not at all sulky, watching Brenda's face for a sign of her reaction.

Brenda saw the eagerness in his eyes. She took her time. "That's a big thing," she told him.

"You were the one who wanted a deal." He was angry and disappointed. He had no sense of the tease of negotiation. He thought concretely and didn't understand how "maybe" could mean "maybe yes."

"I'm not saying I won't do it. I'm saying you're asking a lot."

"So are you."

"If I'm going out on a limb for you, I want a commitment from you."

He watched her warily. He sensed a trick coming. He didn't know whether it had already been laid on him without his noticing. " 'If,' " he mimicked her sarcastically. "If you're going out on a limb. But you don't say you're going to do it."

"All right." Brenda had finally engaged him, eye to eye. "I'll do it." She was looking for a response. But something was wrong here. "If you give me what I want, I won't bring charges that will get you committed as sexually dangerous."

He didn't relax as I thought he would. When a person gets what he wants the tension goes out of his body, he lets out a sigh, he has an inclination to smile. If the negotiations have been hard-fought, he can't resist glancing into the eyes of his adversary. This was the time, when he'd put one over, that I would have expected the hoist of the glasses and the grimace.

But Dave was watchful. His head was tilted defiantly, and his eyes wore a sly expression. I thought, *He's only playing with us,* and my heart sank, thinking of the girl.

I risked a glance at the detectives, and they looked uneasy, too. Wolpert stared at the suspect with slitted eyes. Dempsey had turned away from what should have been the center of interest toward Brenda, as if to catch her eye.

"So," Brenda prompted him. "What do you say?"

Dave pursed his lips and considered a spot on the table a couple of feet in front of him, pantomiming a tough decision.

Brenda was leaning forward, overly engaged, too attentive. She sensed something was wrong, too, but she was part of the process, while the three of us, spectators, could see something else unfolding.

Brenda was impatient. She said, "This is what you wanted, right?" She should have waited him out. He had to come to her now.

"Part of it," Dave said slowly, as if he were still thinking things over.

"Well," Dempsey said, out of nowhere, ignoring the glare from Brenda and her chopping hand signal to cut her off. "We'll toss in your own bunk in the special skinners' PC unit."

Dave was confused, too. This wasn't in the script. The look he gave her suggested he was tempted to tell the cop to go fuck herself, but in a short time, if things went wrong, he could be living in her world, and he checked the impulse. Since he hadn't been to prison, he didn't know that he was a skinner or that PC stood for protective custody, the special unit for pedophiles, gangland informers, and priests. But Dempsey's message was intended for Brenda, not the suspect.

Jerry looked mystified. "Is that some kind of joke?" he asked Brenda. "We're here to negotiate in good faith. I don't appreciate these attempts to intimidate my client."

"I made an offer," Brenda reminded him.

"I agree, it's a start," Jerry conceded.

"You mentioned negotiating in good faith. I've made an offer. Now I want something from your side."

"You don't own the store just because you tossed in some spare change," Dave said.

"But I have to know you're serious."

"What do you want?"

"A token."

"What?"

"I want the name of the other guy."

"I thought you said you already knew him?"

"We do."

"Then you don't need me to tell you."

"We don't. But when you tell us his name, on the record, I'll know we're talking seriously."

"What if I don't know it?" He gave Brenda a coy smile.

"Look," I began, glancing in Brenda's direction to make sure that she wouldn't object to me taking over from her. Interrogation is like a tag-wrestling bout, and we needed someone new in the ring. "None of us has time for wrangling," I said.

"I'm not the one playing games," Dave said.

"No one's playing games here," I agreed. "We had a report from a doctor about Danielle's condition. In this heat, she won't last long without water."

I talked more about dehydration, hallucinations, coma, how people die, and watched Dave for signs of distress. He wasn't cold to the needs of other people. When we'd talked before, he had shown rudimentary concern for others, and he didn't strike me as a sociopath. I kept my description factual and stayed away from lurid details, and watched to see what he did with it.

He looked away. He shifted in his seat from one side to the other. He shook his head in poorly feigned disbelief.

"That was three hours ago," I said, "when the doctor gave his report. Since then, her condition's only gotten worse."

"Unless you know different," Wolpert said.

"This is the way it is," I said, ignoring the detective. The last thing I wanted was everyone jumping in for a free-for-all. "This is what we all want to avoid. But we don't have much time. We don't know how hot it is where she is. We don't know how dehydrated she was before she disappeared. What the doctor says is only an estimate. No one can know for sure how long she'll last in this heat. He says she might last through the night. But she might die tonight, if we don't find her."

I let him sit with this. Brenda glared at the detectives, guarding the silence while Dave sat turned away from us, a silly smile on his lips and his forehead furrowed with a frown.

"No one wants Danielle to die," I said quietly, regretfully. "Least of all you, her friend."

I felt Dempsey shift in protest beside me as I connected victim and perpetrator by an affective tie, the pedophile's rationalization.

"She's a lovely girl, with her whole life before her," I murmured.

The silly smile was fading as the reality of Danielle's predicament came through to him. He loved her. However grotesque, however repulsive the thought, Dave loved Danielle.

"You're a gentle soul," I told him. "But the other guy . . . We don't know what he might do. How he might hurt her."

He abruptly thrust himself away from the table, as if he could physically break free from the emotions I evoked. "I've had enough of this shit!" he said.

"Me, too," I told him.

He was angry. "I'll tell you something," he said. He waved his index finger in the air threateningly. I hoped he'd know why he was angry. He was angry because he was worried about Danielle, not because I'd manipulated his feelings for her.

"Go ahead," I told him.

"Wait," Jerry told him.

"You think you know the way it is, but you don't." His face was contorted by the effort of holding back tears. "You don't know what it's like. Do you think I don't care . . . ?" Dave cut himself off.

"Maybe this is something we need to discuss first," Jerry suggested ineffectually. "In private."

"No!"

It took Dave several seconds to gain sufficient control of his voice to continue.

"If no one finds Danielle, you've got nothing." For a moment he looked into the abyss of Danielle's murder. "You've got no witness. You've got no case. All you've got is circumstantial evidence. They can't convict you on circumstantial evidence."

"But if we find her, you might walk. And Danielle lives."

"If she's still alive. She might be dead by now."

A chill went through us. Dave was the only person in the room who knew whether Danielle had the necessities of life, and he was dooming her. Even Jerry was aghast.

"You said so yourself," he said. "Doctors can't predict."

"So you'd let her die?" asked Dempsey.

We were stunned by the stark reality of a man who was willing to sacrifice an innocent life to save his neck.

"Is that something you can live with for the rest of your life?" I asked him.

His head was down. With the back of one hand he scraped away the tears that shamed him.

"No," he sobbed.

6:35 P.M.

I didn't want to hang around the police station. The atmosphere was dispiriting, with uniformed police returning from fruitless canvassing of the neighborhood. Every now and again I'd catch one of the cops with a familiar look in his eyes that meant he was about to ask, "Hey, weren't you the guy . . . ?" Then he'd stop, because I wasn't quite "the guy who killed the state police lieutenant," and there wasn't a way to ask the question.

I walked the two blocks back to New Beginnings. The sun was low in the sky, but the day didn't seem to be cooling off, and I was glad to duck into the cool of a sub shop to pick up a sandwich and a couple of cold sodas to share with Abby. I'd missed lunch, and I suspected she hadn't eaten, either.

Under normal circumstances, most of the staff at the agency would have gone home, but three of the social workers were clustered around Nan's desk in the lobby as I entered, and they asked me for news.

"Nothing yet."

I tried to put a positive spin on the words, but my expression told them more than I wanted to say, and they turned away without asking more, quietened and disappointed.

On the second floor, I passed the open door of an office in which two women were huddled in conversation. They fell silent as I passed.

The police had moved on and Abby had reclaimed her office. She was sitting at the desk with her head on one hand, and when I entered she turned as if I'd startled her.

She stood and scrutinized my face for news as the others had done, as if this were a more effective means of communication than words, faster and more immediate. She sagged and let out a sigh as she half sat on the edge of the desk.

"Nothing at all?"

"No."

"He told you nothing?"

"Not yet."

I put the brown paper bag on the desk behind her and started to unpack the sandwich and containers of soda.

"I don't know if you got any lunch," I said. "I brought you a tuna sandwich and a Diet Pepsi."

She took the soda and the straw without noticing what her hands were doing. She was still struggling to read my face, frowning as if a spelling mistake were interfering with the sense of my expression.

"I don't get it," she said.

"I know."

"He wants a deal. Right?"

I shrugged. "Maybe."

"Sure he does. Of course he wants a deal. He's not some Charlestown tough guy."

"He's not tough in that way. But he's sly. He's savvy. It's easy to underestimate him."

"What are they offering him?"

"This is just between the two of us, okay?"

"Oh, come on, Paul!"

"Everybody's so hungry for news. They see me talking with you, shut up in the office with the door closed, and they're going to assume you know something, and as soon as I leave they'll start pumping you."

"Okay." She thrust the straw like a dagger through the perforation in the plastic lid. "So what did you offer him?"

"That he'd still be a young man when he got out."

"What does that mean?"

"That's what Jerry Papandreas jumped on."

"Jerry!" she scoffed. "He should talk!"

"He's raising procedural objections and generally getting in the way."

"Then get him out of the way."

"I can't blackmail someone's lawyer."

"Why not?"

I sighed in exasperation.

She grabbed me by the arm. "Why not?" she demanded.

"I don't think this discussion is going to get us anywhere."

She let go of my arm with a dismissive gesture. "I'll tell you what I think. I think all bets are off. It's not a question of what's ethical anymore."

"There's still the rule of law."

"It's the law of the jungle. Kill or be killed. You use whatever you've got against these animals."

"The law's what keeps us from being the same as them."

"Screw the law! The law's just a game that lawyers play."

"But even lawyers play by rules."

"Their rules."

"There aren't any others."

"That's why you make your own." To Abby, it was as if I'd made a compelling point in her favor. All this was obvious, if only I'd open my eyes and see. "If you let them do things their way, Danielle will be dead by the time this Dave Feldman tells us where to find her. We've got to take a shortcut. We're going to get there one way or another, but we need to get there now. Tomorrow's too late. So we need Jerry to step aside."

"So you want me to tell him: 'Look, Jerry, either you get your client to make a deal pronto, or I turn you in as a child pornographer.' Is that it? Is that what you're saying?"

"Yes."

Once more, she stared into my face, searching for something more than the yes she wanted. I felt she'd set a test for me. We were standing so close that her gaze went back and forth, from one eye to the other. She was frowning, almost in horror at what she couldn't find there.

"It's easy for you to say that."

"No, it's not!" she shouted.

I hadn't realized the intensity of the anger that she'd been holding back during the last few minutes. The cup of soda in her hand was shaking; I was afraid she'd crush it.

Abby's emotion was too fraught, too desperate to be the result of a concern only for Danielle. I wanted to get her to see that the threat to Danielle's life was a lens that brought the unresolved feelings about Adrian's death to an unbearable focus.

I reached to touch her shoulder and was shocked when she shook me off with a rough, violent gesture.

Abby turned away.

We stood in excruciating silence within inches of one another. Adrian's absence was like a cold stone slab between us. I couldn't see her, much less hear or touch her.

She made a flipping gesture with her hand as though she were tossing away the anger that had erupted a few seconds before.

She said, changing the unspoken subject, "It's not like we're railroading an innocent man." She cleared her throat of some residue of sadness that had lodged there. "Dave Feldman did it. Right? Is there any doubt about that?"

Always, I thought. But I said, "No."

"Then what is this about?"

She knew what I'd say. And I knew I'd sound weak and mealy-mouthed, but I had a sentimental attachment to the truth. "Principle," I said, as though confessing.

She turned away with an exhalation of impatience. "Principle!"

I heard contempt in her voice for the first time. I could hardly believe she could feel that way about me. Perhaps she was only now revealing an attitude that she struggled to keep hidden. A marriage can't survive contempt. Even hatred is better. Hatred is a passion that binds. Even boredom allows a kind of zombie relationship to plod from one day to the next. But contempt corrodes the ties. It eats into memories, even, and disfigures them.

"Principle?" She looked at me incredulously. "When a girl's life's at stake?" she demanded.

"Don't you think I know that?" I was angry, too. I wasn't sure what feelings of my own might surface now. "Do you think I like it?"

"You don't have to be a fucking Boy Scout every day

of the week!" She was going to say more, but caught herself. "Not now. Not today."

"We don't choose the—" I was going to say "ideals" before Abby cut me off. She'd already repudiated the notion.

"Rules?" She scoffed. "Good God!"

"You can't change your principles to suit what kind of day you're having. That's why they're principles." I felt I was explaining how the Earth might really, in spite of all the images from orbiting satellites, actually be flat. I seemed, even to myself, primitive and undeveloped.

"I know," she said wearily, with the exhaustion of someone who has used up all hope of compromise. "You are who you are."

Her tone suggested this was a condemnation, the hopelessness extending beyond the moment, beyond Danielle.

Our marriage was disintegrating before our eyes. I thought I loved Abby. But how much was this love for the woman I'd married nine years ago? And how much was something less, an affection based on a routine of touches, hugs, kisses, lovemaking? As I struggled to come together again with Abby, maybe I did fake it sometimes, in the hope that by going through the motions I'd provide the emotional kindling, that the real thing would somehow, unpredictably, miraculously, spark and catch fire.

"This has been hard," I began.

"Don't patronize me."

"I know you were fond of Danielle . . ."

She was sucking abstractedly on the straw. Her look warned me not to cross the line into the topic of Adrian. I had nothing to lose.

"But don't you think," I asked, "there might be more to your feelings now than just about Danielle?"

She twisted to place the cup behind her on the desk, and when she turned back to me, hand on hip in a defiant stance, her chin was up and her lips compressed as if she were ready to fight. "What do you want to say?" Her eyes were narrowed.

"I'm suggesting that some of your emotion is coming from Adrian. Adrian's dead, but we might save Danielle. She's the symbolic replacement. The undoing of the trauma."

She gave me nothing. Her face was hard and closed.

"That's why it's so vital to save Danielle. That's why you're willing to be so . . . ruthless."

"How can you do this?" She'd been angry at first and now was close to tears.

The implication was that in saying what I had I'd betrayed her, but I couldn't stop now, there was too much on the line. "How can I talk to you about our son?"

"How can you be so insensitive?"

"I'm grabbing hold of the moment."

"I can't imagine a worse time to have this conversation."

"There never is a good time."

"Then let it go."

"This won't bring Adrian back."

"It might make amends."

This was better. "Tell me how."

She started to speak, but a sob choked her off. She held up her hand for me not to interrupt. "We failed him."

I shook my head in bewilderment. "I've gone over the accident a hundred times."

"We should have seen the guy in the pickup truck. We should have seen him coming."

"I wish we could have."

"We should have!"

"He went through the red light at forty miles an hour. Even if we'd seen him—"

"I saw him."

My world went black. "You saw him?" It was unraveling. The immutable past, which was done and over with and could never change, was shifting. Huge cracks were opening in reality. "The guy in the pickup truck?"

"Yes."

"You saw him before he hit us?"

"A couple of seconds."

"A couple of seconds is a long time."

"I blame myself."

"No—"

"I do." She hung her head and breathed through her open mouth to ward off tears. "But there wasn't anything I could do."

I started to move toward her, to envelop her in my arms, to tell her, "Of course not." She held up her hands for me to keep my distance. Her fingers flickered like flames.

"I was going to say something," she said, "but I thought you already saw him."

"Me?"

"I thought you'd seen him. There wasn't time for me to speak. I thought you'd react. I didn't want to interfere with what you were going to do to get out of his way."

"But I didn't see anything: How could I?"

"I did."

Her tone carried the unmistakable accusation that if she had seen the pickup truck, I could have, too. Should have.

A powerful current was sweeping me toward the opening of an awful pipeline of anguish and guilt. I swam against it, toward the light and what I knew.

"What I don't understand," I said, "is how can you come up with this now, after all this time."

"I know," she agreed.

"We went over it so carefully. Moment by moment. Right after the accident. Looking to see if we could have done anything different. If we could have saved Adrian."

"I think we weren't entirely honest. The loss of Adrian. It was too much, all at once. We had to take it a bit at a time."

"But why now?" I asked. "Don't you think it's unusual, this late after the event?"

"I don't think it's unusual to repress traumatic memories."

"But don't you have to wonder why you've recovered the memory now?"

"I've been working on it in therapy with guided imagery."

Part of our code of silence was that I could ask nothing about Abby's therapy. Certainly it wasn't anything I could criticize, however ponderous and clumsy it seemed, at a distance, to me.

"Guided imagery is subject to the same kind of distortion that hypnosis is. You know how unreliable that is."

"The memory is solid. It's very clear to me."

"But your confidence in the memory—what seems to be a memory—is no guide to how trustworthy it is. All the research shows that."

"It feels real to me."

"But that's the point. Don't you see that?"

"I have to go with what feels real to me. Don't you see that? What else is there?"

"There's the truth." She didn't scoff this time. "What really happened. What we both experienced."

"That's what I'm talking about."

"You blame me?"

She avoided my gaze. "You were driving."

"You blame me for Adrian's death?"

I could hardly bear the words, inert sounds that framed a hypothetical. It was unbearable that Abby should even consider the possibility. She was a long time in answering.

" 'Blame'?" She sighed at the obscurity. "I don't know, Paul. I think we're responsible."

"Neither of us could have done anything."

"I wish I could believe that. I lived and Adrian died."

The memory of his tiny, limp body came to me with all the emotional immediacy of the real event. I tried to turn away from the memory that followed, as I caught sight of his crushed head.

"Nothing could have saved him," I said. I felt certain of this.

"You don't know. You just don't know. That's why you have to do everything you can possibly do."

She was watching my face very intently to see what my reaction would be.

"You mean for Danielle."

"It's the only thing that matters now."

I wanted to ask, "What about us?" but I said, "How can there be only one thing that matters?"

"It's the only thing that matters to me," Abby said.

6:50 P.M.

W e have a problem," Brenda told me on the phone. "At least, I think it's a problem."

She sent a state car to drive me the five blocks to the courthouse. I found her pacing in the marble lobby.

"Jerry Papandreas wants off the case," she said. "You can't blame the guy. But a change of attorney now will totally screw up any negotiations with Feldman."

"Are they ongoing?"

"We're not clear. We're hoping he's mulling things over. He's sitting in a holding cell downstairs with a big, hairy drug dealer in the cell on one side and a crazy guy on the other. We expect this to help him focus on what his future life could be like."

"How's he taking it?"

"You want to see him?"

"He had some simpatico with me when I talked with him alone. Maybe it would provide leverage."

"I'm tempted. But I don't think we can allow that without his attorney. On the other hand, there's nothing to stop you strolling along the corridor and peeking in on him. Maybe you could check out the schizophrenic man in the cell next door while you're at it."

Five cells in the basement of the courthouse held prisoners awaiting trial and those who had just been sentenced and were awaiting transportation to prison. A court officer let me through the heavy steel door at the bottom of the stairs and then a barred gate.

"I'm back here, if you want me," he said and returned to the other side of the barred gate to take a seat at a desk, leaving me to continue along the corridor on my own.

I asked myself what I was doing here. By what mandate, in what role, under whose auspices, was I about to employ my professional skills to trick a scared and lonely young man into betraying himself? The answer was, none and no one. I'd kept the privileges of my calling at the same time as I'd forsaken its principles. I'd gone native and taken my bag of tricks with me.

But the end justified the means. A life was at stake. This wasn't a time to stand on principle. Abstractions couldn't be allowed to trump life.

Abby was the supreme pragmatist. "Be practical!" she was constantly urging me when I balked at her arguments from expediency. "Come down out of your ivory tower."

But none of these arguments worked on me as I walked the corridor in the court lockup. My father had been a judge and he had instilled in me an unshakable belief in the primacy of enduring, eternal principle. It was etched in silicone. I knew that every step I took was wrong.

I'd do it anyway, because I couldn't stand aside while Danielle died. Abby had said I could have acted to save Adrian. I didn't believe that a true memory, after all this time, had suddenly surfaced, but it didn't make any difference. As it had for her, the imaginative possibility had a force that transcended mere truth, enough to wound me. Abby had stuck a knife in me, and all my convictions were bleeding out.

The air in the lockup was cool and dank, and smelled of men's sweat. A broad corridor ran in front of the bars of the cells. On a busy day, they would be full, with several men in each cell shouting back and forth to men in other cells; but today, in the doldrums of what was becoming a summer evening, with the court's criminal cases disposed of, the basement was unusually quiet. The three prisoners heard my approaching footsteps on the concrete floor.

Only the drug dealer appeared interested. Two muscled arms curled languidly around the bars of the last occupied cell.

"Hey," he called as the court officer returned to his desk. "You my court-appointed attorney?"

I took his question as a pretext to walk slowly the length of the corridor, checking out the other two occupants as I passed.

In the first cell, the schizophrenic man appeared to be talking to hallucinations. His lips moved silently, and he did not look up as I passed.

Dave, on the other hand, had already gotten up from his bunk at the sound of the gate closing, and he stood in the middle of the cell expectantly, unsure whether it was better to come to the bars or to remain safely out of reach.

He was slow to recognize me as I came level with him, and I had almost passed him when he called out, "Hey, Doctor!"

I kept walking and stopped in front of the drug

dealer's cell. He was a large Hispanic man with a mane of black hair and a Frank Zappa moustache. We looked at each other the way two mammals do when they're on different sides of a set of bars. It makes no difference whether it's a prison or a zoo: you can't make any assumptions about which one of you is on display. We eyed each other coolly, as specimens that had not yet been allocated a place in either system of classification.

"Hey," he said, "you ain't no lawyer."

"No," I said, "I'm not. I was looking for someone else."

I turned and walked back slowly. He didn't want to let me go. People locked up always have a use for a person outside the bars, but he couldn't figure out whether I was in law enforcement or a neutral.

I nodded hello to Dave and kept walking.

"Wait!" he called and came to the bars. "Just wait a minute."

With a show of reluctance, I stopped, out of politeness, it might have been. I gave him the caution, but it was done in bad faith and it didn't make me feel any easier. "You know," I said, "you really shouldn't talk to me without your lawyer present."

"Don't do it, man," the drug dealer told him. His head was pressed against the bars so that one eye could bring me into focus. "Don't say nothing without your lawyer."

"I just have like a question," Dave said.

"You're making a mistake," the drug dealer said.

He stayed at the bars to listen to our conversation, but since he'd given his advice and Dave had ignored it, he didn't intrude.

Dave made an attempt at humorous conversation. "Hey, what's up, Doc?" he quacked, Donald Duck–style.

"I don't know," I said. "You're the man."

"But, what I mean is, what's going to happen next?"

I turned to study him for the first time. He was scared, certainly. They'd left him his glasses and they magnified the white of the sclera that showed with the retraction of the upper eyelids. In the space of ten seconds, his eyes involuntarily flicked twice in the direction of the big drug dealer.

I shrugged and started to move away. "That's up to you," I said as I passed from view.

I stopped in front of the next cell. The psychotic man was holding an important dialogue with presences only he could discern, and, oblivious to my presence, looked about himself, turning to address them first in one corner of the cell and then, it seemed, through the wall into the next cell. He did not appreciate an interruption from me.

"Yeah, yeah," he told me dismissively when I asked him how he was doing.

I caught a glimpse of Dave at the bars of the next cell.

"But I wanted to ask you something," Dave said. He sounded close to tears.

When I didn't immediately leave, the schizophrenic man waved me away.

"I wanted to make sure everything was okay," I persisted.

"Beat it," the man said.

Dave had inserted his arm through the bars to get my attention. "What I said in that meeting . . ." He whispered as though the drug dealer wouldn't be able to hear.

I didn't turn to Dave, but I didn't make any further attempts to engage the man in the cell in front of me.

"About not being able to live with it." Dave's voice had a catch in it like a hiccup.

When I didn't leave him in peace the schizophrenic man asked belligerently, "Which part didn't you understand?"

I took a step back from the bars of his cell, out of reach. "I'm not going to bother you," I told him.

This move brought me into Dave's view. It seemed legitimate, as a psychiatrist, to listen to him if he was trying to express some suicidal thoughts. I was searching for a technicality, a moral fig leaf, to make my presence here right.

"I'm not sure what you're saying," I told Dave.

I glanced in the direction of the schizophrenic whose paranoid glare intensified now that he saw I was keeping an eye on him, too. I hoped he wasn't going to go on a rant.

Dave was hesitant and shy. For the first time, he was experiencing the total absence of privacy that is as much a defining characteristic of prison as the bars themselves. "If anything," he began. He wanted me to say the rest for him. "You know. If anything bad happens. You know what I mean?"

"Go on," I told him.

"Like you said at the meeting: if anything bad happens, can I live with it? Well, no, I can't."

"Has something bad happened, Dave?"

His eyes moved back and forth as he activated different parts of his brain. The lips made tiny rehearsal movements. I was sure he was going to tell me something about where Danielle was.

But we both heard feet, descending, on the metal stairs. I turned back to my alibi and found the schizophrenic man still watching me. Down the corridor, the officer had his key in the lock of the metal gate; behind him stood Jerry Papandreas.

Jerry seemed relieved to see me. He smiled and started down the corridor, then turned anxiously when he heard the officer lock the gate behind him. All three of the prisoners were now peering through the bars, trying to see, without success, who the new arrival was.

Jerry had a second thought and stopped, then beckoned me to join him at the other end of the corridor. The insistence of the gesture, and the uncalculating way in which he revealed his need, suggested the degree of distress that Jerry experienced, and as I closed in on him, I knew I wouldn't hesitate to take advantage.

He'd arrived at a pivotal moment, at the point when Dave seemed like he was about to give up Danielle's location, and I felt a flare of anger. It was unreasonable and unfair, but I decided that Jerry should be made to pay for his interruption.

As I approached him, I saw that his eyes were almost glazed in panic. He perspired freely; the handkerchief was gone, and he swatted drops of sweat that ran down the side of his face with his open hand.

He spoke in a hoarse whisper. "What's your opinion, psychiatrically?" He hurried on before I could raise an objection. "I know you haven't properly examined him."

"That's right."

"But all the same, you must have some idea."

He was overwhelmed and desperate, ready to turn to any port in a storm, even to the DA's psychological advisor. I figured he'd had his first experience of trial by ordeal in front of the horde of reporters and camcorders. It was nasty, being the only man in the world on the side of a potential child killer. He wanted out. All thought of his client's interests was shoved aside as Jerry tried to extricate himself.

"It depends what the issue is," I hedged. I wanted to spin him out, to see how far he'd go.

Jerry flicked his fingers conspiratorially to bring me closer and dropped his voice until it was almost inaudible. "I'm withdrawing from the case," he said. He took a deep breath. "I have to."

I didn't ask him why or nod my head in understanding, because Jerry was desperate and I didn't have to give him anything.

"I'm petitioning the court."

"Is that a good idea?"

He made a helpless gesture, as though the argument weighed so heavily in favor of his decision that the burden lay in deciding where to begin. "The question," he said, "is which is the least bad alternative."

"I see."

"That's why it's great that I've run into you."

"Where do I come in?"

I called to the court officer to let me out.

"Can he take it?" Jerry persisted. "Will he do anything?"

"You mean . . . ?"

"I don't know." Jerry licked his lips.

"So, if he was going to do something, you'd stick with him?"

"I can't." He raised his empty hands, palms up. "I can't help it."

The officer unlocked the gate and swung it wide.

"You have to realize that this is a very delicate stage of the negotiation," I said, stepping across the threshold. "For all of us. Especially for Danielle."

Jerry crowded after me. "I know," he said, in the tone

that acknowledged a point that nevertheless would not influence him.

The officer unlocked the door, and as I started up the stairs, I said, "A couple of days from now, it won't make any difference."

"But by then, I'll be in the case too deep."

Jerry was having trouble keeping up with me, but I didn't slacken my pace. In two days Danielle could be found dead. And Jerry would be the attorney who'd stood in the way of a deal that could have let her live. But he'd be off the case by then. Long gone. Forgotten.

I turned to confront him as he emerged, breathless, into the courthouse lobby.

"This guy—" I pointed downward to the cells below. "He's on the edge. It wouldn't take much to push him over."

"Suicide?"

"If you desert him now . . ."

"That's a mental health issue. I'm not qualified to deal with that. That's not my department."

He started to back away, but I took him by the shoulder. I came in close to him. My mouth almost touched his ear. For an instant, I was struck by how easy it would be to kill Jerry.

"You should hang in there," I said. "Give it the old college try." I stepped back, away from him, and made a hammering gesture with my fist. "Go Fort Wayne!"

The phrase had been loaded in the frontal lobe speech centers like a bullet in a gun, ready to go on the twitch of a finger. I fired before I'd even thought about it.

I took another half-step away from Jerry. I was shocked by where the impulse had brought me. I was astonished by this action that was so entirely out of character, but at the same time I was pleased at discovering a skill that though new was intuitive and effortless. Then I came rapidly to a focus as professional scrutiny took over.

Jerry blinked hard, as though I'd slapped him. His eyes, which until now had been fastened helplessly on my own, swerved aside, came back, bobbled as his brain activated in panic. "Fort Wayne" had caused his memory banks to put out a high-level alert, and it was going to take his conscious awareness a full second to figure out what the danger was. When it did, his eyes came back to me for the first take: not appealing, not worried, but calculating.

"I don't quite get it," he said.

What he didn't get was whether he'd misheard, whether the phrase came out of my mouth by dumb coincidence, or whether I'd mentioned the phrase knowingly and deliberately. If the third possibility was the correct one, he had to find out what I wanted.

I maintained a stranger's encouraging smile. I knew my eyes wouldn't match the mouth. Even professional actors have trouble getting the tiny muscles around their eyes to contract so as to give the crinkle effect of the spontaneous smile. My eyes were cold.

"What?" I asked with an air of mild puzzlement.

I was provoking Jerry to take the high-risk path. If he demanded I explain the reference to Fort Wayne, he put a spotlight directly on what he wanted hidden. Or he could let it go. But if he let it go, he'd never know whether I knew his secret. And if I knew, who else did?

"Fort Wayne." He smiled, strained, struggling to remain polite. "I don't get what you mean when you say, 'Go Fort Wayne.' "

"I don't know." I pursed my lips and shook my head, at a loss. "It just came to me at that moment. Are you from Fort Wayne? If you are, no offense intended."

"But it could have been anywhere."

My voice hardened and I met his eyes in a challenging stare. "It could have been, yes."

He was starting to realize this couldn't possibly be coincidence. "But you said, 'Go Fort Wayne.'"

His mouth hung open. He was short of breath. A whole new vista was opening before him.

"You're right, Jerry. I could have said anything. For example, I could have said, 'Go Fort Wayne High.'"

We watched each other, eye to eye. The "I know you know" recognition at such moments is like an electrical charge sparking across a gap. I didn't want to give him time to catch up with what was happening to him. He was already starting to figure out the implications of his new future. His lawyerly mind was already creating extenuations, adverse circumstances, alibis.

"There are a lot of things I could say," I told him. "But I don't see any need to do that. I believe our interests are the same: everybody wants Danielle back alive. I want that, the DA wants that, the cops want that. Everybody watching TV wants that. It's what your client wants. It's in your client's best interests. That's why you need to stay on the case and bring these negotiations to a successful conclusion."

7:45 P.M.

Jerry stayed on the case, but my novice attempt at blackmail backfired.

"What could I do?" he asked me as we entered the corridor from the judge's chambers.

I walked fast, unwilling to make any concession to Jerry's bulk or his short legs. "It's done," I tossed off irritably.

"I don't think I had any other option. Do you? I mean, he more or less implied he was suicidal."

I passed through the swing doors to the lobby and let them backhand Jerry as he came after me. I wanted to catch up with Brenda. I was hunting, and Jerry was no longer part of the chase. I'd crossed a line I'd never before come close to. I had committed several clinical infractions, but I wasn't inclined to any soul-searching now. I was ready to shrug off rules left and right in the desperate search for Danielle. My life had narrowed to this single focus.

Jerry slowed to breast the doors and skipped after me as we entered the marble lobby of the courthouse. This was a short no-man's land before we left the building and came to the mob of reporters gathered outside on the courthouse steps. Whether he liked it or not, Jerry was going to have to make a statement. Once we passed through the doors, I'd be lost to him for good. He grabbed my arm to hold me back.

"The court psychologist agreed," he said. His eyes begged me to be merciful on the other matter, made all the more urgent because it could not be mentioned.

I turned on him angrily. "You said he wasn't competent. You set this in motion."

"Give me a break! How can a client work with counsel if he's suicidal? I have a responsibility to make sure he's safe."

"You have a responsibility to save the girl," I spat at him.

We both knew this wasn't true. Jerry had no responsibility to anyone, any principle, any ideal—nothing, save his client. But he wasn't about to argue with me.

"Look," he said. We were coming to the doors to the courthouse. He still clung to my sleeve. Beyond, in the fading daylight, faces on the other side of the police detail bobbed up to catch a glimpse of whoever might be approaching the doors.

"They've seen you coming," I told him maliciously. The notoriety that awaited him beyond the doors was a fate Jerry richly deserved.

"Look," he said in a rush, "my client will talk with the DA. We will negotiate. I personally guarantee it."

"You've put him out of play, you bastard!"

"We can still do a deal," Jerry pleaded. He was horrified by the possible implications this held for his secret. "There's time. I'll go down to Sanders. I'll meet with Brenda at Sanders."

"How can Feldman make a deal if his lawyer says he isn't legally competent?"

"The other thing—"

I went through the doors without hesitation, into a barrage of questions.

I jerked my thumb over my shoulder in the direction of the corridor in which Jerry was hiding. "He's on his way," I told them.

Because Jerry had stayed on the case, Dave Feldman was sent for psychiatric evaluation to the Sanders Institute, effectively putting him beyond the reach of Brenda and the detectives. The commitment was for a period of twenty days, but our time scale was in hours, and as far as we were concerned, Dave might just as well have been sent to Devil's Island for all the use he was to us now.

Arthur had been under surveillance, but he was no fool, and no matter how discreet the state police unit was, he knew they were there somewhere, even if he couldn't see them, and he hadn't budged from his house.

An hour ago, about the time when Dr. Kerensky's survival line had started to take its plunge, they had decided to bring him to the Cambridge police station for questioning.

I leaned against the back wall of the observation room beside Brenda Gorn. State and local police officers crowded the narrow space; the technical people recording the interview sat up front before the console next to the one-way mirror.

On the other side of the mirror, Arthur Hodges sat in the interrogation room. The chair he sat on was bolted to the floor. In front of him, an empty desk was placed obliquely facing two chairs, which were not bolted to the floor.

I'd been on both sides of the mirror and I knew what it felt like. You know there are people on the other side of the mirror and you know they're watching you. You think if you turn your head to catch the light a certain way you ought to be able to glimpse them, but you can't. I watched Arthur in this maneuver. He coughed and tried to shift his chair and discovered it wouldn't move. Then he looked away, uninterested.

Dempsey came in with Wolpert. Wolpert told Arthur his name while Dempsey sat back from the table and riffled a dossier in her lap.

"Are you arresting me?" Arthur asked. He was polite, helpful, and unruffled. "Only, you see, my wife Molly is disabled on account of the arthritis," he told Wolpert, "and she needs me at home. Don't get me wrong—I want to do everything I can to help find this poor girl—but Molly has very limited mobility and she relies on me a lot."

"As of this moment," Dempsey said without looking up, "we have no plans to arrest you."

Arthur slowly nodded his understanding.

The news that he wasn't going to be charged told Arthur that our case against him still remained incomplete. If we'd turned up compelling evidence—a witness who put him with the girl—he'd be in handcuffs. But when he received this vital information, he didn't blink, or bring his hand to his face, or suppress a smile, or show any of the relief signs typical of subjects when an important area of doubt is removed.

He was going to be a very difficult subject to interrogate, and I turned to Brenda to whisper this to her, but she was staring intently at Arthur with a puzzled frown, and didn't glance in my direction.

"It's not like I have to rush off," Arthur said. He had a bumbling charm, an engineer's bonhomie. "Molly's good for about three hours. But after that—well, I don't think I have to spell it out."

Dempsey sat stone-faced. "We'd like you to tell us everything you did this morning," she said.

Dempsey, with her blunt, almost brutal style of questioning, was a foil for Arthur's more courtly manner. She'd badger him until the good-natured veneer cracked and he retaliated. Then she'd provoke him some more, and as he got angrier and distracted by the more immediate need to reassert his dominance over this woman, he'd misplace his core agenda, which was to tell us nothing.

"Sure." He spread his hands generously. "From . . . ?"

He'd give us nothing he didn't have to, all the time extracting every snippet of information that would give him some indication of how much we had on him. Now, by making us define the parameters of the time period we were interested in, he'd find out where he had to focus his story.

On our side, we needed something to tie him to Danielle's disappearance, something that would convince him he had to deal with us. He had been at the scene of the crime. We had a witness who placed him with Dave Feldman, who knew Danielle, who had one of her T-shirts. Arthur knew this wasn't enough to convict him. Even if we found the leverage we needed, any deal that Arthur would be offered was also a trap that would put him away in prison. Whereas Danielle dead removed the prime witness. As I watched him from the other side of the mirror, I was convinced that Arthur could live with that resolution.

"From the time you left your house," Wolpert said.

"Start with getting into your vehicle in the garage this morning."

"That would be eightish. Maybe eight-thirty," Arthur began.

"You decided to go for a ride in the middle of rush hour?" Dempsey asked.

The detectives had to bluff their way out of the bind they were in. The more specific Dempsey's questions, the more she told him about the gaps in our knowledge. But the more open-ended Dempsey made her questions, the more Arthur could run out the clock, mixing generalities about his daily routine with the minutiae of today, "trying to be helpful" by reciting a list of irrelevancies until the detectives' patience gave out. As he shared with them the particular way Molly liked her morning tea, I had an image of a parched Danielle, barely conscious, straining in the darkness for sounds of rescue.

I had caught glimpses of what might lie behind Arthur's good-natured mask when we first interviewed him in his home, and as I watched him in operation I became more certain that we were dealing with a sociopath—a man whose down-to-earth good humor was a disguise that concealed the absence of a conscience or any capacity for empathy for other human beings. He could pass himself off as normal. His devotion to his wife was an important part of that façade. The crippled Molly was a convenient prop who could be counted on to stay home, out of the way. With Molly on display, how could anyone say Arthur was uncaring? Who wouldn't think twice before accusing this kindly man of being a child rapist? I'd seen the hesitation in the eyes of Dempsey and Brenda Gorn, hardened professionals.

It wasn't his callousness or the ruthlessness that worried me now. I was concerned about another quality of the sociopath: his lack of emotional reactivity. The sociopath's heart rate doesn't jump in response to stress. He doesn't sweat when he lies. Deception is second nature. He loves getting one over on other people. The sociopath can flatline a polygraph. So, under interrogation, the sociopath may not emit those tiny emotional clues that tip off the questioner when the subject says one thing and knows the truth lies somewhere else entirely.

He was fussing now, smiling obsequiously and acting slightly flustered as Dempsey took him to task for bogging them down in details. Arthur looked puzzled and slightly hurt. He was doing his best, for gosh sake.

Behind the mask, Arthur was cool and calculating. Occasionally, his eyes, their kindly twinkle extinguished for an instant, flicked over involuntarily toward the reflective surface, unable to penetrate to the silent watchers who remained outside the charmed circle in the interrogation room.

Dempsey, calm and stealthy, had interrupted him to fast-forward through their meandering tour of the old Cambridge neighborhood. It seemed that each minute of narrative took a minute to tell. Wolpert was showing signs of restlessness. His attention was wandering. Twice he'd glanced up at the clock on the wall, and Arthur had picked this up.

Arthur made an expansive gesture. "We've got time," he said. "When you're retired, you've got nowhere to go. You don't worry about rush hour."

"You were driving around just for the hell of it."

"Well, I don't know about that. But, you see, Molly doesn't get out too often, except for doctors' appointments—and let's face it, that's not a whole lot of fun—"

He half turned to the mirror, as if my presence behind it were part of everyone's unspoken assumption and he'd momentarily forgotten this and needed to make sure I didn't take offense. He turned back to Dempsey and Wolpert, but he'd revealed the quality of awareness he brought to the interrogation. He wasn't Dave, who could hardly keep up with a single track. Arthur operated in multitrack surround sound. He processed several data streams simultaneously. He was formidable, but he was vain, and vanity is the sociopath's major vulnerability. Once Arthur was engaged in the process, it wasn't enough just to get away with it. He had to let the dupe in on what he had pulled off. To hint, at the very least, at what had just gone over. And if Wolpert was starting to daydream and Dempsey's patience was fraying, Arthur was beginning to show off to me.

"Anyway, from time to time we like to revisit the scenes of our youth, when the fancy takes us." He resumed his itinerary, then interrupted himself. "But this is stuff I've already told you."

"I'd like to hear it again."

He jabbed an accusing, teasing finger at her. "Of course you would."

"Yeah?"

"To see if I'll make a mistake."

"That's right."

"How am I doing?"

"You tell me."

"You're all questions and no answers." He chuckled to show that he had no hard feelings.

Dempsey waited a couple of beats for this to go by, then picked up again where they'd left off.

"You went for coffee at Doosy's."

"You know we did. I told you that before. And by co-incidence, we were right there, in Dracone Park. But—this is the part I love—how the heck could you know that?"

He was very confident. But he didn't know whether our evidence would stand up. We could place him at the scene of the crime, but he had to know we didn't have a witness who'd seen the abduction.

"You were there. You admit you were there. There's nothing else you need to know."

"I'm curious, that's all."

"Okay. Let's go back to Dracone Park."

"You're not going to tell me?"

"No."

"This isn't going anywhere," I whispered to Brenda.

"It's developing."

"He's good at this. He's got his story down. He's not going to put a foot wrong."

"Dempsey's pretty good, too. We've got cards we want to play. She's waiting for the right moment."

"Whatever she's got, she should unload it now."

"We tracked down Arthur's open and gross from nineteen-ninety. The victim was Caitlin Moody. His niece."

She scanned my face for a reaction, and I felt I had to nod with a show of enthusiasm. But this wasn't the kind of revelation that would shake Arthur. He knew what we had. He was waiting for us.

I tried a fresh tack with Brenda. "I'm thinking, Molly's sitting at home alone. This would be a good time to talk to her."

"We tried. Without her husband, she won't let us in the door."

She held up her hand to cut me off. Dempsey was playing the open and gross card.

She played it well. She took her time, letting the story develop, forcing Arthur to release snippets of information about his relations with Molly's sister's family and the eight-year-old Caitlin. But in the end, all she got for it was a shrug.

"So?" Arthur asked. "What's your point?"

And when Dempsey started to make her point, he cut her off: "It was a charge, not a conviction. An unsubstantiated charge that was dismissed. She wouldn't testify!" It was the only flare of the inner Arthur we were allowed to see. "There wasn't anything to testify to." Quickly, he dropped back into his previous mode of obstructive helpfulness.

I gave Brenda time to drive to the end of this dead end and turn around, and when I judged she was emotionally on her way back, I tried again.

"If the doctor made a house call, Molly might talk to me."

Brenda massaged her forehead with the tips of her fingers. She looked exhausted and discouraged. "Why not," she said without enthusiasm. "I'm staying here with this one." She looked around at the detectives in the viewing room to select one to accompany me.

"How about Wolpert?" I suggested.

"He works with Dempsey."

"Right now, he's working with Dempsey on a side show."

"Why do you want him?"

"I don't. But if anything's going to happen in there, we have to shake Arthur up. Look at him."

Arthur leaned back in his chair with a tiny, complacent grin on his face. He talked on autopilot while his main mind watched the detectives, took in Wolpert's fiddling with a stray paper clip, Dempsey's damned-up ferocity, the blank mirror behind them where impotent DAs and psychiatric advisors fought off boredom.

"I want him to know that while he's bullshitting Dempsey, we're alone with Molly."

We agreed that Wolpert's replacement would enter the interview room after Brenda called Dempsey on the phone to explain the move to her.

Dempsey was furious at the interruption, answering in clipped affirmatives, eyes averted from the meddlers behind the mirror. She grew calmer as she listened to the plan, but she wasn't placated, and as she hung up she allowed herself a single glance toward the mirror, and I knew that her scowl was directed at me.

Wolpert and the detective who was to replace him played out the transfer, with Wolpert flipping open the file on the desk in front of Arthur, then running his finger down the page as if to check Arthur's address.

The captain sent a female officer with us so that we would be chaperoned if we managed to get into the house to interview Molly. She introduced herself as Sue Ryder and she drove the unmarked car, with Wolpert sitting up front beside her. I sat alone in the back. Not knowing the history between Wolpert and me, she tried to start a conversation, making eye contact via the mirror, until Wolpert shut her off.

"You remember Lou Francone, the state police lieutenant that was murdered?"

"I heard about it, sure."

Her eyes came up to the mirror to check me out, and she looked startled when she recognized me from the newscasts. Until that moment, I was out of context, sitting in the back of the state police cruiser as if I'd been one of them, and now, in one sentence, I'd been redefined. I saw her frown in concentration and she started to ask a question, then thought better of it.

We drove in silence until we turned off the highway.

Then Wolpert asked, "Okay, Doc, how do you want to do it?"

"I'm hoping we can work together on this."

We had turned onto Pond Meadow Drive. As if to emphasize our lack of preparation, the driver slowed the car as the entrance to the Hodges' driveway came into view. Wolpert turned around in his seat. I hadn't realized, until I saw his face full on, how angry he was.

"You got me into this fucking wild-goose chase. It's all yours. You own it." He turned back so that I had to respond to the back of his head.

"Look, I'm sorry to pull you out of the other business. But I think we have a better chance here."

"That's your professional opinion?"

"Yes."

"So, tell me, Doc, how come you get to call the shots in this investigation and you don't have one day of investigative experience? How is that?"

"Pull over," I told Detective Ryder.

She hesitated, then looked to Wolpert, but he remained staring stonily ahead. She did as I said.

"Please turn around," I told Wolpert. "We have to talk."

When he wouldn't move to face me, I leaned forward and spoke quietly in his ear.

"Listen to me, you self-indulgent fuck. I'm about to conduct a critical interrogation. You're either part of the process, or you're part of the problem. I don't give a damn whether you like me, or respect me, or whether you still believe I killed Francone, because that's all irrelevant right now. I want to find the girl. If that's what you want, then act professionally. That means you turn around to talk to me, because even though you don't like me, we're working together."

He let out a long sigh, like steam under pressure escaping through a valve. Then he turned, and I saw, to his credit, that his face bore no sign of truculence. "Okay," he said. "What have you got?"

"The most difficult thing is to get Molly to let us in. I'll handle that."

"And then what? You want me to smack her around? You want me to threaten to torch her house? What?"

"I want you both to keep a low profile. You follow my lead."

As we approached the front door, I kept an eye out for a twitch of the lace drapes on the front window. Molly had heard three doors slam when what she wanted to hear was the hum of the garage door opening and the van's engine reverberating in the garage.

She would read the signs: her husband remained, perhaps in custody, at the police station, while the police had come to her. Perhaps they had bad news to break to her. She would be very worried, but she would want to find out what was happening with Arthur.

I had two tasks, and they had to be accomplished quickly one after the other. First, I had to talk my way into her house. Then I had to answer a question: Was Molly a full accomplice in the abduction and rape? Or was she a conscious enabler who aided her husband but didn't herself engage in the sexual abuse? Or was she an unconscious enabler, a liar kept in the dark as to Arthur's real purpose?

It was hard to envision the delicate Molly participating, even as a voyeur, in the nasty business of raping a child, but I'd been caught in this error before, and I'd learned that appearance and personality tell you nothing about a person's sexual craving.

More likely, Molly was part of the acquisition team. It's not uncommon for pedophiles and serial killers to use wives and girlfriends to scout for prospects and to bring the victims within reach. The child who's been told to watch out for strange men may go willingly with a woman, particularly one who raises no suspicion, such as someone in a wheelchair. And though their motives are not sexual, these women are ruthless. I'd assessed women who sacrificed their own children in order to keep their men. All the same, I thought it was unlikely that Arthur had brought her along in the van when he'd taken Danielle. Molly could have been useful in luring the girl, but she was too slow for an operation that depended on a quick snatch.

Most likely, Molly was unaware of her role in the abduction. She'd provided an alibi, and that was all. She hadn't been to Dracone Park with Arthur. Maybe he'd parked her in a coffee shop and picked her up after he'd abducted Danielle and stashed her in his hiding place. Or she'd never left home.

Arthur would have provided her with a near-innocent account about why he needed cover. Some minor scrape with the law, perhaps. A hit-and-run accident. A pedestrian clipped near a crosswalk. "My word against his, but because he's black . . . You know how it is nowadays. All you have to say . . ."

Molly wouldn't have looked too closely at the story. She'd have glossed over inconsistencies, skipped gaps. Her loyalty was to Arthur. She was totally dependent on him. But I didn't think Molly had bargained on child murder.

Each one of these Mollies—the perpetrator, the accomplice, the stooge—had different vulnerabilities. I had to decide which one she was before I could decide on my interview strategy. Molly the perpetrator would be formidable. Molly the accomplice would hold tenaciously to the alibi, too. But I was confident that if I could get inside her house, I could turn Molly the dupe. The gap between what she half-knew and what she chose not to know was the place to apply leverage. I wouldn't give a second thought now, with night falling and Danielle's chances shrinking by the minute, to exploiting any opening poor little Molly exposed. I'd break her if I had to.

Arthur had built a little Plexiglas shelter for the intercom by the front door, with a sign reading, PLEASE RING THE BELL, which I did.

After a moment Molly asked, in a shaky voice, "Who is it?"

"It's Dr. Lucas," I said. "I talked to you this morning."

"Oh, yes." The rising inflection made the words both an acknowledgment and a question.

"I wonder if I could have a word with you?"

She paused, anxious that she might give offense. "What is this about?"

"It's about your husband, Arthur."

"Oh, dear," I heard her say to herself. Then, "My husband says I shouldn't let anyone in when he's not here. For security reasons."

"I understand. You can never be too careful. Arthur knows me, though. I was here earlier talking to you and your husband."

"The doctor."

"Yes."

"Doctor, couldn't you just tell me now, over the intercom, what it is?"

"I don't think I should."

"Is it a medical matter?"

"Yes," I said, without hesitation. It was easier to lie if I did it quickly, without thinking.

She steeled herself to ask the question she feared most, and in that pause, I realized that she'd given Arthur the alibi because otherwise he'd be taken away and she'd begin the terrifying progression that would end in a nursing home.

"Is it about Arthur?" she asked.

"Yes," I told her, injecting into that single syllable all the medical portentousness I could muster.

There was a buzz as Molly released the latch, the door clicked open a crack, and we were in.

I went briskly to the front parlor and cupped the gnarled hand she held out to me in both my own. I took a chair from beside the table and swung it so that I sat immediately in front of her wheelchair, blocking her view of the detectives.

Wolpert had picked up the remote from the small table beside Molly. Slumped in the armchair to my left, it didn't take him long to find a channel that was running the video of Danielle.

Abby was asking, "And what's an emergency?"

"Like, someone having a heart attack?"

"Right."

"Or a dog gets hit by a car."

At a nod from me, he muted it. Detective Ryder settled on the sofa and discreetly took out her notebook.

Molly seemed bewildered by the change of channels. She peered at the TV with a puzzled frown. Then her eyes came back to me.

"Tell me what it is," she said. Her eyes searched my face for signs of calamity.

"Arthur's in a jam," I told her, keeping my face level with hers, no more than twelve inches away, locking gazes with her, using the grim voice of the doctor signaling bad news coming. "As you know."

Her eyes flinched, then came back, but it was enough to tell me that she wasn't Molly the perpetrator. She didn't have the toughness to take a child and deliberately, systematically abuse her.

"You said it was a medical problem."

For a crazy instant I wanted to tell her the medical problem was that her beloved husband would be shanked in jail if he didn't do a deal in the next couple of hours. I wanted to pick up this china-doll woman and throw her with all my strength against the wall and crush her.

"Yes," I continued in the same sympathetic tone. "I did want to talk to you about his medical condition."

"He doesn't have a medical condition. Except his cholesterol. But he's on a diet for that."

"He does have a mental condition, though, doesn't he?"

She flinched again. "We've all got our little eccentricities," she said with a nervous laugh, as though this was a joke.

But she hadn't recovered entirely. When her eyes came back it wasn't to meet mine, but to scan my face with a wild, fearful gaze.

I didn't say anything. I let her read the solemnity of the doctor's professional concern. It was the silence that follows the patient's question of, "It's just a stomach ulcer, right, Doctor?" The silence that follows, "Well, no, it's a bit more than that." A pause that allows the patient to catch up to the dismal diagnosis.

I manipulated her without compunction. I told myself the end justified this gross misconduct. It was an exception. A temporary detour. Tomorrow, after Danielle had been found, I'd return to the straight path. Tomorrow, I'd be whole again.

I waited for Molly to find her worst fears confirmed, and when she'd reached her conclusion and looked briefly down and away to integrate this information, I nodded my head in confirmation.

"We all have our . . . things," she said. She gave an extenuating wave, signifying lightness. "It doesn't necessarily mean anything."

I let this go. She'd do the work herself once I got her started. I shadowed her, nudging her on, jogging her forward. Once I got her past the brink, Molly's wheelchair would pick up speed of its own accord; it would roll all the way down the hill, faster and faster, careening down the slope toward the awful truth that lay at the bottom.

"You must have wondered," I suggested.

"I don't know what you're talking about."

"Things you came across."

Somewhere, sometime, during the last thirty years, she'd stumbled upon a detail—perhaps the ambiguous picture of a child, naked but not lewd, with whom neither she nor Arthur had any family tie—that had puzzled her briefly. Perhaps she had wondered, in passing, why they spent so much time beside the swimming pools of theme parks. Perhaps it wasn't one thing, but the hundred times she'd followed Arthur's gaze toward eight-year-old girls. But these events couldn't forever be relegated in memory to the folder marked "unfiled." Once you recognize a category, it fills suddenly, of its own accord.

"I believe in privacy," she said firmly. "I would never go through his stuff."

"Those times he went away," I suggested, changing topics before she could begin to resist me on the old one.

"They were business trips," she said quickly. "He had

to go there on business." She was looking down, her eyes fixed on her lap as she sorted through these trips, reallocating them to new possibilities. "His company sent him."

I thought of all the places in the world where a few dollars would buy a child. I glanced at the mask on the wall and remembered an oriental fan in the hallway on the way in. "Thailand," I said. "Indonesia."

She nodded.

Then she gathered herself. "But I never wanted to know what he did when he was away from home," she said with resolve, meeting my gaze with a new challenge.

"I understand. A man's entitled to his privacy."

"I don't ask questions about stuff I don't need to know about."

"Arthur's a very careful person."

"Oh, yes." She made a comfy, settling motion of her shoulders against the sling-back of her wheelchair. "Always considerate."

This was Molly the dupe. She didn't know about Arthur's sex life. Didn't want to. Never asked. If there was something there that wasn't quite right, she pushed it to the periphery and managed never to bring it into focus. With practice, she never thought about it.

Time was pressing. I had to take shortcuts.

In my pocket, a gnawing presence, I carried the pictures Danielle's mother had given me that morning. I took them out now and shuffled through them thoughtfully, letting the previous business pass, waiting for her curiosity to be aroused.

"This is her here," I told Molly in the tone of a proud father shamelessly boring an acquaintance with pictures of his kids. "Danielle."

"Oh, yes." She seemed pleased and not at all discomforted by images of the victim. Her mood at once changed, and I marveled at her extraordinary capacity to disconnect parts of her life. "What a little cutie-pie!"

I shifted my chair and took hold of the bottom corner of the photo so that our heads came together in alignment.

"Of course," I said, "this was taken three months ago."

"She looks just like Caitlin, when she was eight years old."

The name had popped out, because Molly was always looking for cheerful segues. Before she could see where this might lead, I asked her, assuming the slightly sentimental smile that people put on when they ask about other people's children, "And who's Caitlin?"

"That's my niece." But her face was already firming. Her eyes were troubled. There was unpleasantness down this path. Better not go there. "But we don't see as much of her as we used to."

"How old is Caitlin now?"

"You know what teenagers are like," Molly said, the twinkle in her eye restored. "Too busy with their friends down at the shopping mall!" I didn't remind Molly that Caitlin must now be in her twenties, because she was off. "Now that!" She jabbed her knobbed finger at Danielle. "That is lovely!"

This was how she did it. This was how she lived with a monster. Her emotions were uncoupled, and thoughts simply dropped through a hole in the bottom of her mind. Our allusive discussion of Arthur as a sicko might never have taken place.

"Arthur loves children."

"I know," I said softly, gently.

Out of the corner of my eye, I glimpsed Wolpert turn away in disgust at my complicity. For a moment I saw myself through his eyes, and I felt a sudden urge to escape this filthy house with its frigid air-conditioning and run outside to draw deep breaths of hot, steamy air. But true emotion was a luxury I couldn't afford.

"I'll bet he liked Caitlin," I suggested.

Molly was judging how best to answer.

"When she was younger," I supplied.

"Oh, yes."

"Young girls are so affectionate. You don't have to tell them twice to do anything. Then they become teenagers."

I carried the conversation on the topic of girls passing through their teens, keeping the terms of reference general, without mention of names. Molly was going down the Caitlin path, whether she wanted to or not. She didn't know it, but she was walking down that path with me. At a moment of my choosing, I'd rip off the blindfold and she'd recognize where she was.

"Do you have any photos of her?" I asked. After all, I'd shown her my family pictures.

"Who?"

I chuckled. "Caitlin, of course."

"Well, I don't know." She was not alarmed. It was a practical matter. Her eyes tracked back and forth as she searched an inner representation of her home.

"I'd love to see one."

"I'm not sure I could put my hand on them just like that."

To an interrogator, there's no such thing as "No comment." You phrase your question, you pick your spot. When you ambush her, the subject may refuse to answer, but it doesn't make any difference. However scrupulously she might try to assume an expression of unconcern, the human brain is inherently reactive. It will betray you every time. It just can't help changing gears, throwing off a blink, a flinch, a muscle contraction around the eyes, a hand-to-mouth, a tiny shift in posture.

Molly was smiling into my face when I asked her, "Did Arthur have pictures of Caitlin?"

She turned aside as if I'd used a nasty word. "Well . . ." She recovered. "I suppose so. After all, she was his niece, too."

"Did you find them?"

She turned again. "I don't know what you mean." I saw fear and regret.

For a moment, her eyes actually closed over the memory. I knew if I didn't do something she'd throw us out when they opened.

I pushed the picture of Danielle in front of her. "Danielle's the little girl who's missing."

"The one you told me about."

The topic had gotten too hot, and with the interview in jeopardy, I had to work quickly to reduce the emotional intensity. I talked about the TV coverage. When we'd come in, Molly's TV had been tuned to a sitcom rerun, and not, as it seemed to be for everyone else in Massachusetts since Danielle had disappeared, to one of the local news channels.

"Haven't you been watching the news?"

"I never watch the news," she said proudly. "Arthur does. He watches it all the time. But he tells me not to, on account of my nerves. 'I'll tell you what's up,' he says."

She chuckled with the simplicity of a happy, contented child. If the laughter was a little forced, the humor a little thin, you had to make allowances for the plucky little lady looking on the cheerful side of life. She had let go of Danielle's photo, but I still held it, forgotten and invisible, before her. There were so many ways to change the subject away from darkness, pain, and suffering that it had become second nature to her.

Molly was rebalanced, and I judged her ready for another encounter with reality.

I shuffled the cards and came up with the fetching photo of Danielle in a two-piece bathing suit that her mother had forced on me when she'd grasped my hand in the lobby of New Beginnings. The fabric hung on Danielle's upper body, and her girlish figure contrasted with the pose of a glamorous fashion model as she threw her hips out and hammed for the camera. You didn't have to be a pedophile to notice the latent sexuality of the image, a sexuality that the girl in the photo had no more understanding of than if it had been a foreign language.

"Here she is again," I said, forcing the photo in front of her.

Molly didn't want to look, but politeness prevented her from turning away. She glanced at the photo. "Oh, yes," she said, with an air of boredom.

"This was taken earlier this summer," I said. "Look." I waited, insisting she attend as I pointed out details. "That's why she's hardly wearing anything."

"Young girls don't nowadays, do they?"

"Do you think she's sexy?" My guiding finger brushed her bare thighs, tickled her naked midriff.

"I don't know. I'm sure she will be. A pretty young thing."

She turned away, looking for something, anything, but I still had her attention.

"I wanted to ask you something."

"Yes."

"Do you think Arthur would find her sexy?"

If Molly had been a hardened skinner's moll, she'd

have brazened it out. She'd have taken the picture out of my hand for a closer appraisal, told me her frank opinion.

She blinked. "Sexy?" She showed a tiny grimace, little more than a tic, as the skin around her eyes contracted in momentary discomfort.

She wasn't tough. She had reacted to the oblique suggestion that her husband found female children sexy, but not with the panic or fluster of someone with guilty knowledge. She'd reacted with mild alarm, as people do who habitually push raw facts from notice. She didn't know Arthur was a pedophile. She didn't know why he needed an alibi for this morning. She did know that Arthur had a secret life. It could be anything. She just didn't care to know what.

"If we don't find her soon, she's going to die of thirst."

Molly's eyes involuntarily went to the photo, but I'd covered Danielle's picture in my hand. I wanted her to remain an abstraction until the chosen moment.

"Arthur won't tell us where she is."

She turned on me angrily, in protest. She was horrified. She didn't know it yet, but she was beginning to roll down the slope toward the ugly truth. Tears started suddenly and inexplicably at the inner corners of her eyes. She blinked, but they wouldn't entirely go away. "Arthur doesn't know where—"

I held up the picture of Danielle, demure and clothed, sitting upright on the edge of her bed, surrounded by ranks of her stuffed animals. Molly was fixated by the girl. She started to speak, but her eyes couldn't leave the image.

"He would never . . ."

"There was that trouble before."

Her eyes came to mine, searching and afraid to find what she feared.

"He was accused of interfering with Caitlin."

She knew about the charge. Her lips moved silently, unable to gain purchase on words that would extenuate, salve.

"Arthur loves children," I supplied.

"He loves them." Her eyes were filling. She was submerging beneath the pity of it.

I pulled her back. I said, "He would never hurt her."

"Never."

"But there's someone else who would."

She was terrified. "Arthur would never be part of that."

"I think perhaps things got out of control. They went further than Arthur planned."

"How do you mean?"

"The other man."

"But that's not Arthur's fault."

"Arthur was there. He was stopped by Dracone Park when Danielle was taken."

She hung her head. Molly was thinking. She seldom went beyond the immediate implications. She didn't like to think things through to their painful conclusion. Now she made the effort to figure out where this road led.

She turned to me, the doctor, with more certainty. "This is what you came to tell me?"

"Yes."

"What's going to become of me, Doctor? Arthur said—" She cut herself off.

I waited to see if she'd finish the sentence. "That you'd be put away?"

She nodded, her lips pursed tight to hold in the sob.

I took a risk and touched her hand. When she didn't pull it away, I took her twisted hand in mine.

"Your social worker—"

She shook her head. "Never had one." She coughed to

clear her throat and looked away. "Arthur said he didn't believe in them."

"So you never had anyone come in to help you?"

"Arthur did it all. He didn't like people coming into the home."

"You can have an aide help you get dressed in the morning. You could have a nurse come visit you here."

The question of whether she could live independently in her own home was too crucial for her to entirely trust what I said, but it was food for thought. I didn't want it to distract us at this moment.

"Right now," I said, "Arthur's in a jam. He needs you to help him get out of it. He's—I hope you don't mind me saying this—Arthur is stubborn."

"Oh, he is!"

"You're not part of this."

She shook her head. It was beyond the realm of possibility.

"So you can't lie for him."

She showed shame for the first time. "I know."

"Did you see Danielle at Dracone Park this morning?"

"No," Molly said. "I haven't been out all day."

I hovered in the background of Molly's living room while Wolpert carefully took her statement and Detective Ryder wrote it down. Wolpert was gentle and respectful. I waited to swoop, in case, at the last minute, Molly balked.

Once, in the middle of reading through her statement, she looked up to ask, pleadingly, "Am I doing the right thing?"

It needed only a nod to put her back on track.

She didn't ask again what would become of her husband. With the self-absorption of the chronically ill, for whom every day was a challenge to be overcome, she was focused on the practical arrangements of her daily existence.

Laboriously, she drew out her signature at the bottom of the page, with Detective Ryder crouched beside her to hold the clipboard.

Then we were gone. The detectives packed up like caterers at the end of a wedding. It wasn't objects they stowed, but the emotional elements from which the interrogation had been constructed. Whatever atmosphere had existed a moment before Molly signed—the solicitude, the willingness to accommodate her pace, to tolerate her repetitive need for reassurance—was replaced by a brisk professional coolness.

At any moment I expected the walls of Molly's comfy parlor to be removed like the scenery of a movie set to reveal the elaborate deception. Molly herself sat openmouthed, unable to keep up with our departure.

"I just have some questions," she said, but the detectives, even the nice lady detective, weren't paying her any notice. "Doctor!"

"I'll call you about that social worker," I promised, hoping to give her something that would slow her down.

I saw the detectives walking swiftly down the driveway to their vehicle. They had to get back to the police station before Arthur's interrogation petered out. They weren't going to let me slow them down. They'd be happy to have an excuse to ditch me.

"But . . ." She gestured helplessly at her surroundings.

"I'll have them send someone." I was at the door.

"Doctor!"

I ran to the car and we took off even before I'd slammed the door.

Wolpert was speaking on his cell, reporting, I assumed, to the chief of detectives.

"We got it . . . Yes . . . Here it is: 'Contrary to other statements I may have made to the police, I have not left my home today. I did not accompany my husband Arthur Hodges to Dracone Park in Cambridge.' That pretty much does it, right?"

Wolpert listened, and I couldn't hear the other side of his conversation. "The doc . . . ," Wolpert said reluctantly. "He did the talking . . . I don't know." He gave a dark chuckle. "He fucked with her mind, I guess."

Not that I expected any appreciation from Wolpert and Ryder. I was still on the outside. When we were on the highway, lights flashing as we sped through the darkness, I felt Ryder's eyes on me, but when I glanced at the mirror, she'd already returned her attention to the road.

They didn't like my way of doing things. They'd have preferred to break her down by force of will. To their way of thinking, my allying with Molly, getting inside her head by seeing the world through her eyes, was devious. Wolpert, who would have been happy to whack a suspect on the side of the head with the telephone directory if he could have gotten away with it, regarded my manipulation of that poor, sick lady as dirty pool.

I wasn't happy with my performance, either. I was used to a sharp line that divided black from white. I was on one side or the other—a defense expert, or a witness for the prosecution—and no one could have any illusions about where my loyalties lay. But I'd misled Molly. I'd wormed my way into her confidence.

I told myself that this was a one-day war and that Molly was an enemy combatant. I was fighting lies with lies. She'd tried to trick us, but I'd tricked her. She'd exploited the privileges of the sick person, and I'd exploited the privileges of the physician. You take the enemy's fight to him. You match his methods. If you fight by the Marquis of Queensbury rules, you can't win.

But I'd presented myself as a doctor, and I couldn't wriggle free of the stern injunctions that defined the role. Do no harm. Take no advantage. But I was a doctor trying to save a life, I argued. I continued in this silent debate with myself fitfully, and I was glad that neither of the detectives cared to engage me in conversation. When we arrived in Cambridge, the result remained inconclusive and

I was left uneasy. However I twisted and turned, I couldn't shake a nagging sense of shame.

When we came to a stop in the parking lot I jumped out of the car and kept close to Wolpert, slipstreaming behind him through the back door of the police station to avoid the media crowd who blocked the front steps. People greeted him or nodded as we went by, and no one questioned why I was there.

Only once, when Wolpert stopped briefly to run off some copies of Molly's statement and we stood facing one another on opposite sides of the copy machine, did he show any inclination to acknowledge me. Even then the compliment was ambiguous.

"You're something, Doc," he said, with eyebrows raised and a bemused smile suggesting that whatever that something might be, it lay outside his system of classification.

I followed him into the observation room behind the one-way mirror.

It had grown more crowded since I'd left. Some of the people in suits looked like politicians, and I recognized Brenda's boss, Randall Ford, the District Attorney for Exeter County. I wondered whether he'd come because he'd heard there had been a break in the case. They greeted Wolpert like a conquering hero. I didn't begrudge him the glory. I was pleased that Brenda's confidence in me had been borne out, but the only person I wanted to impress was Abby.

I'd give her my own blow-by-blow account later, when we finally had a chance to sit down to supper. Maybe we'd celebrate by opening that very expensive bottle of wine she'd given me for my birthday that had always been too special to actually drink. If we found

Danielle . . . My thoughts ran on to where that might
lead. The future had been foreshortened by this possibility. It loomed so large that nothing else existed. Everything came down to this one thing. If we found Danielle,
anything was possible, even Abby and me.

We had the leverage now that we needed to bring
Arthur to the bargaining table. Wolpert flourished Molly's
statement, and there was such a burst of excited chatter
that Brenda had to remind people that there was an interrogation going on the other side of the glass. Wolpert
was about to make a mock-ceremonial presentation of
the papers to Brenda, but Randall Ford stepped in and
took the copies. He handed the original back to Wolpert
and took his time studying the statement while those
around him tried to read it over his shoulder without being too obvious about it.

"This is great," he announced.

He asked Wolpert his name, nodded thoughtfully as if
committing it to memory, looked around the room as
though he could now safely leave it to us to clean up the
details, and made his exit.

We'd broken Arthur's alibi. I'd cracked the case for
them. It wasn't the kind of situation where you could
say, "Okay, all you have to do now is x, y, and z," but
now they really had something on Arthur. He'd been
placed at the scene of the crime, and he'd been caught in
a phony alibi. Any competent interrogator could take
that and run with it.

On the other side of the mirror, little had changed, except that someone had had the excellent idea of bringing
Arthur coffee. It sat in a big polystyrene cup with the
Doosy's logo prominently displayed; beside it, also untouched, lay one of their specialty donuts, the kind

Danielle had been fetching for the social workers at New Beginnings.

Dempsey and Arthur seemed to have run out of things to say to each other. He had twice asked to leave, Brenda told me, once soon after Wolpert had taken off to see Molly, but Dempsey had stalled him. Brenda referred to Dempsey as Carol, and I took that to indicate that Brenda felt I'd earned my place as an insider.

Wryly I thought, I'd sold out as a doctor, so now I was eligible to join Dempsey's crowd.

We waited with the expectancy of a theater audience as Wolpert made his entrance into the interview room.

Dempsey and Arthur sat like an unhappily married couple around the kitchen table, their bodies angled away from one another. Arthur slumped in his chair, staring at a spot on the desk in front of him. He appeared inert, but I could see his eyes respond to any movement on Dempsey's part. She sat wearily with her chin on one hand. She looked desperate for a cigarette. As if she needed the activity to remain engaged, she broke in without apology as the other detective was in the middle of a line of questioning.

"So tell me again where you parked when you pulled up to the curb by Dracone Park," she asked brusquely.

Arthur stirred impatiently and gave a deep sigh. He looked like he was about to tell her he'd had enough and wanted to leave, but then Wolpert made his entrance.

Arthur didn't change his posture or his bored expression. He scarcely moved his head, but he looked intently as Wolpert relieved the detective beside Dempsey, who at once got up and left the room.

He was intensely curious about the paper that Wolpert passed to Dempsey. His gaze followed it and then fixed on Dempsey's face to learn her reaction as she studied it.

There was no triumph in Dempsey's face. She read the short statement and then looked away as if she were considering if she'd left anything off the shopping list. When she'd read it again she slipped it away in the manila folder in front of her.

"Let's take it—"

"Oh, no!" Arthur groaned.

"This is the last time we're going to do this."

There was an ominous tone in her voice that Arthur missed.

"There's a limit!" he protested.

"That's where we're at."

He got it this time and sat silently, attentively, and very still.

Dempsey changed the phrasing of her questions from request to command. "I want you to tell me what you did, starting from the time you left your house."

"Like I told you." He sighed, but it was more for show. "My wife fancied a run. She wanted to go out, so I drove her to Cambridge to this place we go. Doosy's."

A few minutes previously, Dempsey would have interrupted him to ask for details, but now she waited for him to finish. Then she waited some more, sitting across the desk staring impassively at his face.

"What is this? The silent treatment? Come on!" He didn't ask her to give him a break, but he sensed that the balance of power had changed and that he might just need a break around now.

"Were you alone when you drove the van out of your garage this morning?"

"No. My wife was with me. She was sitting in the back, so no one could see her, you see, because—"

"Your wife told our officers that she hasn't left the house today."

"And she also told your officers that she went with me in the van to Cambridge. I know, because I was right there when she told them."

"This is her signed statement." She plucked the paper out of the file and rotated it on the desk so that it was the right way up for Arthur to read, but she kept her hand in place so that it covered most of the text. "This here is your wife's signature, isn't it?"

He tilted his head to look at it from different angles, stalling so he could extract as much of the statement as possible from between Dempsey's short, stubby fingers. "I'm not a handwriting expert."

"Take my word for it."

He sat back in his chair, relaxed all of a sudden, giving up the struggle over the paper. He raised his hands, palms up, in a gesture of acceptance. "What can I tell you? Molly gets confused. It's all the damn medicine she's on. Sometimes she can't remember one day—"

"She wasn't confused when she gave this statement to our officers. I know that for a fact, because we had a clinical psychiatrist go with them to make sure she was in her right mind."

Out of the corner of my eye, I noticed Brenda glance toward me. I hadn't reckoned on being a witness in this case.

Arthur launched a tirade. "You took a shrink down to see my wife? Without my permission? Without her permission? You took a psychiatrist to manipulate that poor, sick woman? What kind of devious, underhanded behavior is that? No wonder she gave you the statement!" He gestured contemptuously toward it. "That won't stand up. It's not worth the paper it's written on!"

"Cut the crap," Dempsey told him. "We want Danielle. It's time to cut a deal."

Arthur's outrage had dissipated as suddenly as it had begun. He sat deep in thought, in the pose of a chess player considering his next move, elbows on the desk, fingers interlaced, upper lip resting on the knuckles.

"I want a lawyer," he said.

"You'll get one. Right now I'm placing you under arrest."

Arthur waited, head down, for Dempsey to finish the Miranda warning.

"Are you done?"

"For now. We'll pick up again when you get your attorney."

"I don't think so."

Dempsey shrugged. "That's up to you."

"Who around here do I tell I'm suicidal?" Arthur asked. "How about that psychiatrist you took to see my wife? Is he still around?"

"You're no more suicidal than I am."

"I'm suicidal," Arthur pronounced, "and I want to go to Sanders to receive psychiatric treatment."

He spoke robotically, like a soldier who had been taught what to say in the event of capture, and I wondered whether this was a strategy he'd worked out in advance with Dave Feldman.

"I'm telling you I'm suicidal. I think I'd know, wouldn't I? I'm telling you, if you put me in a cell, I'm going to run against the wall and bash my head in." He turned right around in his chair so that he faced the one-way mirror. "Do you want that on your record, Doctor?"

Nothing upsets wardens more than prisoners who kill themselves before they get to trial, except an escape. Suicide is a kind of escape. The accused has evaded the long arm of the law. Justice cannot be served. Plus, when someone suicides in jail, the press persecutes the prison administration. The governor's office calls. There's a mortality review.

For this reason, when a prisoner awaiting trial says he's suicidal, there's every incentive to pack the problem off to Sanders. With a high-profile prisoner like Arthur, the process was over in minutes. All it took was a brief examination by the court psychiatrist and the signature of an on-call judge, and Arthur, handcuffed and shackled, was packed into the blue van and on his way.

I passed them on the highway at ninety miles an hour.

I called the moonlighter who covered the hospital through the night and learned that Dave Feldman had already arrived.

As I crossed the Sanders parking lot, the mosquitoes that swarmed the orange floodlights sensed my warm body and began to close on me. The lot had been built on a leveled landfill, and they were a militant breed, mutants raised in pockets of water deep within the strata of ancient refuse. I walked quickly, brushing away insects that persisted, and was glad that the correctional officer buzzed open the outer perimeter gate so that I didn't have to wait outside at their mercy.

In the front trap, a booth surrounded by bulletproof glass, sat three officers whose job it was to monitor people entering and exiting the institution. One of them, I was surprised to see, was Lieutenant Kovacs. He didn't work the evening shift.

Under surveillance of the officers in the trap, I entered the eight-foot space between the next two doors and submitted to a search by the officer stationed there. Once he was satisfied I wasn't bringing in a cell phone, medication, liquor, or any sharps, he signaled for the second door to be buzzed open, and I passed through into the administration corridor.

Kovacs came out of the trap as I passed. He had made it seem coincidental, pausing to look down the corridor to the shift commander's office, then changing his mind, but he wasn't a man who left things to chance. We fell into step as we crossed the wide grassed yard around which the buildings of the Sanders Institute were grouped. A few stars were visible through the surreal orange glow of the floodlights. Beyond the wire was the impenetrable darkness of the forest.

"I thought you'd have gone home by now," I said, to make conversation.

"Oh, no. I'm shift commander."

"They made you work a double?"

"Could be a triple, the way things are shaping up."

"What happened to Captain DaSilva?"

"He came in. Then he had to leave. He went home sick."

"Nothing serious?"

"Something he ate, I expect. He was feeling a bit under the weather. I told him to go home."

I didn't ask Kovacs how, since he'd been working the day shift, he'd have been around to tell DaSilva to leave. Or why the lieutenant was telling a captain to go home sick.

"And you're working the graveyard shift, too?" I asked, still in the style of casual conversation. "I thought the union had rules against that sort of thing."

"I volunteered."

Kovacs hadn't asked me why I'd returned to Sanders so late. I'd never before turned up for work at ten o'clock at night. I had no business there. The moonlighter would take care of the new admissions. I didn't have to put in a special appearance because we had a couple of men receiving media attention. Every week, Sanders received a high-profiler of one kind or another.

Nor was there a good reason why, by unspoken agreement, we were both heading toward the Intensive Treatment Unit. We understood each other. Whatever purpose each man had, it was his own business. Talking served only to put things on the record.

Kovacs was first to the front door of the building that housed the ITU, and as he held it open for me we came face to face for the first time.

"Lucky for the administration you happened to be here when the need arose," I said.

He shrugged modestly. "Times like these, you have to step up to the plate. Know what I mean?"

I didn't answer his question. I didn't think I knew what he meant. If his tone had suggested another, sinister meaning, I wasn't going to speculate about it. But I thought, *This is Massachusetts. This is a state institution. There are checks and balances. There are cameras in ITU monitoring every move. This is normal for us. Life goes on at Sanders as it always has. No reason for Kovacs or anyone else to step out of character now.*

I followed him down the dingy corridor and we waited together at the heavy steel door that was the first of the pair leading into the ITU. A buzzer mounted beside the door would alert the officers inside to your presence, but it was considered polite to wait until they spotted you on the TV camera mounted obliquely above.

We didn't wait at all. Nor did Kovacs expect to. He precisely anticipated the electrical release of the lock by grasping the handle and leaning his weight against the door at the instant the buzz signaled the lock's release.

We entered the compartment between the doors, a small enclosed space for two men, six feet by five. I'd always thought of it as a compression chamber where you prepared for a deep dive into the depths of human nature. Kovacs stared ahead, mind fixed on what had to be done when the door opened. In the closeness of that small space I was aware that whatever impassive expression his face might assume, however much he cultivated a relaxed stance for his powerful body, Kovacs was breathing hard.

The lock of the inner door buzzed open and we entered.

Inside, everything was quiet.

The ITU was a T-shaped structure. At the junction, the control center had views of the stem and both arms. We stood at the bottom of the stem, a broad corridor lined on either side with single cells for patients who were too dangerous to be released even to one of the maxes. These patients were impulsive, disorganized, delusional, ranting at voices, enraged. They often set one another off. One patient yelling would irritate the patient in the cell opposite, who in turn would shout abuse, which in turn would recruit other patients who believed themselves to be singled out in the verbal melee.

But this evening, a sullen silence pervaded the unit.

You develop a feel for the emotional atmosphere of a psychiatric unit as soon as you enter it, and at first I couldn't put my finger on why the absence of noise troubled me. As I walked the corridor, faces as usual appeared at the small windows of the cell doors. Dave Feldman was one of them, but I didn't want to make eye contact with him. At the end of the corridor, in a bay, a patient from my admissions unit, too violent even to be placed in locked seclusion, lay secured to a bed by four-point restraints. He raised his head at the sound of footsteps, but when I waved hello to him he let his head fall back again without a word.

Collectively, the ITU was most often angry. Sometimes depressed. Occasionally manic and giddy. It wasn't until I came to the end of the corridor that I realized that the pervasive emotion was one I had never encountered in this place before: fear.

Even the psychotic patients sensed something. Those who would usually have given free vent to their raving held back. The sociopaths hiding out in Sanders to avoid the problems that awaited them in their prisons were watchful, ever on the lookout for opportunity.

"It's quiet," I mentioned.

Kovacs shrugged. "Yeah," he replied indifferently, though in his way he was as sensitive to the emotional vibes of the place as I was. Kovacs was a hunter, and though he affected a negligent, macho manner, he was tuned in to the subtle changes in the environment in which he moved, whether the cinder blocks of Sanders or the pine trees of Maine.

We came to the end of the corridor and entered the control center. Four officers lounged in front of a bank of TV monitors that lined the wall; below the monitors, a bank of switches controlled the opening and closing of the doors as well as the lights and the water supply of each cell.

The officers returned my hello perfunctorily. The crew on the day shift liked to josh with me, but these guys seemed withdrawn and preoccupied.

ITU was the hub of the institution, where problem patients were contained. Over the years, we'd evolved some degree of mutual trust, so I was puzzled by the coolness with which I was received. Two men I'd worked with for half a dozen years studiously avoided my eye as they examined the monitors.

"Feldman's on number twelve," Kovacs announced before I'd had an opportunity to ask.

"When did he get here?"

"Couple of hours ago."

"He said he was suicidal."

"That was just to keep himself out of jail."

"But he hasn't done anything?"

"He hasn't said anything, either," one of the officers said and was silenced by a look from Kovacs.

"He hasn't done anything," Kovacs said. "But you never know. He's a keeper, I'd say." It was a statement phrased as a suggestion: Kovacs wanted him to stay in ITU, under his control. He glanced toward me to acknowledge that it was still my call.

"Okay," I agreed.

If we released him from ITU, the convicts in Admissions would torment him mercilessly. We didn't want him showing up at his next court appearance black and blue from a beating.

"We'll give him a couple of days to toughen up," I said.

If Danielle died, someone would try to kill him. He was an easy hit, a sure way for a prisoner with nothing much to lose to raise his status in the prison community.

"He'll need more than that."

"He's never going to toughen up," I said. "But he might benefit from a time-out."

I thought two of the officers exchanged looks, but I could have been mistaken.

"The other one's on his way," I said.

"Hodges. We heard."

I said, "All of a sudden, he became suicidal, too."

"That's bullshit, though, isn't it, Doc?" one of the officers at the monitors asked.

Kovacs answered, "Soon as they get arrested? They

both become suicidal, get themselves sent to Sanders? It's a setup. They arranged this beforehand."

"So, they're getting set to serve their time here?" the officer said. "Instead of in a regular prison where they belong? That's not right." He looked sick and turned away. "They let the little girl die—"

"She's not dead," Kovacs said.

I turned my attention to the monitor. We all stared in silence at Dave Feldman. He sat immobile, head down, on the edge of his bunk.

I had no right to observe him, of course. I shouldn't even have been there in the ITU. He was a patient in this hospital, not a suspect. And I wasn't a doctor; I worked for the police. I had no therapeutic role. I certainly didn't feel in a therapeutic frame of mind. I wanted to send the officers off on a diversion, pull the connection on his camera, and get into that cell with him. As he sat on his bunk, in the relative cool of the ITU, with the remains of his supper on the floor at the corner of the screen, a tumble of empty milk and juice containers on a polystyrene tray, Danielle lay bound and gagged, dying molecule by molecule. I wanted to torture Dave.

Psychotherapists are fond of telling their patients, "Yes, we all have thoughts like that. It's absolutely normal. Just so long as you don't act on it."

But it's a fine line between thought and action. After years of questioning men who cross that line, I'm not sure I know the difference between those who do and those who don't. Of all the million men in Massachusetts who think of killing their wives, I see thirty a year who actually do. Most of them aren't any different from the guy standing behind you in the checkout line at the supermarket.

I knew I would never do it. I thought I did. "I'd never torture anyone," I told myself. It was a given. An absolute. You might discuss it with good friends over dinner, after the second glass of wine, but only to dismiss the possibility. "Besides, it doesn't work," someone would point out, although no one could cite the double-blind, placebo-controlled study that showed that. Torture was something that rough, stupid, impatient people did. We, on the other hand, were confident that the strength of our convictions would keep us out of harm's way. If we discussed the possibility, it was as an academic exercise. A reductio ad absurdum that returned us, unaltered by the process, to our true, our bedrock premise. The fact that you discussed it showed that you were secure in not doing it. Because, really, it didn't bear thinking about.

Except that I was thinking about it. But I was thinking about it because I knew I'd never do it. I couldn't not consider the possibility of torture. A girl's life was on the line. Not to think about it would have shown moral cowardice. An act of bad faith. Not to consider all the possibilities open to one in a given situation constituted a betrayal of one's existential freedom.

What if a hurricane cut a swathe through New England, leveling Boston and everything around Sanders? What if a terrorist attack stopped life as we knew it? Would the same old rules still apply? Or would we have new rules for the new, more primitive setting? Wasn't this a situation like that? Wasn't this—on a different scale—just such an exception?

What bothered me was that I didn't feel in the slightest bit philosophical. I wanted to go into that eight-by-twelve box and hurt Dave until he told me where Danielle was. I wanted to hurt him as only I, the doctor, knew how to hurt people. And I knew I'd want to keep on hurting Dave even after he told me where Danielle was.

But I'd never do it.

I drifted out of the control center down the other arm of the T with the intention of turning around when I came to the door to the disused cell block that housed the tiger cages. I was simply pacing as I thought, standard institutionalized behavior. Kovacs got ahead of me to unlock the door, though I had no purpose in mind.

"Hey, you want to stick around for dinner?" Kovacs asked. He'd never invited me before. I'd never seen him so congenial.

"No." I didn't know what I wanted to do. I stepped into the auditorium-like cell block. "Thanks," I said as an afterthought.

"We're sending out. There's a Thai place down on Route Thirty-one, just after the rotary."

"Thanks, I'm not hungry."

"Me, I'm hungry. Know what I'm going to get?"

"No." He was beginning to irritate me with this talk of food. I thought of the sandwich I'd shared with Abby that afternoon and longed to be home.

"Chicken satay. It's really good. Know the kind I mean?"

"Yes. Sounds good."

"Kind of like a shish kebab. Except it comes on these bamboo skewers."

"Yes," I said.

"I used to eat it when I was in Laos. Except it wasn't chicken then. You never knew what it was. Some things you don't want to ask about."

He jerked his shoulders, hammed a spooky shiver. I waited him out. Kovacs was a man of few words and limited sociability.

"But you still have a taste for it," I said. "Whatever."

"You know what? The thing that takes me back isn't the meat, but the skewers it's on. In Laos, we used them all the time."

We had been standing side by side, facing the cages, and he glanced now at my face to see if I was catching up to where the conversation was headed. He rocked forward on the balls of his feet.

"There are certain moments when I almost get nostalgic thinking about those bamboo skewers."

"I'm sure they had their uses."

I wanted to break free, but you didn't just walk away from Kovacs. He held me, fascinated.

"The thing about the bamboo skewers is that they're real sharp. They go right into the meat and through, clean. You think they're smooth, but they're not, once they hit something hard."

He paused to let me consider. The effect is always more powerful when the recipient fills in the blank from his own vocabulary of fears. Something hard: bone.

"I get it," I said.

We faced one another now. He was staring at my face, reading off my reactions to his words.

"When that bamboo hits something hard, it splinters."

Kovacs waited politely for anything I might care to say.

I wanted to ask him if he was kidding, but Kovacs had never shown much of a sense of humor. I was afraid he'd tell me what he planned to do with the bamboo skewers once he finished his chicken satay.

It was something like a standoff.

But, I thought, kidders like to draw it out. There's often a sadistic element to putting one over on you.

He smiled, in so far as he was capable of, and chucked

me on the side of the arm, and the tension broke. In unison, we turned and strolled back the way we'd come.

He didn't tell me, "Hey, you know I was just pulling your leg back there!"

His creaky smile, the physical contact, implied this. But he hadn't reassured me.

"You hanging around for Hodges?" he asked.

I shook my head. I'd had enough of Arthur. I felt beaten. I wanted to go to Abby and get some comfort, but I knew that wouldn't work, either.

We'd reached the control center and I stuck my head in to check out Dave's monitor. He hadn't moved.

When Kovacs walked me to the steel door at the end of the corridor, it felt as if he was escorting me off the premises.

"There's nothing for you here, Doc," he said, almost kindly. "Go home."

10:45 P.M.

When I was back on the road, I called Brenda to get an update.

"Nothing yet," she said. Her fatigue sounded through the tone of strained optimism. "We're following up everything—cranks, psychics, suggestions from the media. We've enlarged the search area. We've got cops going house to house. They're checking garages, basements, storage lockers, anything they can get into without search warrants. The overtime will bust the budget, but the mayor says do what it takes."

"You never know when things are going to turn your way."

She started to say, "We could catch a break tomorrow," then stopped, because tomorrow would be too late. She said, "I pray Danielle's somewhere with access to food and water. If we can just have a little more time, sooner or later, something's going to turn up."

"It's possible there's someone else we don't know about who's looking after her."

"That's a mixed blessing. He might be giving her water, but that comes with a price. And with all the media attention, he could decide at any time he's better off without the witness."

I felt guilty and ineffectual that I had both suspects in my hospital and I couldn't get a simple address from them. "I wish we could have had a shot at Arthur Hodges," I said.

"They had everything planned in case they were arrested."

"Don't you think their trips to Sanders were coordinated? I think they're laying the groundwork for serving time there."

At the other end, Brenda paused, and I thought we'd been cut off. "We're going to have a hard time convicting them, you know, on the evidence we've got. Without Danielle."

When I pulled into the driveway of our home the lights of the kitchen were on. I wondered if Abby had eaten since the sandwich that neither of us had had much appetite for.

When I came in, she stood expectantly in the middle of the room, waiting for me. Behind her on the counter, the small TV was tuned to the local news channel, and I could hear that they'd just finished reporting on Danielle's case.

"Anything on the news?" I asked.

She sagged in disappointment. "I was hoping you'd have something for me."

"I just came from Sanders."

"You saw them?"

"One of them. Dave Feldman."

"How is he?" Her scowl told me she wasn't inquiring after his health.

"I didn't speak to him."

She started to ask me why not, and gave it up with a shrug of futility.

"I can't," I said.

She didn't dispute this, but I saw a look of accusation in her eyes. She turned back to the cutting board, where she was making a sandwich, tossing slices of ham and fragments of lettuce haphazardly onto a slice of bread, spreading a dollop of mayonnaise unevenly over the lettuce. "Want one?"

"No thanks."

I thought of Kovacs eating chicken satay and felt the stirrings of uneasiness I hadn't entirely been able to suppress on the ride home.

"I know," Abby said. "I'm not hungry, either."

She stared indecisively at the sandwich, unsure now what purpose it served.

"What are they going to do with them?"

"They'll keep them in seclusion as a precaution."

"I mean, will they give them a beating?"

"We don't do that anymore."

" 'We'?"

"You know what I mean. I was never involved in that."

She raised an eyebrow. "Never?" It wasn't a casual question. "Honest?"

"Never."

"They might work these two over."

"They might like to. But there are cameras now. They're everywhere. They record everything. Anyway, that isn't going to do any good."

"How can you be so sure?"

"Beat it out of them? Torture them till they tell us where Danielle is?"

She looked up. "No one said anything about torture." She was suddenly interested, as though, for the first time, I'd given a response she hadn't expected. "I was talking about a good old-fashioned beating."

"This kind of case brings out the worst in us."

"I think you have to fight fire with fire."

"It's not about revenge. It can't be about revenge."

"Who said anything about revenge? I'm talking about roughing them up a bit so they're more inclined to give up Danielle."

"Their lives depend on Danielle . . ." I didn't want to complete the sentence, to spell out to Abby the stark reality of the case.

"Their lives depend on not talking," she said confidently. "I know that. But people talk anyway. Isn't it true that no one can stand torture indefinitely? Isn't that something you'd know about?"

"For God's sake!"

"But isn't it? Isn't that your area of expertise?"

"I don't know about torture." I was angry at being characterized as an expert of that kind.

"You know about interviewing. You know interrogation. No one knows more about that than you do. Isn't torture just a logical extension of interrogation?"

"I don't have anything to do with the dirty end of the business."

"They ask you, though."

"They ask." I shrugged to concede a point that had no compelling significance. "A couple of times a year some spooky acronym organization calls offering me grant money for a research project they don't want to specify. I tell them no thanks. That's as far as it goes."

"So they think you know something."

"I make it my business not to."

They didn't need my expertise at Sanders. I remembered one time when I'd come upon Kovacs manning the rear trap on a slow afternoon. Kovacs the sniper was flipping through *Gray's Anatomy,* shopping for new targets the way he might peruse an L. L. Bean catalogue for a new pair of hunting boots.

"I know where you're going with this," I said. "I don't think we should even be talking about it."

"I'm not telling you to do anything. There can't be any harm in discussing it, surely?" She looked at me curiously, sensing I was holding something back. "Can there?"

"I don't want to talk about it."

"You're the one who says we never talk. Now you don't want to talk."

"This is different."

"You complain we don't talk when it's something you want to discuss. But when it's something I want to talk about, that's different."

"This isn't about us."

"Not you, maybe. But it is about me."

She glared at me in a fierce confrontation.

You can be hot and angry with the person you love, and you can be cold and angry with a person you don't much like. I'd never before seen that cold, angry look in Abby's eyes. I turned away.

She contemplated the crumb she'd been pushing around the counter at the end of her index finger. It was a spiky crumb, dry and hard, that had been there since the morning. She was silent, considering, head to one side as she regarded the crumb. She brought her fingertip over the crumb and very slowly applied pressure. I imagined the sharp edges of the bread sticking into her fingertip. Not enough to hurt a lot, but enough to cause a sensation of pain. Then the crumb burst into powder.

She looked up abruptly with a new resolution. "It's not complicated," she said. "If we don't do something, Danielle's going to die."

"I can't."

"You can do anything you want."

"It's not who I am." I raised my hands in a gesture of regret. "You know that."

"You can be anything you want to be. You're always saying that."

"But not torture. There are limits."

"You've stuck things into people. You've cut people. You did it all the time when you were an intern."

She cut me off before I could return her argument. "No, it's not!" she burst out. "It's not different from cutting someone in surgery. It's precisely the same. You don't have to enjoy it. Of course you're not meant to enjoy it, because you have to be cool and dispassionate. You're trying to save a life, just like you would in surgery. It's just that the person you're cutting isn't the patient you're trying to save."

Was this Abby? Here was a whole new person whose existence I'd never suspected.

"Are you listening to yourself?" I asked.

"I'm listening to you and I'm not hearing anything that's going to help Danielle."

"I'm a doctor, for God's sake!"

"Who are you kidding?" she shot back. "You're no virgin, Paul."

I waited a moment in case she wanted to take back what she'd said in the heat of the moment. Sadly, I searched her face for the person I thought I knew. "That was below the belt," I said quietly. But I saw no sign of regret.

Instead, she asked, "You don't like to fight dirty?"

I stared at her in disbelief. This wasn't an impulsive outburst. It was no aberration.

"Who are you to talk?" she demanded. "You damn near stabbed a man to death!"

"In self-defense."

"Exactly!"

"It was him or me."

"Don't you get it? That's the point I'm making. In extreme situations the rules no longer apply."

The truth was that I longed for her, by some magical stroke, to release me from the obligations that caged me. Impossibly, I hoped to be justified. But I wanted the sinuous logic of the Serpent in the Garden, not the stark expediency of Realpolitik.

She had reined in her anger. She spoke to me calmly, as you might to a stranger. "I've been thinking about this since I left the agency this evening. I've struggled with this, Paul. I'm not a lynch mob." She paused to see how far she had carried me along her line of reasoning. "I think this is one of those extreme situations."

"Okay," I said reluctantly, in acknowledgment, not agreement.

"We have to do what we can do."

"But, Abby . . . This is crazy."

"It's not crazy," she said, patiently, reasonably. "It's just outside the bounds we operate in day to day, that's all."

"Look, it's been an emotional day—"

"Don't patronize me!" The anger she'd held back flared again. Her eyes were filled with tears, but not of sadness or despair. She shouted, full in my face, "You think I like begging you? If I could do this myself, I would. I can't get to them!"

"Listen," I said, trying to calm her, "Sanders is shut

down for the night." I reached over to touch her hand, but she saw me coming and pulled it back. "I probably wouldn't be able to get in myself."

But, in stereo, I was considering what she said in spite of myself. Would Kovacs let me back into the institution? He might welcome my medical expertise. Or he might not want another witness. But Kovacs wasn't serious. He was on some fantasy trip reliving the Laos days of his youth as an Army Ranger. He was yanking my chain. There was nothing Kovacs liked better.

"You can get in," Abby said. "In an emergency? They'd have to let you in."

"This has to do with Adrian," I said gently.

She laughed bitterly. "Don't tell me that this isn't going to bring him back!"

"Nothing's going to bring him back."

"Danielle's still alive." She challenged me, as if to disagree was to condemn the girl to death. "We can save her."

"I know this is vitally important to you." Danielle sat on the fault line of our marriage. Whether she tumbled into the abyss or was saved might seem like a test, but I wanted Abby to know that whatever the outcome, if, for all the right reasons, I failed the test, our marriage had already been decided elsewhere. I began, "I know—"

"I don't want you to explain it to me."

"Abby, I just can't do it." I heard the note of apology in my own voice. "It's a matter of principle." The words sounded petty.

"Paul, extraordinary times demand extraordinary measures."

"That's what the Nazis said."

"And that's exactly what the liberals say whenever anyone tries to change the rules."

"I thought we were liberals."

"Not today, I'm not."

"But principles, ideals . . ." I had to swallow to finish the list. "Ethics. They don't change. They are who you are."

"I want you to do this for me."

"Abby—"

"One life against your principles." She demonstrated the balancing with open hands. The principles were light as air.

"I can't."

"People are making sacrifices, Paul. Did you ever think of that? Men and women are dying. They're sacrificing their lives in Iraq. Okay, it's a stupid war. But the people in the army believe they're defending our country. You showed me the pictures of blast injuries in your medical journal. They're risking horrible wounds. And maybe we have to make sacrifices, too. We're not going to be injured by a roadside bomb, but maybe we have to accept another kind of sacrifice. Maybe we have to sacrifice some of our principles. Maybe that's what our contribution has to be."

"It's a question of loyalty," I insisted. We were speaking across a divide, without the possibility of contact. "I have to be true to what I believe in."

"I don't think you realize how arrogant that sounds. I know you don't mean it that way, but you make it sound like you're up in an ivory tower, surveying the world of ordinary mortals from some lofty height. We have to come down to where everyone else is."

"I wish there was something I could do. Really. Something I could legitimately do."

"I'm sorry for you, Paul." She looked at me wistfully. As if I were receding toward a distant horizon. It was a good-bye of sorts. "I think you've lost touch with yourself. You're so good at assuming the point of view of the person you're interviewing that you've become a chameleon. You don't have any convictions. The substance has dropped away. All you're left with are these abstract principles."

Alone in separate rooms in the huge house, we tried to distract ourselves. We were restless. We moved about and crossed paths and made polite gestures of glancing contact. We'd never sleep. With sudden dread, I realized we wouldn't sleep until Danielle was dead.

Finally, I went for a run along the back shore. A faint, humid haze obscured the stars. A quarter-moon shed just enough light to see where my feet went on the road. On one side, the surf rushed at the rocks and drew back. On the other, cicadas chirped, suddenly fell silent, then anxiously started up again as I passed. I ran hard, trying to tire myself enough to sleep. The sweat streamed down my face and stung my eyes, but however I pushed myself I couldn't achieve that endorphin rush where the worries of the day faded as the body took over.

It was after midnight when I returned home. The light was on in our bedroom. I took a long shower, finally turning the lever all the way until cold water splashed on my head and ran down my shoulders, but I couldn't feel refreshed.

The run had been a mistake. I wasn't in the least ready to sleep and I felt now that I'd never cool down. I went out onto the terrace with a towel wrapped loosely around my waist. I couldn't settle. It wasn't sleep that I was avoiding. I couldn't face lying next to Abby.

I didn't know who she was anymore. It was as though I'd suddenly discovered that she could play the piano or was a member of the Communist Party: a gradual process that had taken place away from notice emerged as an abrupt, astonishing change. We'd gone about our daily routines side by side, but we'd been living a parallel existence since Adrian's death. When we'd been eating breakfast, talking after work over a glass of wine, catching each other's eye while dining with friends, sleeping in the same bed, Abby had been gradually, imperceptibly veering away.

I was convinced that her desperate need to rescue Danielle at any cost was driven by the unconscious striving for restitution. She'd said so herself: We can't bring back Adrian, but we can save Danielle. When your beloved child is killed, it cannot be meaningless. The event is so encompassing, so crucial, that you can't allow it to be allocated to blind, numb chance. An event of that magnitude can't be left out there in the absolute zero of the cosmos. It must be tied into the nexus of human character and motive.

Her desperate advocacy of torture, I thought, was part and parcel of this same process. I felt some solace in this, because it placed the question of torture in a context. It was a clinical phenomenon that yielded to a well-established psychological explanation. The issue was neutralized. If only it would stay in that box.

She blamed me for the accident that killed Adrian. Not that I was responsible for it—the drunk in the pickup truck was responsible—but I hadn't prevented it. Every professional instinct told me not to return to the past. It was a crime scene that had been meticulously and thoroughly examined, that thousands of cars had driven over, that street cleaning machines had passed over, that had been snowed and rained over and repaved, and now Abby was claiming to have found this piece of evidence that contradicted all previous constructions of what had happened at the intersection. It was unverifiable. To lend credence to it was to open a bitter debate with oneself that was without hope of resolution. But I couldn't help myself.

Above me, on the second floor, Abby turned off the bedroom light. I decided to wait half an hour until she'd fallen asleep, but tonight Abby wasn't going to sleep, any more than I would. I decided to wait half an hour until, in silent complicity, we could pretend that she'd fallen asleep.

I crept into the bedroom, careful to make no noise that could give her an excuse to wake, and lowered myself carefully onto the bed. The windows were open and the fan blew what should have been cool ocean air into the room. As it scanned the bed, its oscillations sent a breeze that climbed my body, disappeared, came back. I concentrated on this rhythm and tried to empty my mind.

We communicated even in our shallow state of drowsiness. It started gradually. We tossed and turned individually, each one jarring the other from the brink of sleep. Then we began to turn in concert, until the fiction of going to sleep was no longer plausible. We lay parallel and still, awake and aware.

In a normal conversational voice, as though picking up a discussion that had recently lapsed, Abby spoke into the darkness. "It's hard to imagine what she's going through tonight."

"I only hope she's still alive."

"Oh, she's out there somewhere."

We were silent for a few moments, each in his or her own thoughts. I could have reached out in the darkness, located some part of her, found my way to a hand to clasp or a cheek to caress. I could have touched her, except that we were strangers now. We were two people passing the time while waiting for the trains that would take us to our separate destinations.

I thought, *So this is what it feels like when your marriage comes to an end*. Half of the process was making a decision that it was over, half perceiving, all of a sudden, how things really were. I had learned today that Abby had already come to her own conclusion.

She broke the silence, hesitantly speaking her thoughts aloud. "Before, I asked you to do it for me. That was wrong. You should do what's right. I believe that the right thing is that we should do everything in our power to save Danielle."

"You know how I feel about that."

"I don't think you want to feel that way. I know you want to be free of these inhibitions. You want to act."

"I don't think of them as inhibitions."

"But they are. I'm not even sure they're yours. They seem more like your father's."

"Please!"

"You can do anything you want."

I launched myself off the bed angrily, hardly thinking what I was doing, wanting only to break free from these emotional currents. It wasn't that she'd mentioned my father, though Abby had chosen an effective trigger. A dangerous resolve was hatching in my mind. It wasn't rational, and I didn't like it. I paced, indecisive, beside the bed, my heels thumping on the wooden floor.

"What?" she asked, though she already sensed what my trajectory would be.

"This is crazy," I said, referring to the impulse that was gathering strength and definition, even though I didn't fully see what it was. I was succumbing, all the same.

"What are you going to do?"

"I don't know," I said. "I'm going to Sanders."

She touched my shoulder, as a friend reassures you when you're about to embark on a course of action that can't entirely be explained.

I drove fast, eager and impatient to come to grips with this new assignment. I told myself I wasn't going to do anything. It was exactly the opposite. I had to go to Sanders to prevent Kovacs from doing anything. I was filled with a guilty thrill that was inconsistent with that goal. I was taking a first step, neglecting to notice the next step in the sequence, much less where the pathway led. This is how you plunge headlong into some dizzy love affair, or fall off the wagon, or commit a crime. First you convince yourself you're entering the wrong place at the wrong time for the very best of reasons.

2:35 A.M.

I'd never worked in Sanders during the graveyard shift. I didn't know the correctional officers staffing the front trap. They didn't know me from Adam.

"Who?" the sergeant asked, as if I was a bad joke.

Instead of my handing the ID to the officer as I passed through the double doors, he told me to pass it through the slot into the trap. Routinely, he checked the photo against my face, then turned the card over to examine it for tampering. He passed it to the other officer to check. Then, unusually, he got on the phone.

I figured he was checking with Kovacs. As shift commander, he didn't have to let me enter the institution. He could declare a lockdown. It happened all the time, when a fight broke out and they temporarily suspended all activities in the institution, including entrances and exits. Tomorrow I could protest to the superintendent all I wanted, but by tomorrow it would be all over.

On the other side of the bulletproof glass, the sergeant looked me over dispassionately as he described my height, weight, age, hair color, and manner of dress to Kovacs. There followed an animated conversation during which his eyes kept returning to me. I thought he was conveying my mental state, and I assumed a suitably patient, respectful stance.

He nodded acknowledgment and replaced the phone, and I knew I was in. Instead of putting the ID in the wooden rack, empty except for the single card of the moonlighting overnight doctor, he kept it in the trap, tossing it facedown on the counter. He didn't write my name and time of entry in the logbook.

Then I waited for five minutes. I wondered if they had to clean up the evidence in ITU before I could be allowed to enter. Then the steel door on the other side of the corridor opened, and Kovacs sauntered in. We regarded each other through the greenish tint of two layers of bulletproof glass while he stood on the other side of the trap considering his options. The officers waited expectantly for his decision, and when he gave a nod of his head, the sergeant's thumb came down promptly on the button to buzz me through the doors.

"Couldn't stay away, huh, Doc?" he asked as I emerged into the administration corridor.

"Guess not."

He nodded understandingly.

I hadn't realized that he was blocking my way until he didn't turn when I expected him to.

I was going to avoid any challenge to Kovacs. "I thought I'd go to ITU," I said in a matter-of-fact tone.

He nodded thoughtfully. The corridor, a hub of activity during the day, was unnaturally quiet. Effectively, we were alone, having a private and privileged conversation.

"Let me tell you right off what my problem is."

"Okay," I said. "Let's deal with your problem."

"I don't know who you are."

"Sure you do."

"I know who you are on the day shift. Dr. Lucas, straight-shooting, straight-dealing psychiatrist. Fucking ace, when it comes to getting to the nitty-gritty of what someone doesn't want other people to know. But now you're off-duty."

"I'm working overtime, like you."

"But you can't say that for sure, because you don't know for sure who I am, either."

"Maybe not."

"You know the story of Dr. Jekyll and Mr. Hyde. Here's what the problem is: Are you Dr. Jekyll? Or are you Mr. Hyde?"

"I see."

"Now you understand my problem."

"You're only giving one of those gentlemen access to the ITU."

"You got it."

He waited for me to declare my allegiance.

As I opened my mouth to speak he cut me off, biding his time in order to interrupt at precisely that moment. "Don't fuck with us, Doc."

I started to speak and again he cut me off. He didn't glower at me or raise his voice. There was no need for histrionics. I knew Kovacs and he knew I knew what he was capable of. I was struck, though, by the passion revealed by this most circumspect of men.

"Every one of those men in ITU tonight is a good guy, someone I can count on. And they count on me. We stick together. We don't go running to grand juries. If I take you in there, anything you see, anything you hear stays there. I don't have to tell any of those men what the rules are. And they don't have to remind me of my responsibilities, either. They know anything you say is like I said it, because I brought you in there. Anything you do, it's on me. If there's any spillage, I clean it up."

The emotional intensity didn't come from the threat but from the suppressed ferocity of the loyalty that bound him to the other officers. It was as much of a tirade as I would ever see from him.

He found himself momentarily unguarded and caught himself. He took a breath and let out a long sigh. He shook his head in disbelief that he had let himself go. And if he was becoming unpredictable to himself, what about me?

"Go home, Doc. It's late. Go home to your wife. Get some sleep. Forget this ever happened. You were sleepwalking. Tomorrow it'll all be just a bad dream."

He looked at me wistfully, perhaps even slightly enviously.

"Good night, Dr. Jekyll," he said with a faint smile, turning on his heel and starting for the big steel door.

He had the flat of his hand on the door, and the buzz of the lock retracting almost drowned out my words.

"It's Mr. Hyde," I called after him.

His action was suspended for a moment; then he stepped back and let the door swing closed in front of him.

"Say again?"

"I want to go to ITU," I said. "You won't have to clean up after me."

He took two measured steps, looking at the floor, and planted himself in front of me, feet apart, slightly closer than was comfortable, inside my personal space.

He still wasn't looking at me. He spoke in little more than a murmur. "There's no going back on this."

"I know."

"You're sure?"

His eyes came up to mine, and I didn't flinch.

People think that if you look hard into someone's eyes you can read in his face whether he's lying, but it isn't true. If you come close enough, if you stare long enough, if you frown hard enough, everyone looks shifty and uncomfortable. Of course they are. Normal reactions tell us nothing. What's common is a useless indicator.

No one knew this better than I did, and yet I felt transparent under Kovacs's gaze. The reason I passed this lie detector test was that I had nothing to hide. If Kovacs had been able to read my mind, he wouldn't have found any deception there, for the simple reason that I didn't myself know what I thought.

I didn't know what I was going to do. I was willing to join Kovacs, and I'd keep my mouth shut. But on the bigger picture of torture and principle, I still hadn't decided my allegiance. Maybe I was the mole who would subvert their mission. Even that made it seem more thought out than it was, because I was traveling on impulse. It wasn't what Abby called acting from conviction, but it was something close to it.

"Okay," he said, apparently satisfied. "You're in."

I knew that Kovacs was too canny to trust me or anyone else. He'd take the consequences of letting me pass through the door, but he'd have no illusions about my loyalty.

"We can use what you've got," he said. "But understand: You're not running this show."

He waved a finger and the door instantly buzzed open. I followed after him, and we walked together silently across the yard.

When we came to the first steel door to the ITU, Kovacs didn't wait for the officers inside to notice us on the camera, but put his thumb on the red buzzer and the first door opened, with the second in sequence so that we passed through hardly breaking stride.

Inside, it was quiet. A couple of faces came to the windows of cell doors as we passed, but they said nothing.

"It's half empty," Kovacs said. "We sent everyone we could back to their units."

"Where's the on-call doctor?"

"He did rounds early. He's holed up in his room. We told him we had a security situation and it wasn't safe for him to come out without an escort."

At the end of the corridor, three officers came out of the command center as we approached. They seemed uneasy at the sight of me and came toward Kovacs to take him aside. He lifted a hand in reassurance, but they weren't satisfied, and as we entered the command center, I felt their hostility.

Also, all the monitors were blank.

"Cameras are down," Kovacs mentioned. "Electronics snafu. They can't locate the guy to fix it."

One of the officers asked me, "Hey, Doc, you brought your truth serum with you?"

Another cut him off with a scowl. "We have to talk," he said.

"Yes," Kovacs said, "we have to talk." He turned to me with a gesture of apology. "Would you mind?"

Their conduct was very professional. There were no officers on a rant, threatening mayhem and smacking fists into the palms of their hands. They were jacked up, but they were contained and disciplined, and Kovacs had them under his control. Besides the excitement of action, the officers were also anxious. They would pay a price for what they were doing, because unavoidably some of this would come out. The prisoners, if they survived, would make formal complaints that would be investigated. At a minimum, even if everyone stonewalled the investigation, they'd sustain damage: suspensions, demotions, firings, and the expense of lawyers' fees. If there was a breach in Kovacs's band of brothers and it all came out, they'd do state time. We'd all do serious time. If Dave or Arthur died . . . It didn't bear thinking about.

I walked to the end of the corridor of the short arm of the T to the Medical Room and perched on the edge of the examination couch. Around me were the familiar chrome and black upholstery of the stools, the shiny metal cabinets with glass windows holding rows of dressings and medications, and I breathed in the anti-septic atmosphere. Examining rooms like this one had been my natural habitat for almost my entire adult life. I reflected that likely as not, I'd lose my license to prac-tice medicine. We lived in extraordinary times. We all had to make sacrifices.

I was telling myself it wasn't too late to step out when Kovacs entered. He closed the door carefully and leaned against it. In his left hand, dangling casually, he held a roll of gray duct tape.

"I told them you're not here for the scenery. I told them you're here because I want you here, because you have skills we need and no one else has."

"As an interrogator."

"As a doctor."

"You want me . . ."

"Forget mind games. We want you to get physical."

"You want me to inflict pain, as a doctor."

I noticed for the first time the bamboo skewers that stuck out of the breast pocket of Kovacs's fatigues. He saw my eyes go to them, but he made no comment.

"This isn't a spectator sport," he said. "They want to

see you in there doing something. We want to see you
with your hands dirty so later you can't say you were
only a witness."

"Fair enough."

From down the corridor came the rumble of a heavy
object moving on castors, approaching rapidly. It stopped
outside and a knock sounded on the door. Kovacs told
them to come.

In the corridor, two of the officers from the command
center leaned against a dental chair that they had trun-
dled from the dentist's office at the end of the corridor.

"Where do you want it, Lieutenant?"

Kovacs surveyed the room. "Over there. Move the
trolley so it'll go under the lamp."

The men strained to get the heavy dental chair back
in motion, then let it come to a stop under the examination lamp.

Kovacs took his seat in the chair. He ran his hands
thoughtfully over the arms and settled back to get
comfortable. Finding the configuration unsatisfactory,
he stepped out to make an adjustment to the angle of
the footrest, then settled once again.

When the door closed behind the two officers, he
continued. "When a high-profiler dies in custody, with
telltale bruises, et cetera, it attracts a lot of attention. A
dead body could even bring the Feds in. No one wants
one of these sick fucks to die in the process—we do, we
all do, but you know what I mean."

"You want me to make sure they stay alive."

"It's what you do, isn't it?"

I looked at the EKG machine on the trolley and the
blood pressure cuff hanging on the wall, and for an instant wondered if I'd gone psychotic. The composition of
my surroundings hadn't changed a jot, but their comfort-

able familiarity had been replaced with a bleached stark-
ness that was so physical that it seemed like a trick of the
lighting. I was on the brink of succumbing to an irrational
outburst of laughter.

"You going to hook him up to this stuff?" he asked.

"Who are you going to start with?"

"The weakest link: Feldman."

"Sure." I indicated the medical devices on view.
"We'll hook him up to everything we've got. Make him
think the entire capability of modern science is focused
on what he's thinking. It'll be like a medical procedure:
cool, clinical, and irresistible. The only problem is, he
may not know where the girl is."

"That's right, you already talked to him for the police."
He gave a tight smile that couldn't hide his tension. "We
have our sources."

"I don't think he knows where she is."

"That makes it tough on him."

"Why waste time on Feldman? Why not go straight to
Hodges? He knows for sure."

"Feldman will tell us something. He'll give us something we can use on Hodges. When we come to him,
we're going to need something to get him going."

Outside in the corridor the lights were turned off. A
moment later, distantly, I heard the hum of a cell door
opening.

"We'll hook him up," I said, "and then I'll talk to
him. Okay?"

He shook his head pityingly. "You're hoping you'll get
lucky. You're hoping you'll scare the shit out of him with
this science fiction and he'll spill the beans, and you
won't have to get your hands wet. Get this straight. You
can't go into this hoping you won't have to be nasty. They
sense it. They feel your hesitation. Your credibility's

blown. That's why, straight off, the first thing you do, for no reason that's apparent to the subject, you demonstrate that you're ruthless and pitiless and cruel."

"Like what?"

The machinery hum began again, followed by the faint thud of the cell door closing.

Kovacs shrugged, lips pursed as he surveyed the options in his mind. There was any number of them, apparently. "Feldman?" He considered. "There's a blow that's delivered to the sternum with the flat of the fist." He stared into the middle distance, remembering. He might have been describing a restaurant at a favorite vacation destination. "It doesn't sound like much. It hurts a bit. Of course. But the pain isn't the main thing. What the blow is about is the fear of death. When you get it right, it's the next best thing to reaching your hand into the man's chest and squeezing his heart shut. He skips a beat or two. Maybe he passes out. Either way, he feels like he's dying. It gives him a taste of death. A preview of a coming attraction."

I heard footsteps approaching very slowly, from the direction of the command center.

"You might as well tell me what you're going to do with those."

He drew the bamboo skewers out of his pocket and reached out over the arm of the chair to drop them into a metal kidney dish on the white Formica counter. "These are for Hodges."

He bounded lightly out of the chair to the door. He listened for a moment before opening it cautiously. Then he gave instructions softly to the approaching group, and the slow, shuffling progress came to a halt.

He closed the door again.

"All right," he said, brisk and businesslike. "It's Feldman. He's got a laundry bag over his head, so he can't see anybody. He's seen me; he's seen the others; but he won't see us here, in this room. The main thing is, he hasn't seen you. So don't speak. If he doesn't hear your voice, you're in the clear. I'm the only one whose voice he'll hear."

"I want to interrogate him."

"Look, you're good at what you do, but your box of tricks won't work through a laundry bag."

"Take it off."

"Then he sees you."

"I'll take the risk."

"It's not a risk, Doc. It's a certainty."

"Screw it." Nothing else in my life mattered. The mentality of exceptional circumstances held me in its grip. I'd jettisoned my biography. Everything came down to one thing: Save Danielle.

"This was a mistake," Kovacs said. I thought I saw a flicker of concern light up his face for an instant.

"No, I'm okay. This is right. I'm ready."

"You do this, you're fucked as a doctor."

"We'll do this my way first."

"No one said anything about a deal."

"Come on. Good cop, bad cop."

He looked at me sadly, shaking his head. But I knew he was wavering. He didn't want to throw away his life any more than I did. If I could get what we wanted without violence, we'd take years off our sentences.

"It's worked for interrogators for hundreds of years," I said. "It's a classic."

"I'll humor you."

"Okay." I looked the room over with a new sense of possession. "Let's lose the dental chair. We don't need the examination light shining right in his eyes. And we can skip the punch in the sternum."

"You've got twenty minutes."

We glanced at the clock on the wall above the steel cabinet. It was five of three.

"That's not much to work with."

"It's all I can give you."

"What about the chair?"

"The chair stays. He's going to be secured in the chair. That way he knows this is something different from the run-of-the-mill interview. We need the light so if he turns around he can't see the rest of us. If he tries to turn around, I smack him." He was heading swiftly for the door. "You ought to let him know that."

"You don't have to punch him straight off," I said. "I'm the good cop, right?" He paused momentarily at the door. "Give me something."

He turned back with a warning finger. "When I hit him, you'll both know the twenty minutes is up."

It was dark in the corridor beyond the open door. A bundle shuffled into view and was made to turn left by one of the officers at his side. As the light from the examining room struck him, I could see that the laundry sack covered Dave all the way to his handcuffed wrists. His feet below the ankle shackles were bare, and he wore only a gray pair of the institution's boxer shorts.

He stopped at the threshold, sensing the light through the tight weave of the sack, and one of the officers shoved him forward. He moved compliantly, and when he came to the dental chair and they held him back and turned him, he was docile. The only reaction came when they pushed him backward, and he gasped in alarm. For all he knew, they might have been pushing him off one of the tiers.

He sprawled, out of alignment, half on, half off the seat of the chair, and didn't seem to recognize what was required of his body. No one wanted to speak to tell him what kind of object he was in contact with. After a few seconds, the officers manhandled him into position.

Kovacs tossed a couple of towels at the bottom of the door to reduce sound traveling beyond the examining room. He found a radio and tuned it quickly, randomly, to a classical music station, then turned the volume up. I recognized the music as a Mozart string quartet, the "Dissonant," and I knew I would never be able to listen to it again. The realization brought home to me for the first time an emotional understanding of how my life would change—how certain things would simply disappear from my day-to-day existence because of what I was doing at this very moment.

They took off Dave's shackles and used strips of duct tape that Kovacs silently passed to them to bind his ankles in place; then they secured his wrists to the armrests of the chair. When they were finished they looked to Kovacs for further instructions, but he'd decided the hood was mine to remove, and they took up position out of sight behind the chair, slightly back from Kovacs.

He jerked his head toward the clock to indicate that my twenty minutes had begun.

I wound the blood pressure cuff around his arm and then reached under the laundry bag to stick a couple of EKG leads on his chest. I let Dave listen to my leisurely footsteps across the hard floor and then the squeak of the wheels of the metal examining stool as I pushed it from the other side of the room. It made a squealing noise that jibed as a kind of protest to the string quartet. I took my time because I wanted him to know that I wasn't the one under pressure.

When I sat down I nodded for Kovacs to draw up the sack that covered Dave's upper body.

They'd taken his glasses as a security measure, and he blinked in the glare of the examining light that shone down on him. His electric hair stuck out at odd angles from his head. He passed a dry tongue over his lips, and I wondered if they'd withheld water from him.

He screwed up his eyes, blinking continuously as he tried to adapt to the bright light, trying to bring me into focus.

If we thought that Dave had been intimidated by this lead-up to the interrogation, we were wrong. He hadn't lost control of his bladder in the last few hours, as some new admissions to Sanders did. He wasn't even trembling.

He looked down, puzzled at the duct tape around his wrists, and tried, experimentally, to move his arms. Then he tugged at them angrily.

He was furious. "I want my lawyer!" he spat out. It was laughable how little appreciation he had of his predicament.

"Your lawyer isn't here," I said. Even if his eyes were still dazzled by the light, he'd recognize my voice soon enough. "Your lawyer can't reach you here. He can't do you any good."

He stared at me, frowning in disbelief and confusion. He knew he'd seen me before, but now I was out of context, and he couldn't figure out just who I was. None of this was making sense. Gradually the furrows flattened as he began to understand.

"It's just us," I told him levelly, without sarcasm, without malice. "No lawyers. No law. Nothing, nobody, but you and us."

"You're the doctor with the police." Relief broke over him. "You got them to send me here."

"I'm not your friend. And I'm not a doctor."

He thought this was a joke. He was waiting for me to tell him the punch line. "Well, what is this?"

I spoke quietly. "This is where you tell me where Danielle is."

"Hey, give me a break! I can't talk to you without my lawyer. You know that."

He had become so cocooned in his inviolable rights that he couldn't conceive of being without them. It was like walking naked down Massachusetts Avenue—something you might dream of or see in the movies, but for that very reason, something that couldn't actually happen to you.

"You're outside the law now," I told him. "No one can help you. It's just us. You have to deal with us. It's much better you deal with me. If you don't, then you'll have to deal with the people behind you."

He didn't turn to see who they were. He still didn't entirely believe what I told him. He was uneasy, but far short of the terror that was needed to get him to start talking against his best interests.

"This is bullshit," he said, with a confidence that made my heart sink. "I want to go back to my cell. I want to see a real doctor."

I had sparse leeway to make him realize that he was in real, mortal danger.

"Listen to me."

He shook his head, denying preemptively what I was about to tell him.

"Listen to me, Dave. If you don't tell me where Danielle is, these people are going to hurt you real bad. Then you will tell us where she is. But if they do that stuff to you, then they're going to have to kill you. Because they can't leave you as a witness."

He understood this contingency, of course, and the

symmetry between his fate and Danielle's started to bring home to him that the cozy arrangement of rights and lawyers might not hold. People crossed the line, just as he and Arthur had.

"You can't kill me. You can't get away with that."

He was focused on disposing of the witness, not the torture. The one was dependent on the other. If we weren't in a position to kill Dave, then we couldn't cross the line to torture him, either.

"This is a prison," he said. "People are going to know."

"People hang it up here all the time."

"I'm not suicidal, though." He realized his mistake and moved to correct it. Then he wasn't sure that it was a mistake. "I know I said . . ."

"You said you were suicidal. You said so in front of witnesses."

"I know—"

"So if they find you tomorrow with your underpants tied around your neck, no one's going to think twice about it."

"There'll be the crime scene. They'll investigate. DNA. Latent fingerprints. They can find out stuff."

"These guys are professionals. They know how to handle themselves. There won't be any traces. It'll be just another jail suicide."

He had a childlike belief in experts, and this took some air out of him. "The police will look into it," he said. He was starting to be afraid. "You can't fake them out. They'll find some clue. I saw it on TV."

"No one's going to look too hard at what happens to you." I wanted to present him with a statement of fact, and I worked to subtract any hint of animus from my voice. "You're a sex offender. If you end up dead, no one's going to care."

"Fuck you!"

With great agility, Kovacs emerged from the darkness behind the dental chair. With one hand he covered and averted Dave's head. With the other—he paused for a split second to gauge the target, the force necessary—he pumped his arm through twelve inches, into the middle of Dave's sternum.

The blow made a dull thud, like punching a firm mattress, and Dave coughed as though it had squeezed the air out of him. His face filled with a look of terror and amazement.

It hurt, of course, but it had to be more than that. Slamming a car door on your fingers causes intense pain, but it's out there at the periphery, a long way from where you live. It's not like core pain, like getting kicked in the testicles or the pain of a heart attack. Core pain is far more primitive and alarming. It consumes you. It bypasses thought. Core pain carries this special component: your body is telling you you might die.

For an entire minute, Dave was lost in this vortex of suffering. I was afraid he was dying. His face was ashen, and when I glanced at the EKG it was plain that his heart had stopped for a moment, then jumped back with a disorganized, irregular pulse, then reverted to normal sinus rhythm. When I took his blood pressure, his arm was cold and clammy.

He was blinking, returning to full consciousness, trying to open his eyes, to comprehend, as he emerged through the all-encompassing pain, what had just happened to him. He groaned. I was relieved to see his heart settle down to a tachycardia—fast, but regular.

He tried to speak. His mouth gaped and his lips moved, but he couldn't give form to his protest. His eyes fixed on me in anguish, and the fingers of the hand closest extended as he tried futilely to reach out to me.

I wanted his attention, and there wasn't any point in speaking when he remained preoccupied with pain. I waited for my moment: when the memory of the blow was still fresh and immediate, but when he had sufficient wits about him to appreciate the converging forces of his predicament.

I heard a restless movement from Kovacs in the shadows, and Dave started and began to turn.

"Don't do it," I warned. "If you try to turn around you're only going to piss him off."

He stared at me. He was still dazzled by the pain, but it was waning, and the realization of his true situation was starting to dawn on him.

"He'll do it again," I said.

"Please!" Dave whispered. "Don't let him do it."

"I don't know if I can. He wants to do it again." I sighed. "He likes it."

"Oh, God!"

He looked like he was going to cry, and the last thing I wanted was for him to break down in some self-pitying, inaccessible mess.

"Listen up," I told him sternly. "I'm your best shot."

"You're in charge?" His voice was husky.

I shook my head in slow motion and watched the pleading expression in his eyes change to horror.

"You're the doctor," he insisted.

"That was this morning. This is different. This isn't a normal situation." I paused as if reluctant to go on. "You have to understand: things have gotten slightly out of control here."

Finally, like a dying person who must first struggle

through the psychological stages of denial and bargaining before he can reach a point of acceptance, he understood that his existence was entirely without safeguards. He tried several times to speak, and when he couldn't find the words, he started to plummet into despair.

"Open your eyes," I ordered. "If you don't pay attention to me, he's going to take over."

"But you'll help me?"

"I'm all you've got."

"You'll stop him? You can keep him from hitting me?"

I had been standing in front of him, and now I took a step to the side so that I effectively blocked the direction from which another blow from Kovacs might come.

"You have to help me," I said, more softly than before, as if speaking in confidence. I put one hand on the rest behind his elbow and leaned in toward him. "I can't do anything for you if you don't give me something. I have to keep him happy."

"Well, what do you want?"

I stood up. My tone stiffened. "That's exactly the kind of smartass response that's going to get him mad."

He squirmed in his seat. "I'm sorry." He started to turn to apologize to Kovacs directly and then realized that turning around would make his precarious situation even worse.

"Well?" I asked. "What have you got for me?"

His mouth was open. I could visualize the frenzied activity in his frontal lobes, as the subunits offered up one plan after the other only to have the central processor throw them out and resume the frantic ransacking of memory. There were no good options. If I'd been able to read lips, I might even have known his inner speech. I waited, aware for the first time that the breathing of the three officers behind the chair was synchronized.

"Okay, then . . ." Dave hesitated, stopped, blurted out, "We did it."

Immediately I said, "We already know that. Give me something I don't know. Something new."

"I don't know!"

I came around from the side of him, hooked the wheeled stool with my toe, and spun the seat so that I sat directly in front of him, close and eye to eye. I needed everything I could get. I'd accomplished the first objective: Dave was convinced the rules had been cancelled. He was scared and he'd talk. What I had to find out was whether he knew where Danielle was. I needed to find out quickly, because we couldn't waste time. If Dave didn't know, we had to move on to Arthur. But Dave was a compliant subject and he'd tell us whatever he thought we wanted to hear—anything he thought could save his skin.

I said, speaking slowly and calmly, "Tell me what you did."

"It was John."

I was starting to understand the laziness of torture. I thought of slapping his face: it would have gotten his attention and provided negative feedback on his last response all in an efficient, one-second burst of action. How easy it was to slide into brutality!

He must have seen some of this in my face. "Arthur, I mean," he added hastily, as if jolted by memory.

"I want you to tell me about what you did. Only what *you* did."

He became distressed, his face screwed up, about to protest. "Look, I—"

I realized that he was about to tell me he had no idea where Danielle was. "No!" I said harshly, almost shouting to cut him off and leaning into his space to block out anything else that might get his attention. At all costs, I had to prevent him rehearsing his answers. "You tell me what I ask you. Nothing else." I wasn't ready to ask him where Danielle was. When I did, if he attempted to lie to me, I wanted a virgin lie.

"Get it?" I demanded.

He was confused and didn't respond. There was a hurt look on his face.

I spoke clearly and loudly. I wanted him to acknowledge this important rule. "You answer the question I ask you. Nothing else. Do you understand?"

"Yes," he said humbly.

"How did you meet up with Danielle this morning?"

"I knew Danielle. She and I used to talk sometimes. Like when I took a break. It was the same time she came for the coffees for the people at the office where she helped out."

"Today. Tell me what you did with Danielle today."

"I didn't do nothing!"

He meant that he hadn't sexually molested the girl. The promptness of the outraged response was its best quality. It was automatic and unconsidered, and that was hard to fake. The tone of his voice, a mixture of protest at the charge and slight anxiety that he wouldn't be believed, was complex and well nuanced. His eyes came quickly up to mine to read the expression that accompanied my words, without secondary evasion, and without the telltale boggle that indicates activation of other brain regions that have no business being activated. Most impressive to me was the immediate stifled gesture of the hands that were taped to the arms of the chair: the elbows lifted slightly and the fingers were fully extended and separated with the agitation my question had evoked.

I couldn't be certain he was telling the truth, of course, but given what we knew of his movements that morning, it was very unlikely that he'd had an opportunity to molest Danielle. And his behavioral response was of very high quality—far too good a simulation for someone of Dave's limited cognitive resources. For all intents and purposes, this was what the truth looked like.

I knew he'd misunderstood my question, but it suited my purpose to go along with this. "I'm not accusing you of anything," I said mildly. "I just want to know what you did today."

Kovacs was growing restive, and a glance at the clock told me I'd burned seven of the twenty minutes.

"Let's start with you meeting up with Danielle. You were on break. She was on her way back to the office with the coffee."

"See, Danielle is very helpful."

The use of the present tense, even in someone who was as careless about language as Dave, gave me an unreasonable burst of hope. I was encouraged, too, by the uneasy look on his face. This was the point in the chain of events when Dave had crossed the line, and I thought he was hesitating because he was ashamed. I waited for him to get over it. He swallowed and went on.

"I said, 'Hey, Danielle, that guy in the wheelchair looks like he's having a problem.'"

"That was Arthur."

"Right. But she didn't know him."

"But Arthur knew her."

His voice shook slightly as he said, "He would watch her. He used to come in the van with his wife. He used to go into Doosy's to get coffee. Then he'd sit in the van and drink his coffee and watch her go by." He hung his head, and I filed that away, too, for use later: Arthur's motivation in the abduction was different from his, rougher and more crudely sexual: This troubled Dave.

"So she went with you."

"She trusted . . ." Again, a twinge of shame erupted like a hiccup and as quickly dissipated.

"Because she trusted you and she was a helpful person."

"Arthur was in his wife's wheelchair. He'd gotten it jammed in the door of his van. He made it seem like he was stuck. Someone had come by and tried to help him but he told him to get lost."

"Then you and Danielle came along."

"I said, 'Let's help him.' "

"What happened to the coffees she was carrying?"

"They were stuck in this cardboard carrier, and Danielle needed both hands to hold it, so Arthur said, 'Here, let me take that for a moment.' And she handed it up to him to hold."

"What did he do with it?"

It was a question of no great emotional significance; nothing hung on the answer; he had no reason to lie: another sample for me of what telling the truth looked like.

"Well . . ." Dave looked up and to the right. Then the memory came to him like a flash of inspiration. He seemed pleased and his eyes lit up with the achievement of memory. "He reached round and put it on the floor behind him."

It was hanging together like a truthful narrative. Not too many details, but no bland generalizations, either. Liars don't realize that people telling the truth often don't remember details; they have gaps in their memories, and so Dave's search of memory was authentic.

And Arthur had stowed the coffees as though he meant to keep them rather than kick them out of the van once he had Danielle in his power. I reflected that he might have

tossed them out the window at any time during his drive
to the hiding place, but there was a chance he might have
left this large store of fluids with Danielle.

"Then what?"

"Arthur and I worked it out so me alone wouldn't be
able to get the chair unstuck. Of course, I wasn't really
trying. But I made it look like I was."

"So?"

"So, that's when I said—no, it was Arthur."

This was the first lie. His hesitation and backtracking
told me the lie was coming, and I was glad to have the
opportunity to study Dave as he told it. In midsentence,
immediately before he hesitated, his eyes bobbled as he
changed the access source: if the information he's about
to deliver is coming from memory, from the temporal
lobes, why change gears? Why stop, disengage, switch
on another brain region? Unless, of course, you're no
longer remembering, but inventing.

Then, after the lie, came the signature gesture. He
couldn't raise his finger and he had no glasses to push
up his nose, but his brow furrowed and his upper lip
curled in the ticlike snouting expression that would have
accompanied that action.

"Arthur said, 'Honey, hop up here, will you? I think
my chair's caught on something behind me.' Danielle
didn't think twice about it. She climbed up into the van,
just like Arthur said she would."

I had both templates now, for truth-telling and for lying. When the time came—it had to be soon—to pop the
question of where Danielle was hidden, I felt confident
I'd make the right decision.

I took Dave quickly through the mechanics of the abduction.

"Arthur had this remote. Like a TV remote. Smaller,

though. He could control the van by pressing buttons. So after Danielle got into the van, that was it. He closed the door."

"Then what?"

"I went back to work."

"What about the van?"

"Arthur took off."

I wanted to ambush him with the question rather than lead up to it in sequence, so I asked, "Who was around, in the square?"

"A few regulars. People passing through on their way places."

"Was there anybody nearby when Danielle got in the van?"

"Just a bag lady."

"Where is Danielle now?"

He hesitated. But it wasn't a pause to bring other brain resources online, because there was no eye-boggle associated with it. He was searching for words, not ideas: I was certain of this because I saw his lips move minutely. He paused not to deceive but because he wanted to find words that would convince. He didn't evade me by looking away and he didn't engage me in the high-intensity eye contact that liars fancy looks sincere. During the second after my question, he had been staring blankly into the middle distance before him, and now he brought his gaze to mine and I saw his pleading expression, his fear at the inadequacy of his answer.

"I don't know," he said. "Arthur took her."

"Where?"

"He didn't tell me."

"Why not?"

"Because he said it was best I didn't know."

The string quartet came to its conclusion. In the silence, I waited three bars for the grimace that didn't come.

I stood up. To Kovacs, I said, "Time to move on."

3:20 A.M.

Kovacs stood with his back pressed against one of the tiger cages and his hands grasping the bars. He jerked his weight back, knees bent, like a wrestler testing the ropes. He looked like he wanted to tear the whole structure loose in his frustration.

I'd seen him this way before, all wound up and no place to go, when he'd suited up with the tac team—biteproof jumpsuit, flak jacket, helmet, and curved Plexiglas shield—ready to force entry into a cell where the inmate was holding a shank. Then at the last moment the man had quietly surrendered the blade without a struggle, and Kovacs and his team had no way to work off their adrenaline rush.

"Move on!" I shouted at him, and my voice echoed off the concrete of the empty cell block. I was pretty fired up myself. "We're done with Feldman. He's got nothing we want."

"We don't know that!" He turned on me.

"I know it."

He took three threatening steps toward me. There

was a muscular swagger I hadn't seen before, and I wondered how much else Kovacs kept under wraps.

"Oh, you do?" he asked.

"I do."

He strolled by me, and though my skin tingled with vulnerability as he stared intently at the side of my face as he passed, I didn't turn.

"It's not a hunch," I said, speaking into empty space. "If you want, if you have the time, I can tell you what I base my decision on."

He passed behind me and doubled back. He waved away my explanation impatiently. "I don't want to hear your mumbo jumbo."

He stopped in front of me as if he'd completed a tour on which he should have found the answer to his question. Arms tightly folded, head tilted, he scrutinized my face, but I knew he wouldn't find the clincher he needed for his peace of mind. He took a deep breath and let out a long sigh of resignation.

"It's what I do," I reminded him quietly.

He paced again, away from me, toward the nearest tiger cage, and took up a position, half-crucified, with both arms woven between the bars.

He jerked his head back in the direction of the control center. "They're not happy. They want to make sure."

"We don't have time to make sure. Certainty's a luxury we can't afford. That's why we're here, doing what we're doing. Because we have to take a shortcut."

"They're not going along with a change of plan based on the hunch of some shrink."

"They'll follow you."

He stared at me with a worried frown, but I didn't have

anything more to give him. It was a leap: either he took it or he didn't. He knew that.

"We have to move on to Arthur Hodges," I said.

When he let go of the steel bars of the cage, Kovacs was released like a taut rubber band. It was an outer form of agreement. "Let's do it," he said, letting the momentum carry him toward the door to the chamber.

"Wait," I said. "We're not done."

He stopped, then made a slow turn, glowering. "I don't like this. The whole idea was to keep it quick and simple. Now you've gotten into the act—"

"It's not an act, and it was never simple."

"I like you, Doc, but some people are saying you're becoming part of the problem."

"Well, I'm here now. I'm part of the mix. You have to deal with me."

"That's what some people are saying."

There was no need to explore the implications. Kovacs didn't make idle threats, and I didn't want to be distracted by what might happen to me if this really took a bad turn.

I said, "I've interviewed Arthur Hodges. I've seen an experienced state cop interrogate him. I know him. He's like a safe. You can whale on him with sledge-hammers, but it won't do you any good. You need a safecracker to pick the lock. That's me."

"I wasn't thinking sledgehammers."

"You know what I mean. Physical force."

"Even physical force has its sensitive side. It isn't just smacking people around."

"He's tough."

Kovacs shrugged. From his perspective, toughness wasn't a quality that required any change of plan.

"Not your kind of tough," I said. "Though he may be that, too. Hodges is mentally tough. He's smart and he's disciplined. He's not the kind of guy that's going to be swayed by emotion, even if he's scared."

"We're not here to scare him."

He came close to me, sauntering with a sinister deliberateness.

"Pain isn't going to work with Hodges."

"It's not just about pain. It's also fear and destruction. It's an individual thing. You don't give everybody the same medication. It depends on the individual. Right?"

"Right," I agreed reluctantly.

"Pain, fear, destruction. You take your pick. Then you go to the place where he's at. Young stud, you target his cock. Farmer, his hands. Pain's important in its own right. Pain alone is very persuasive in people like Feldman. Hodges, okay, he's tough. I'll take your word for that. He's got endurance. He can get through the pain for a while. No one can endure it forever."

"We don't have forever."

"That's what I'm saying. In some cases, the pain's just a way of telling him where you are. It gives him ideas about what's being destroyed. Where that person is, that's where the pain should be."

He plucked one of the bamboo skewers from his pocket and held it before me between the tips of his thumb and index finger. I felt a rising panic. I put it aside, trying instead to put myself in Arthur's shoes, to imagine Kovacs holding the bamboo in front of my nose.

"Someone who lives in his head," Kovacs said, "like Hodges, you go inside his head."

I shook my head to dissipate the image. "Oh, God!"

"That's because you live inside your head, too, Doc."

I said, thinking I was illuminating the craziness of this scheme, "So you stick that in his head? Where? Through his eyeball?" I remembered Kovacs poring over *Gray's*

Anatomy: "You slide it in below the nuchal prominence?"

"Through his ear."

"I can't believe you're serious."

"You don't jam it in. You insert it slowly. All the same, it makes a loud crashing noise, like there's a building collapsing inside your head. That's the sound of your ear being destroyed. Then it takes only a tiny movement to spin you around." He demonstrated, rolling the skewer between his fingertips. "It feels like you've been hit by a hurricane."

He nodded as though I might not believe him. I knew he spoke from experience.

"The next thing, everything goes quiet."

Arthur would shrug off threats, however convincingly we dramatized them. He was made of different stuff from Dave. He wouldn't fold just because Kovacs punched him in the chest. He was clear on the priorities. He wouldn't give up the witness who would put him away for the rest of his life, except in extremis. Except, maybe, with a chicken satay skewer through his ear.

I didn't want to go that far. I wanted out.

I said, "There's no way of explaining a prisoner with a skewer in his middle ear."

"You're right. He takes a fall. The side of his head gets banged up. The autopsy can't say what happened when. That's where we'd need your medical expertise."

"I say we put them both in the tiger cages. Play one against the other."

"It's not a freaking circus, Doc."

He turned to go, tucking the skewer back in his breast pocket.

"We use Feldman as leverage to open up Hodges."

"You did good in there with Feldman. I'm not averse

to persuasion, if it's going to work. But Hodges isn't Feldman. You said so yourself."

"You're going to have to break Hodges."

"I aim to."

"I mean, it's going to take time. You'll have a lot of screaming. You're going to have to do things you haven't done in a long time. Your guys are going to have to see things they've never seen before."

"They knew that before they signed on for this."

"You respect them. You think you know what they're capable of. But we're not talking about going up against an inmate with a shank. This man isn't fighting back. He's going to be strapped down. You don't really know—"

He tried to cut me off, but I wouldn't let him.

"You don't really know what their threshold is, not when it comes to torture."

"I know these officers."

"Here, yes. Here, on this side of the line, you know they'll back you up come hell or high water. But where you're taking us—heart of darkness—you can't tell how a man will react."

"I'll take my chances."

"It's not a chance. If we go down your road, as soon as we get an answer or as soon as the seven-to-three shift comes on duty—whichever is first—we have to get in our cars and get down to Logan and get the next plane out to Panama City. Either that, or we spend the next ten or fifty years in the SHU at Concord with pedophiles like Arthur Hodges."

"You have to have the will," he said.

His fists were clenched. We stood face to face, glaring at one another. We were, each in his own way, utterly reckless.

He said, "We have to see the mission through.".

Kovacs was wound very tight. He knew he wasn't the man he was thirty years ago in Laos. He had to wring out any doubt he had about himself. I was the embodiment of doubt. The others would close ranks. He couldn't tolerate any gray area now. I was about to become the enemy. He wanted to deliver a blow to my chest and stop my heart, too, for a second, to remove me from consideration. His fists came up a few inches, to his beltline. His eyes took on a veiled look, still directed at me but unfocused, as he planned action, counteracted the launch of the sternal blow.

He broke away. He made a dismissive gesture of contempt. "You can't start asking questions halfway in."

"This isn't a suicide mission," I said. "No one signed on for that."

"If you don't have the stomach—"

"It's not about balls, it's about brains. We have to think this through."

"Look, if you want, you can go. This isn't your fight."

"This is my fight. My wife was the one who sent that girl to fetch the coffee."

Guilt, even guilt by association, was a passport that granted passage across the line. It gave me rights where there were none. He shook his head in frustration at the persistence of reason.

"You're a pain in the ass!" he cried.

"You owe me."

"Fuck you!"

"You gave me twenty minutes for the Feldman interview. I've got eight minutes left."

My doubt had infected him. It weakened the continuous effort of will that was required to be ruthless.

"Be reasonable," he said. "What can you do in eight minutes?"

"I'll take my chances. I want both of them in here at once. I can play one off against the other."

"You're screwing everything up. We have a plan!"

"You're going to have to bring Hodges in here anyway. If my stuff doesn't work and you have to do your stuff, Hodges is going to be doing a lot of screaming. You'll need this soundproofing."

3:45 A.M.

The officers had brought examination lamps from the various medical offices and balanced them on chairs next to the two cages. The spotlights illuminated each prisoner in a stark cone of light, while the rest of the vaulted space remained in darkness. Kovacs stood in attendance with two of the officers in deep shadow.

The light spilled onto the floor between the two cages, providing a small zone in which I could walk and be seen. I circled each man in his cage, tracing out the sign of infinity, letting them hear my measured footsteps, as if I had all the time in the world. They weren't so much men as shapeless packages covered from head to waist in loose canvas laundry bags.

Kovacs had debated intensely the disposition of the prisoners—what they should wear, how they should be secured, which cages we would use, and how much lighting was needed for my eight minutes. They stood anchored to the front of the cages by the links between each handcuff that ran around and outside one of the bars, so that they were unable to reach the seat in the middle of the cage, or to retreat into the back of it, or lie on the floor, or even to turn away.

I reflected that the scene with hooded prisoners inside tiny cages would have made a fine poster for Amnesty International. I would never, in my wildest nightmare, have expected to find myself here, on the wrong side of this issue. All the ideals, standards, and aspirations that had been inculcated during my years of liberal education had fallen away. I was a man without a past and a man with no future.

"Let's begin," I announced, and an officer reached into each cage and pulled off the laundry bags covering Dave and Arthur.

Dave was like a moth suddenly exposed to bright light, his head jerking about, trying to get a fix on where he was and what might be about to happen to him. He was very frightened. The first thing he saw that made any kind of sense was me.

"Doctor!" He wasn't sure whether to be relieved. "For God's sake!" He tried to reach out his hands in a pleading gesture, and then realized steel bars surrounded him. He began to turn and was made aware of how closely his movement was restricted.

Then he caught sight of Arthur and became even more frightened.

Arthur stood stolidly with his hands between the vertical bars and his wrists resting on the horizontal. His glasses had been taken from him and he blinked myopically in my direction, screwing up his eyes.

"That would be Dr. Lucas?" he asked.

"You're not here to ask questions," I told him sharply. "You're here to answer questions."

He made a gesture of being taken aback, as if I'd said something indelicate and out of character. He stood with his chin up and his expression was composed, but I heard the click of his dry tongue on the roof of his mouth and knew that in spite of his show of confidence he was afraid, too.

"I'm not about to answer any questions without my lawyer present," he said somewhat pompously, clinging to the fiction of business as usual, though he must have realized that things had gone dangerously awry.

"There aren't any lawyers here," I said. "We make the rules."

Arthur started to protest the legalities of the situation, but I walked away. I clicked my fingers, and the light shining on his cage was switched off.

He had become almost anonymous again, his face obscured by deep shadow. He glowered in the direction of the only lit spot in the chamber, Dave's cage.

I wanted to suggest a connection between Dave and I, and I stood as close to him as I could while remaining out of reach, with my hand resting proprietarily on the bars.

I'd intended to calm him, to work our alliance, but it seemed that in the interval since we last spoke Dave had come to the conclusion that I was as likely to hurt him as anyone else. As I drew closer to him, he became even more terrified: on one side, the malign doctor; on the other, the codefendant he had just betrayed. I had thought it would take me several precious minutes to work him around to the point I wanted, but he was already there.

"Give it up, John!" he shouted, still not assimilating the fact, even now, that Arthur hadn't trusted him enough to tell him his real name. "Tell them what they want to know."

Arthur said nothing. He shook his head slowly in calm defiance, as if Dave's outburst was beyond belief.

"I told them."

Arthur looked as if he'd been hit with an electric prod. The leisurely, professorial manner disappeared and a far more vicious Arthur emerged. "You told them what?" The snarl on his face made me worry about Danielle's condition.

"I had to."

His voice failed him and fell almost to a whisper. He was almost as afraid of Arthur as he had been of Kovacs. I was being shown a different and far more sinister Arthur than the one on permanent public display—the devoted husband of the crippled wife.

"Say nothing."

"They fucking tortured me!"

"That's bullshit! Pull yourself together. They're not allowed to do that."

"They did anyway."

"All we have to do is keep quiet and we're home free."

"They said Danielle's going to die if she doesn't get water."

"Shut up!"

"I couldn't help it."

"What? Couldn't help what?"

"What I told them."

"Oh, God." He shook his head in disgust.

I snapped my finger again as the sign for the lights to be turned off, and the chamber went pitch black. I stayed where I was. To my left I heard a cry of fear from Dave as one of the officers cuffed his wrists, then the sound of scuffling as he briefly resisted their efforts to extract him from the cage.

Arthur called out to him, "Wait! Dave! What did you tell them?"

The noise of boots and shuffling feet moved away. He wasn't struggling now.

"What did you say?" Arthur shouted after them.

We saw a slice of light as the officers opened the door and left the chamber with Dave between them. Then the steel door closed again, and in the darkness, the slam of the bolt going home carried an air of finality.

We waited in silence for a moment. It hadn't been part of the plan, but it was a nice psychological touch: Arthur had just learned that we had crucial information; he didn't know how much; now he saw nothing and heard nothing; and he was alone with his thoughts.

I thought of Abby lying awake in bed in darkness waiting for my call. I started to think of Danielle, in the agony of tight binding for more than eighteen hours, dying of thirst, and I found that I was reconciled to the skewers in the event that I failed in what I was about to attempt. If it came to it, I would accept my obligation to help them kill Arthur.

I clicked my fingers, but the light didn't come on, and I realized that I, too, was being given a moment to appraise my position. Kovacs controlled the lights. At any moment, in response to some minor setback or a smart remark from Arthur, Kovacs would lose patience and take over the interrogation.

The light over Arthur's cage came on.

I thought that in the interval of darkness and silence something would have changed, but everything was the same. Arthur stood with his forearms resting on the bar. He might have been a vacationer at a lookout, eyes screwed up as he tried to make out a distant point of interest.

He blinked when I came to stand in front of him. I was hard to ignore.

"I've got nothing to say to you," he said.

I wasn't going to intimidate him as I had Dave. I was starting to see the line I'd have to take; but before that, I wanted to have one last try to feel out where he thought his best interests lay.

"Give her up," I said quietly. "If the girl dies, you know what's going to happen. Natural life. Life without parole."

He stared at me unblinking. He wore a patronizing smirk, but his eyes were cold.

"If she lives—if they find her because you tell us where she is—you'll see the outside world again."

He looked at me pityingly. "You got it all figured out, huh?"

"You may think that if Danielle dies, then there's no witness."

"I don't have to listen to this."

"Yes, you do. You're chained to that steel bar. You've got no place to hide."

He sighed impatiently and looked away, eyelids drooping to hood his eyes.

"You were the last person to see Danielle alive."

"How do you figure that?"

"Dave saw her get in the van with you. He'll testify to that. You were in the wheelchair"—I caught a blink, a slight tensing at the corners of the mouth, but he didn't turn to me—"Danielle got in the van behind you to un-snag whatever you seemed to be caught on. Then—nothing. She's gone. Last seen in the company of Arthur Hodges."

"The van's clean. The police went over every inch of it with Q-Tips. You saw that for yourself. As far as the physical evidence is concerned, she was never near it. The only thing that ties me to this case is testimony from that flake. It's his word against mine. You know how that's going to go in front of a jury."

"There are other witnesses."

"It doesn't matter. This won't do you any good."

"We want that girl."

"You're wasting your time."

"We'll do whatever it takes to get Danielle back to her mother."

"Too late."

He tossed the phrase out like a pebble into a pond, to see what he might start up with the splash. His eyes came over to my face more and more often to see how I reacted to what he said. He wanted to show that even though he was handcuffed, confined to a steel cage, he still had power over me. I wasn't sure what leverage he thought he had, but I was happy to play right along with him. If he was engaged, even in some pathetic power struggle, that was better than his previous isolation.

"I don't think so," I said. I started to say, "It's never too late," but he cut me off.

"She's already dead."

It was too pat. The lie served too obvious a purpose: If Danielle was dead, there was nothing anyone—not even Kovacs—could usefully do, except as an act of revenge. If Danielle was dead, then we'd come to the end of the line.

He'd surprised me, and I had to play back from memory what his demeanor had been. It was a line to short-circuit whatever I might be trying to do. It served a good, practical purpose—to avoid being tortured—but it was also a punch line, spoken for effect. Arthur couldn't resist needling me. His facial expression had been consistent with that: eyes down to disguise the impending delivery, a faint, self-congratulatory flutter of the eyelids, then the gaze coming up obliquely, without the head turning, for the irresistible check of my reaction, the payoff.

"You can't know that for sure," I said, to draw him out.

"Oh, I'm sure," Arthur said. "I have it on good authority."

All Arthur had to do to stay alive was to stall us until the night was over and Sanders returned to normal operations, but he had to one-up me in the process. The coy response—"on good authority"—was frivolous. He'd added decoration where none was needed. And the emotion wasn't congruent with the action he hinted at. If he'd killed a child within the last eighteen hours—killed Danielle with his own hands, or even left her in circumstances where he knew she'd die of thirst or hyperthermia—he couldn't have managed the emotional modulation he was showing now. He'd have been overwhelmed with the surge of excitement, lust, guilt. Even if he was a conscienceless killer, he'd be high, giddy with success. None of this was conclusive, but it was enough to convince me that Arthur was bluffing. Danielle still had a chance.

He'd opened a seam, and I wanted to provoke him further. "You killed her," I said, as though only now coming to an understanding of the way things stood.

I heard stirrings in the shadows behind the cage, although Arthur was too pleased with himself, too bound up in his contest with me, to notice. I worried that Kovacs would be compelled to put Arthur's claim that the girl was already dead to his own test. My time was running out. I had to show progress.

"I didn't say that." Arthur suppressed a prissy smile that in itself, if Kovacs could have seen it, would have been enough to launch him into action. "I said I knew she was dead. Like 'an unnamed source'? 'A high administration figure'?"

"Someone told you?"

"Call it intuition." He looked away, as though bored with a game that his opponent didn't play to his level.

"Intuition isn't certainty. Intuition is guessing."

"Look, let's not get caught up on words."

He surveyed my face. I knew he couldn't really feel the smugness he strove to express. I couldn't scare him and I couldn't persuade him, and as I looked back into his eyes it became clear to me that I'd have to break Arthur. I had to wreck his confidence so that he understood the situation, puncture his arrogance so that all the air that kept him pumped up escaped, destroy the picture of himself as in control.

"What you have to realize," he said, "is you're wasting your time. Because I've got nothing you want."

"You know where she is. I know it. You know it."

"You're not listening, Doctor."

"You're right. I'm not listening. It doesn't matter what you say, because you're not telling me the truth. I'm not listening, but I'm watching every twitch of every muscle of your face and every shift of posture your body makes. That's what tells me what's true and what's bogus."

"Is that the scam you pulled on poor old Moll?"

"No, it really didn't take much to get Molly to tell me what happened."

"You turned my wife against me."

"That didn't take much, either."

"You tricked her. It's not difficult."

"I was straight with her."

"Molly's trusting. She's a good soul. You took advantage of her good nature."

"I told her what you are."

"She knows what I am. I'm a good husband. I've cared for her for—"

"She found the photographs."

"Photos don't mean anything."

"Photos of kids. Girls." He made a dismissive gesture, but before he could speak, I added, "Photos of Caitlin."

He looked uncomfortable for a second. "Family photos. Molly would have understood what they were."

"Not at first. She was troubled, though. But she didn't want to think about what the photos of an eight-year-old niece might mean. Molly doesn't like unpleasantness. But when I told her of the things you did with young girls—"

"You don't know what I do."

"Oh, yes, I do."

"You have no evidence."

"We don't need evidence here. Here you're guilty until proven innocent."

"What did you tell Molly, you bastard?"

"I told her you fucked little girls."

His head went down. It was only a notch, and it was only for a second, but I'd wounded him.

He said, "She doesn't understand that stuff."

"No one understands that stuff, except skinners like you and psychiatrists like me."

He stared at me in hatred.

"Molly understood enough about what you'd do to Danielle. I had to fill in some blanks, but after that she got the picture."

"You had no right to intrude in my family!"

"Some of the blanks didn't need filling in. Others took some time for me to explain. For example, she'd never wondered about all those business trips to Thailand."

He'd been studying me, his gaze fixed on me steadily, but when I mentioned Thailand, his eyes flicked sideways. It was an involuntary shift, like flinching, and I knew that Thailand had a special, dangerous meaning for him.

"What is it you consult to in Thailand, Arthur? Molly never thought about it, but I did, as soon as she told me. You fly out there twice a year. Or you used to. All of a sudden you stopped going. You have a problem there? Is that why you turned to a local girl?"

"You're guessing."

"Call it intuition."

"You've got nothing."

"This isn't your first time. You've done this with young girls before and you've been caught before. You've been interrogated before. Not like this. I bet when the Thai police questioned you, you had a polite young man from the American consulate to make sure they behaved themselves."

"Dream on."

He scoffed, with a laugh that sounded like a cough because his larynx was constricted, and I was satisfied I was on target. I wanted to keep battering at him with Molly's view of his behavior. He might not have been at peace with what he was, but Arthur could live with being a child sex killer. There were only two chinks in his armor: pride in his intellect, and his stature in the eyes of his wife.

I said, "Molly didn't find it far-fetched."

"Leave Molly out of this."

"Once I explained how predatory pedophiles work, a lot of things fell into place for her."

"She had nothing to do with this."

"Molly has everything to do with this. Where would you be without Molly? She hid your secret life. She was your cover. You played out the role of the devoted husband. While all the time—"

"I love that woman!"

"Come on, Arthur. She's a prop. Just like the van. Or the wheelchair."

"I devoted my life to her."

"You've devoted your life to finding little girls to molest."

"I doted on her."

"But it wasn't real, was it? You're a sophisticated man. Surely you don't believe your own shtick?"

"We loved each other!"

I laughed, lighthearted and relaxed, at the impossible whimsy he was suggesting. I took two steps closer to taunt him, putting myself within reach of his hands. He measured the distance. He wanted to hurt me. If he reached, I'd let him grab me. There wasn't much he could do. It would provide a practical demonstration of how powerless he was.

"She was your cover while you took long, leisurely rides through the old neighborhood to scout out prospects." The hatred I'd been holding back was coming to the surface now. I leant in so that he could have grabbed my face if he dared. I was ready to kill him. "And the kids wouldn't worry about accepting candy from such a nice, harmless lady. Why, she could hardly move. You wheeled her around like a ventriloquist with his dummy."

His eyes lit up, but he didn't try for me. The fight was going out of him. Arthur was breaking before my eyes. I wanted to strip him of every shred of illusion.

I said, "Once I started to explain to Molly what her life had been, she saw what she'd really been to you. Then she began to mention things to me that fit the pattern. Your life together started to come together for her in a whole different light."

"You don't know what our life was together. You don't know what I did for that woman."

"Molly does. That's why she turned you in."

"I know how you worked her over. You threatened her."

"It wasn't necessary."

"You told her she lied to the police. You said she impeded an investigation. Right? That she'd get five years in Framingham."

"No one's going after Molly. She's the star witness for the prosecution."

"She can't exist without me. She can't even start her day without me caring for her."

"Molly will be well cared for without you."

"You told her I'd go away forever."

"I promised her that."

"I gave up my life for Molly. I devoted my life to her. What kind of a marriage is that? To a woman who can't have children, can't make love, totally dependent?"

"So you give Molly a bed bath. A little good here. Then you go fuck a little girl. A little bad there. But the one cancels out the other. Is that how the books get balanced?"

"I didn't choose to be what I am."

"Is that it? Is that how you live with yourself?"

"I have done good!"

"Did you tell Molly what the deal was?"

"Don't be ridiculous."

"Did you ask Molly how she felt being cared for,

when everything that was done for her was to pay for what would be done to a child?"

"I never hurt them."

"Hurt them?" I was shouting. "I see these girls ten years on, twenty years on. Sixty years! They never forget. The violation never goes away. Hurt them? You damage them forever. I deal with their suicide attempts and their drug addiction and their flight from one therapist to another, in and out of psychiatric hospitals! This is a wound that never heals!"

Kovacs stood beside me, in the light. I hadn't seen him move.

I grasped the bars on either side of Arthur's head.

"I want that girl!" Fragments of spit hit his face, but he couldn't turn away from me. "I want her now!"

"Maybe . . . ," Arthur began, uncertain how to continue, but it wasn't enough for me.

"Open the cage!" I yelled. "I want in." I was pulling on it, trying to shake it, but the cage wouldn't move.

Kovacs's hand was on my shoulder. "Doc."

I shook it off. "I want that girl!"

Another officer was on my other side as I yanked at the door. They held my arms but didn't try to pry my hands from the bars.

"It's okay, Doc," Kovacs said. "We'll take over from here."

Arthur said, "I'll talk to the doctor."

Later

They didn't open the cage, because Arthur gave me the location of a locker in a self-storage facility ten miles from his house.

Abby was awake when I called. She got there shortly after the off-duty EMTs who had been standing by, waiting for Kovacs's call.

They found Danielle alive, but she lived not because of any provisions Arthur had made. He had bound her wrists and ankles with duct tape and tethered her so that she couldn't reach the pull-down door. He had also taped her mouth.

But he left behind the cardboard holder containing the three coffees—one large regular, no sugar; one medium black; one large, extra cream, two sugars—that Danielle had dutifully carried from the donut shop. He must have forgotten to toss them out the window on the highway, and I suppose he left them simply because it was a convenient way of disposing of the evidence. They saved Danielle's life.

She is a resourceful girl. With her teeth, she eventually succeeded in nibbling a tiny hole in the tape covering her mouth. She located one of the plastic stirrers in the darkness and after a couple of hours managed to manipulate it through the hole in the tape. Then she used this to penetrate the plastic covers of the polystyrene containers, but not before she tipped one of the coffees and felt the precious fluid wash around her on the concrete floor of the locker. She was able to sip enough from the rest throughout the day to keep herself alive during the torturous hours of the night.

When Abby arrived, she found Danielle sitting in the backseat of the unmarked van of Kovacs's EMTs, luxuriating in the air-conditioning that was turned up full blast and with a bottle of Gatorade clutched on either side of her.

The EMTs watched Danielle to make sure she could walk, with Abby supporting her, to Abby's SUV. They told Abby they had to go. They were never there, they said.

Danielle had been terrified, she told Abby on the ride to the hospital, but as Abby asked her about her ordeal, she was able to learn that Arthur hadn't had the opportunity to molest her.

On the advice of his attorney, Dave Feldman has decided to accept Brenda's offer of a plea bargain: he will serve a three-to-five-year sentence in exchange for his testimony against Arthur. He never saw fit to mention the ordeal of his first night at Sanders, but, abruptly, he is no longer suicidal and has been transferred to a regular jail to await trial.

Arthur also no longer feels the need to avail himself of the psychiatric services of the Sanders Institute. He was held awaiting trial at the county jail, where the authorities had great difficulty keeping him from being killed by young gangbangers with nothing better to do. Even now, in the relative safety of the protective custody unit, his attitude engenders conflict. Brenda tells me that in pre-trial hearings he tries to one-up the judge, a strategy that could result in His Honor handing down Arthur's sentences to be served consecutively rather than concurrently. It is also a characteristic that makes it more likely that he will serve the greater rather than the lesser number of the fifteen to twenty years that the smart money is betting on.

As to the events at Sanders on the night of his arrest, Arthur has managed to spear himself with both prongs of the dilemma. The witness is alive to testify against him, and he can claim no credit for her having been found.

In his complaint to the Department of Corrections internal affairs investigator, he gave an accurate description of the infractions committed by Dr. Lucas and unknown correctional officers. But he does not make a sympathetic plaintiff, nor can he muster much credibility when he changes his story from one week to the next. In his first version of events, he claimed that on his arrival at Sanders I convinced him of the evil of his ways, and that he'd had a change of heart. It was he who told authorities the address of the storage locker where Danielle would be found. He had made the disclosure of his own free will, he insisted.

The trouble for Arthur was that the authorities had no record of this information being conveyed to them. And he was at a loss to show how information about Danielle's whereabouts in a storage locker had anything to do with her mysterious discovery on a gurney in a hospital emergency room.

Then, when Brenda refused to accept that he had had any hand in saving the girl, he changed his story. Now he claims he was subjected to the harshest interrogation techniques and tortured. But there are no marks on him, other than some pressure necrosis around the dorsum of his wrists where an overzealous court officer applied handcuffs too tightly. Asked to corroborate this new account, Dave Feldman, on the advice of his attorney, chooses not to respond.

Internal affairs is investigating, of course. They have to follow up on complaints even from floridly paranoid patients. The officers assigned to the ITU noted nothing untoward that night, other than the camera failure. They have a strong union that will see to it that although they are suspended pending investigation, it will be with full pay. They are in no hurry to return to work.

Kovacs sent me a postcard from Montana, where he is hunting bear with a crossbow, signing off, "Keep the faith." Even this friendly salutation carries an undertow of threat.

Inevitably, word of that night has seeped out. I am under a cloud. People who know me well pooh-pooh the suggestion that I was in any way involved in a rogue interrogation. I am a notorious straight shooter. A Boy Scout, as Abby was fond of telling me. But the rumor mill is working overtime. Various administrations, authorities, and licensing boards suspect everything but can't prove anything. They would like to be seen doing something, but the threat of litigation ties their hands.

I have been ordered not to attempt to enter Sanders "until your personal security status has been clarified." Judy O'Donnell, channeling a message from Larry Shapiro, the department chair, has suggested that I take a sabbatical until things cool off. "Check on the state of forensic psychiatry on the Great Barrier Reef. Write a book or something." I'm not fired, she is at pains to explain, so much as indefinitely suspended in a state of academic limbo.

In many ways, I'm on the loose. I have moved out of our home, though it's hard to imagine Abby rattling around in that big house on the ocean all on her own. It will be sold in due course, I expect, but we're both still squeamish about taking these kinds of irrevocable practical steps of separation. This will change once the lawyers get involved. For now, we are oddly solicitous of each other, particularly on the subject of the other's loneliness. We talk every day on the phone, but we haven't yet figured out how you succor an old, dear friend you happen to be divorcing.

Every day, I think about that night at Sanders. I wonder at my actions, but I also wonder that I don't feel more horror. I went native. I behaved like a sociopath. Without principles, we become just another gang warring with people who happen to live on the other side of the steel bars.

I ought to feel ashamed of what I've done, but I don't, and that is a deeper problem. At least, I think it is. I ought to think so. I can't see what I did as an aberration, because I don't believe that we're fixed in who we are. This new freedom troubles me more than anything else. Once you've crossed the line, especially if you've gotten away with it, you know that there never was much of a barrier there in the first place. Just you, talking to yourself. Or not.

Thankfully, I'm grounded in the reality of finding a place to live and a job. I'm not without prospects. The other day, out of the blue, I had a call from a polite young man from a government agency whose acronym I wasn't familiar with offering me a very lucrative consulting package at a U.S. military installation in the Caribbean.